PRAISE FOR **Steve Piacente's**

Bella

getbella.com

"If this first book is any indication, sign me up for Amazon alerts on Steve's future books. Read Bella. You'll see."

— Candi Harrison, Tucson, Ariz.

It took me less than five pages to get hooked into this absorbing story.

— Frank Leyman, Brussels, Belgium

Steve Piacente writes eloquently about a man who steps out in the middle of oncoming traffic without looking left or right and tells us all about it. *— Clare Morris, Columbia, S.C.*

Multi-faceted, compelling and entertaining.

— Ina Blumberg, Jackson, Wyo.

Penetrating character study of a woman few men can resist. Bella unfolds like a Venus Fly Trap. — *Judye Osborne, Rockville, Md.*

I couldn't help but feel an instant connection to the complex, intriguing Isabel Moss. — *Liane Sallada, Charlottesville, Va.*

Bella wraps you around her finger; a most captivating and intriguing story. — *Erinn Wischum, Philadelphia, Pa.*

A must read for those who know the sacrifice and devastation of loss, and the hope of tomorrow.

— *Ashley Elizabeth Graham, Clarkesville, Tenn.*

A stylish and provocative thriller that will make you think — and keep you up way past your bedtime.

— *Susan Pelter, Jacksonville, Fla.*

I would recommend this and any other novel by this author.

— *Joseph Adelman, Hillsborough, N.J.*

A great escape from real life. — *Laura Travis, Newark, Del.*

Piacente's gripping tale of beautiful Bella leaves the reader feeling intrigue, empathy, and fascination with a widow's grief, an Army's secret, and a reporter's approach ...

— *Margaret Gavian, Minneapolis, Minn.*

Couldn't put it down. — *Diane Werner, New York, N.Y.*

Bella

A novel by Steve Piacente

For Ceil, my mother,

For Felicia, my wife,

And for Danielle, Ali and Nick, our amazing children …

Bella

a novel by

STEVE PIACENTE

Bella

Preface

She was, as Frost said, an awakener, not a teacher. Now I am awake, alert even. I am not especially thrilled that my blissful sleep was disturbed. I was, to be sure, hibernating through life, successful at work, happy at home, content to ignore the chaotic swirl of people and events outside my cozy cave. Now that my eyes are open, I find there's too much light. It gives me headaches. I get angry. But I'm smarter, too, for having been awakened. Most of what I learned during my year of enlightenment may seem obvious. You might think, *Just how good a reporter could he be if he thinks this stuff qualifies as news?* Or, you may learn, as did I, that:

Some creamy smooth women come armed like bear traps, treacherous, but not appearing so, lest you're tempted to study one nose to tooth and get yourself snapped in two. Such blessed females are immune to the routine plagues — no pimples, cavities, lisps, bad breath, flakey skin, tics, tummy bulge, eye goo or gas. Cramps don't attack each month, they pay respectful visits. Gray hair and accursed gravity postpone the day of reckoning for decades, and the more serious diseases pass like picky bees in search of sweeter flowers. A mistake, certainly, for no bouquet is sweeter or more captivating. They can be small or tall, almond or round-eyed, long-haired or short, freckled, pale, sweet, sharp, sluttish, or even a little psycho, but each sizzles. They come in a dozen shades, smell wonderful, tan, don't burn, and blaze through life, radiating presence and beguiling everyone from priest to paperboy. They toss their hair and moisten their lips without looking trite or phony, and when they're gone, they linger in the imagination of both sexes. Women mutter Bitch; men murmur Baby, unless the ladies they're with at the moment are their beloved wives, in which case silence is especially golden.

You know the kind of girl I'm talking about, and yes, of course there is a male version, and he's just as predatory. My awakener, however, was a woman, and so it is her story, and mine, that I will tell. Other men who have toed up to the trap know that caution is advisable, as this brand of female will lure, love and lose a man with such ease and nonchalance, it seems practiced. Imagine practicing such a thing. A guy who stumbles upon such high voltage treasure should turn around and haul ass, for though coyotes and other beasts will gnaw off a limb to survive, men, though beastly, are not nearly as brave as coyotes, and the women I speak of have a sense for these things. Really, the government should require warning labels.

You scoff. *Couldn't keep it in his pants and now he's lost it. Serves him right.* You think I'm about boobs, butts, and all the rest that men have lusted after since the first bare-breasted cave-mate of the month appeared, charcoal on sheet rock, all those millenniums ago. I'll give you that, at least in part. Fact is, I've seen a guy wrap his ride around a telephone pole after being blinded by the glint of a belly ring pinned to a taut female stomach jogging down the bike lane. That was my hoops buddy Clay Ohrbach, no dope; dopes don't get into MIT, let alone walk off as engineers in aeronautics and astronautics — *Aero-Astro* for short — and wind up at government intelligence outfits like the National Reconnaissance Office. Clay, tagged *Double A* (more catchy than *Aero-Astro*, we decided) by the

Bella

Sunday morning basketball crew, is happily married with a line of equity ripe enough to build a third story onto his Bethesda Tudor and two great kids who nearly lost daddy to a belly ring. They would have found the poor guy crushed like a plump Italian grape, his NRO *Freedom's Sentinel in Space* T-shirt a seeping black cherry rag.

I'm getting ahead. To understand, know that the girl I'm talking about is a notch apart. Feminist blood will simmer and yes, I'm bitter, but over this past year, I've known a woman who hid the snare within her softness. She wasn't so soft after all, a fact that only became evident once I was caught. Then it was way late. I was helpless as Pavlov's doggy. She rang the bell and I, panting fool, trotted up and dropped to my knees, for on my knees I was closer to her sex. This is the bell that made me drool, and she jingled it as she wished. I was so lovesick and grateful, if I had a tail, it would have beaten dust from the carpet.

It didn't start that way. In the beginning, I was the Dominator, all steely biceps and superior cerebellum. In wispy Dominator daydreams, I signed autographs for busloads of breathless females. *Slide down your top, young lady, so that I may initial your lovely breast.* Then one day it dawned that my clever female friend and I had traded places, and the one who needed a support group and maybe even some cranberry vodka, *Vicodin* and a soft cotton blankie, was me.

The truth I know is that now and then, God gets especially inspired and stacks a brilliant, calculating mind on top of a flawless face already perched above enough lusciousness to seed doubt in the mind of a guy fresh from the closet. In fairness, that lassie should post a skull and cross-bones pennant on the squiggly black antenna of her German-engineered convertible. What could stop a woman who's thus consecrated upstairs and down? Fate? But she's *already* a creature of Nature. What happens in a death match between Nature and Fate? Make the series best of seven,

I'd take Fate 4-3. Nature sends the tornado; Fate decides if it drops you in Hell or Oz or skips by and flattens the next seven houses. Now if Fate *does* fire up a nasty storm or two, be assured she will make it through, and the gal peering out on the horizon once the wind calms will be even tougher. By, say, 27, she has lift and separation, and there is nary a wire in sight.

*A*ttention *please,* because here's the thing. In rare cases, there's an X factor, and you better not miss it the way I did. It was plain as day, but my mind was elsewhere, which is why these days I'm alert and bitter and shoveling down *Crying Tiger* out of mushy Thai take-out cartons by myself here in good old Dumpsville, USA. There's been plenty of time to review my lessons.

See, the terrain changes dramatically if Fate rears up and does something terrible to our blessed girl above, something hideous or irrevocable; something random that cuts or scrapes her pretty flesh so raw, she seems always to be bleeding. If such tragedy visits and the woman survives, she is never the same. After a time, she may look and act as before. The pretense is transparent and a little frightening. She will cry and not realize it. Or cling to her kid when his fidgety pals are waiting with their skateboards. Or stare at nothing for long stretches. Or laugh when everyone else has stopped, or argue out loud with God while wheeling her cart down the paper goods aisle, even though her heart has hardened and she cares more about double-ply napkins and scented trash bags than the Almighty. She will curse the paperboy and priest she once enthralled, the former for being late, the latter for never showing when he was needed most. And then one day she swings quite the other way, adopting a pose that is polite, helpful and overly charming. People begin gossiping about how she's forever helping with the school play or the church raffle, how she always brings the snacks, how she's always hugging and smiling. Kids being kids repeat what they hear at home. They are less artful than their mothers at keeping secrets and she overhears, *The woman is strange, like she's made of plastic. Yes, you're right, and we all see how she simply smothers that poor child.*

She tenses. She is fine, given the circumstances. How could anyone know what it's like? Let one of those cows trade places for a day, *then* we'd see. Still, when she checks the bathroom mirror, she sees that yes, oh my, the smile is unnatural, and works it, practices, forces herself to relax. She paces, stops, paces some more. What happened is over. It will not ruin her; she is still young enough. The husbands of the cows check her out plenty … And yet … The primal beat that pounds her temples is relentless, immune to impotent prayer and each drug prescribed by her doctor, and triggered by the tortuous, unending search for answers that haunts her in darkness and light. *Things were so right. And then … Why?* She craves revenge and has no target. Prayer is futile. To whom would she pray? The God who took everything? Spinning class does not help, or talking to friends, blind dates, cherry-vanilla swirl, beading or delicious bargains at the *Rack*. Will it require hurting someone else to ease her pain? She grips the edge of the sink until her hands get cold. The mirror shows wavy veins pulsing in her forehead. She vows to silence the drumbeat, relax away the ugly veins. Control is the key, not a shrink, as some have quietly suggested. *Must get on top of it.* She shakes her hands and feeling returns, and yet still the slender fingers tremble.

Several weeks pass. She feels better. Tonight she will go out solo, make herself have fun. She calls the sitter.

The makeup goes on light; she never needed much. A sip of chardonnay. A simple black dress that accents without bragging. Small white gold earrings from Italy, with matching flat *Omega* necklace and heart ring. And one more practice smile. She drains the wine and brushes her teeth. Then she is off, tightly wrapped, ready to tangle. She tests the doorman and he responds in kind, loudly tooting his whistle even though a cab is hugging the curb. The cabbie hops out and the two middle-aged men nearly bump bellies trying to be first to open the passenger side. The doorman's joy at winning is short-lived; his dream girl is about to drive off with his rival. The cabbie thinks she cannot see as he scoots around the car and winks lasciviously at the doorman. She smiles her old smile and settles inside. The night looks promising. Tangle yes, entangled, no. A few laughs, maybe more if the band is tight and the right guy shows. A slight snicker. Perhaps, she muses, she's teaching herself to think like a man.

All the signs say keep your distance, and, as is probably already plain, I never saw one of them.

This is the true bear trap woman — exotic, self-absorbed, hurt to the core and only partly healed. Her scars do not show, but they hurt, and because of that, she is dangerous, certainly no one you'd want for an enemy. You probably don't even want her as a friend. Worst of all would be to fall in desperate love with such a woman.

Bella

Chapter 1

The first time Isabel Moss called, I tried to blow her off. I am called and emailed all the time by people trying to peddle stories. Politicians, candidates, press secretaries, communications directors, even college interns slaving away for trade associations or think tanks get hold of some media directory and call every reporter from Abrams to Zorinsky. Pitching stories used to be an art. Today's practitioners are indiscriminate as spam. Nine of ten times their ideas don't mesh with my readers, or else the so-called stories are self-serving crap. *Collapsible snow shovels? Tampa's in Florida, lady!* So I developed a clever routine for saying no thanks. Basically, the system is I let them yak until they're winded, then tell them no thanks. The only flaw is that the strategy takes time and patience, not my strong suits. Isabel Moss tested the system on a bad day with predictable results. She got me on the phone and started jabbering. I waited for a pause. None came, and none seemed to be on the horizon, where the predicted black clouds were beginning to mass, I saw from my office window on the 12th floor of the National Press Building. *Shit, gonna' get soaked running for the Metro.*

Look, miss, said I, the diplomatic Washington correspondent, your story's really interesting, but I'm buried in a piece that could affect public health and a lot of people, so I don't have … She cut me off. She said her story was more important.

You don't even know what I'm working on!

Whatever it is, this is more important.

I guess I groaned, though the sound that emerged was more like, "Self-centered bitch." She called me rude, which was rude in itself and showed little consideration for the hovering guillotine that was my deadline. Each day we reporters set our heads on the block, and are only granted amnesty once the stories are in, edited, and approved. I said as much and she invited me to shove my story, deadline and nasty attitude down the crapper. She actually said "down the crapper." Had it not been for the editor I imagined tapping his watch down in the newsroom, I would have egged her on some more for fun. As it was, time was too short for an insulting woman who didn't understand the risk of disrespecting deadlines and guillotines. Annoyed now, I suggested she take her load of BS and ship it off in a letter to the editor. "Or I'll give you a number and you can buy an ad."

She disregarded both ideas. She phoned him instead and next thing you know, he's telling me, "Take her call, Danny. Could be a good one."

The phone rang again nearly as soon as I hung up. I was incredulous.

"You called my boss?"

"Let's not get off on the wrong foot, Mr. Patragno," she said.

No one called me Mr. Patragno except Alana Lipinski, my kid's first grade teacher, who still had the red-bumped chin and cheeks of the geek who works for fun in the high school nurse's office. On *Meet the Teacher Night* at Forrest Glen Elementary, I would sit with the other parents in

the little chair and desk sets and feel like an idiot calling her *Ms. Lipinski.*
Has Robin stopped roasting ants with his magnifying glass, Ms.Lipinski?
I was 36 and Washington correspondent for the *Daily News* of Tampa,
an ambitious, medium-sized paper with a squad of medium-talent editors who thought they knew best how their lone Washington reporter
should fill each hour of each day. *How 'bout 14 inches on congressional*
pets, Danny? Sure, boss, while I'm thinking, *How 'bout I lay this 14-inch*
crowbar across your kneecap? The hours totaled about 70 a week when
you tossed in all the Saturdays and Sundays I had to work. My job was
to hound the congressional delegation, sniff for local angles on national
stories, write features, tell what goodies were stashed for Florida in the
agriculture, education or tax bills, and come up with a column for the
Sunday paper where I could tell what I really thought about the bullshit
that went on all week. Like the time the rookie Tampa congressman,
Eddie Dwoark, got sucker-punched by his own party during a close vote
in the House. Dwoark, aka *The Dork* by most Florida reporters, had been
ready to turn thumbs down on a tax bill favored by his party. During the
15-minute vote, four Republican cronies, clearly more experienced in
the art of politics, asked for a minute to make their case. He agreed, they
button-holed him in a corner, and the debate ensued. When he finally
realized he'd been a willing, almost gleeful victim in his own kidnapping,
it was over — the sand had run out. Dwoark didn't get a chance to vote,
and the Repubs won by a margin of three. The headline on my column
that Sunday read: *Dork Absent for Key Vote.* Funny thing was *The Dork,*
aka by me as *Dorkman,* told me the story himself. No one would have ever
known, as reporters aren't allowed on the House floor. Guess he thought
it would make him look folksy.

Papers like the *New York Times and Los Angeles Times* have legions
of reporters covering Congress, the White House, Supreme Court and

the feds running the agencies, but mid-sized dailies depend on wire service reports from outfits like *AP, Reuters, and Gannett.* When a regional paper sends a guy to D.C., the mission is to customize coverage for the hometown readers. Hence, when the Transportation Committee rolls out the highway bill, a correspondent from Florida zeroes in on what money is buried inside for Sunshine State road and bridge projects. If there's an eruption about shady overseas trips taken by the House speaker from Texas, the Florida correspondent turns to the travel records of lawmakers from Miami, Tallahassee, Tampa and Jacksonville. *How about that — the Senator flew to China courtesy of the lobbying firm that represents Joliet Sugar down in the Everglades. But Danny, it was a fact-finding mission. Well, Senator, I'm sure the voters will understand once I explain the facts.* It's like being a plumber. Something was always leaking, rusted or in need of replacement. You could work 24-7 if food and family didn't get in the way. Mine didn't.

Robin, the ant-barbecuing student under the tutelage of Ms. Lipinski, was surlier than most budding first-grade sadists, probably because my wife insisted on giving him a girl's name. *Robin Patragno ...* To me, it still sounds like a new bird discovered in the Galapagos. *Look, Carlos, it is not in the robin anthology. I weel call it the Robin Patragno.* Ellie insisted. Uncle Robin died less then a year before our son was born. How do you argue against a favorite uncle taken out by colon cancer? All I could do was call my boy Robbie and glare at anyone who used the girl-bird name. Which meant glaring a lot at my wife of nine years, who treated any variation as a slight to the departed Uncle Robin. Ellie started off as a high school English teacher and eight months later found herself wanting to smack kids who didn't know a Minotaur from a metaphor and who couldn't care less. She dispensed considerable punishment and they hated her for it. So she became a personal trainer, did the same thing, and found her chubby new students loved her for it. And paid plenty for the privilege of being tortured. She sweated alongside her adoring charges and pulled in about 10 grand more than me a year. Sometimes I'd overhear when they called the house. She answered like a substance abuse counselor, all tough love and sarcasm. *You want to look like Shamu this summer, Margaret? Go right ahead; have the jelly doughnut. Have two. Wash it down with a nice vanilla shake.* Ellie's stomach was hard as the hood of a '69 LeSabre. Mine was like a punctured kickball.

Chapter 2

I didn't want to find Isabel Moss or her story interesting. I didn't know much, only that her husband was a Florida soldier killed in action overseas. Our military reporter had written something about it. I'd already decided she must be a whack job who couldn't handle the grief. She'd found some sort of cause because she couldn't bring back the poor bastard. It was pitiful and not without precedent in my years on the job. I'd covered another story where the father of a murdered nine-year-old couldn't move on and took his grief to Tallahassee and made the legislature toughen up background checks for childcare operators. In the end, after the governor signed the bill, the father cried, not because he'd prevailed over a stubborn lobby representing the providers, but because he finally figured out no new law was bringing back his kid. After the champagne, after everyone had left, including his wife, he put his head in his hands and cried. *My boy*, he said, over and over. I can still hear it. Best quote I never used. I assumed fast-talking Isabel Moss, who had tattled to my boss, would eventually reach the same place. We arranged to meet in a third-floor conference room in the Dirksen Senate Office Building that turned out to be just like every other room I'd been in up there. Heavy wood-paneling, leather chairs with seats big enough for double-wide asses, and thick, gold-framed paintings of no one you ever heard of. Everything smelled like cigars, even though smoking was prohibited, by federal law no less. I could almost see the senators playing poker late at night, a pungent *Cohiba* in the hand holding the cards, a hefty tumbler of scotch in the other. Someone would make a joke about smoking being illegal and they would laugh and drink to the terrific fun of making laws that covered everyone but members of Congress.

When the doorknob turned 10 minutes later, I didn't stand. She was late.

"Sorry, I finally got hold of Newlin — you know him? North Dakota? Bad skin? Tries to hide it with that beard? Doesn't work; he looks like a goat; someone should tell him. I've been trying to get him for three weeks. He runs the subcommittee. The Army's stonewalling. I swear those tight-assed, tiny-peckered officers are the most condescending men I've ever … *Poor little widow. She's crazy with grief, boys, act like you understand.* One of them patted me on the head. I almost kicked him in the … Newlin can make them cooperate. And really, he should help me. Good publicity; he's up against a strong Democrat next year. The aide said if I wanted to talk to him, I'd have to walk alongside to a hearing that was like a half-mile away. It's so hot out. It's hotter than Florida, for gosh sake. Then I knew I was late for *our* meeting, so I ran all the way back. In *these* heels. *Look.*"

She thrust a leg forward. We were less than two feet apart. Now, I don't know Cagney from Lacy when it comes to women, but it struck me as a move she'd pulled before, designed as sudden and innocent when it was really calculated and a little naughty. Fine, let her think she's calling the plays, I thought, aware suddenly of a peachy scent coming off the nice curve of her calf. Until then, I'd been imagining wild stories with head-lines like, *Oxygen-Deprived Pixie Lives Normal Life.* How did someone that small suck in enough air to talk so long? Jeez, if she could carry a tune, she should be singing opera. Then suddenly I was face to face with a leg wrapped in fine pearl-colored silk. I don't lie and won't start now. It was a good-looking leg, and it and its upscale partner were connected to the kind of hips you don't see tooling through the Dirksen Senate Office Building, well, ever, unless some ancient senator gets caught with a girl named Bunny on his payroll. *I say, Danny, this ain't no story for the newspapers. Sure, Bunny dropped out of high school in Jacksonville way back when, but she's very good, yes, I say very good at constituent service. No doubt she's providing excellent service, senator. Why was she doing it draped across your desk with her skirt bunched up like that?*

I pulled my tie left-right and down a half-inch and let my neck loose of that hateful top button. I was sitting, but figured if I stood, Isabel Moss would top off at my chest, which would make her about 5-3. She was more striking than beautiful, with flashing black eyes and a girlish way of finger-combing her black hair behind her ears that made me forgive the earlier babble. She wore intricate gold earrings that made me think Aztec and had the berry brown skin of a girl from an exotic island, Fiji, or maybe Majorca, that one off the Spanish coast. Where was she from? Who were her parents? What was her maiden name? I made a show of looking at the shoe, which was a darker pearl than her stockings, and which indeed had a long point at the heel.

I've thought a lot about that moment. Sometimes I think I should have called her on such an obvious play. *What's the flirting about, Mrs. Moss? I thought we were here to talk about a story.* Maybe I should have snatched her knee and raced my hand up her thigh until she was forced to stop me. *What do you think you're doing? I'm showing you I'm someone you don't mess with, lady.* Of course I didn't do anything nearly so bold because I wasn't sure, or maybe I was right and didn't want to discourage her. Honestly, I can't say, even after all this time, even knowing all I've learned. I will say I figured out something at the opening bell, namely that Isabel Moss was a girl with assets she was willing to invest, so long as a decent return seemed likely.

"What's Newlin got to do with anything?"

"His subcommittee funds all branches of the military. They've got staffers who can investigate."

I must have blinked like a mental patient. She waited. I smelled stale cigar and assumed she did as well. I doodled triangles in my reporter's notebook.

"Do you know *anything* about all this?" More strained silence. She sighed, causing a strand of expensive-looking pearls around her neck to expand and relax. This was the first of many times I would see her swing instantly from mischievous flirt to button-downed K Street lobbyist, and to many other incarnations. She reached in her briefcase and pulled out two sheets with dates and notes. "This is the chronology."

The first listing read, *June 7, 2000, Hank turns pro.*

Chapter 3

Hank Moss had achieved the rank of specialist in the Army, which meant there were two grades of soldier below him and lots more above. He was an excellent marksman and, to the surprise of some, was developing into a likeable, natural leader. The reason for the surprise was that Hank's expertise as a civilian was the solitary and sometimes lonely game of tennis, where there are no teammates to help take the other guy's turf. At the time he traded racket for rifle, Hank had climbed to 123 in the world on the men's ATP Tour. That was three years after he graduated from the University of Maryland with a degree from the Robert H. Smith School of Business, a minor in communications, and plans for a career in public relations once the tennis thing had run its course. Isabel confided in her father-in-law, who assured her Hank would be done on the tour "quicker than a 48-hour virus." That's the way it played out at first. He lost badly in second and third-tier tournaments in Knoxville, Cincinnati and Burbank. He had no coach or sponsor, carried his own bags, booked his own flights, and always collected quarters for the nearest Laundromat. He stayed at cheap hotels and took buses and subways to the stadiums whenever possible. He lost first round in Birmingham and second in Waco, 6-3, 6-2, to a 19-year-old from Spain with holes in his sneakers.

Bella

He called home dejected and told Isabel, "Everyone's really good." She reminded him she was home alone, a single parent juggling daycare, her job as a fledgling real estate agent, buying the groceries and paying the rent. But she believed in him, and told him that as well. She told him to forget all of it — money, rankings, fans, even his family — and focus every moment on one thing: the next ball headed his way. "And don't dare come home 'til you win some money." They laughed. Two more disappointing losses followed, and then slowly things began to change. Hank won a match here and two there. He got a good draw and reached the round of 16 in Tarzana. Then he qualified for an ATP event in Scottsdale, won it, and got a mention in *Tennis* magazine. He was signed and began wearing the *Swoosh*. Over the next 14 months, he reached the quarters or semis of several bona fide pro tournaments and blazed into his first major, the Australian Open, where he won three rounds, the third marking his first upset of a player in the top 15. Isabel was in the stands and gave him a pumped fist that raised his spirits whenever he seemed to be foundering. *ESPN* caught their embrace after his best win, a five-setter over a one-time tournament champion, the commentator remarking that hunky Hank and the black-haired beauty made a stunning couple. He took on a full-time coach, a retired pro who had been in the top 20 for seven straight years in the 80's. Others carried his bags and did his laundry. In a span of seven months, Hank skipped from 435 to 123 and banked well more than he would in five years of writing drippy ad copy for wheel rims with silver spinners or French vanilla toothpaste. They were on their way. At 26, he was older than some guys on the tour and younger than others, a 6-2, 193-pound lefty put together like a football safety, fast, rugged and so fierce, he played each point as if the outcome would decide whether he ate that night. The commentators liked to say Hank's desperate scrambling around the court made his sneakers talk. Fans would shout, "C'mon Hank, make 'em talk." Some called him "Screech." Two other things separated Screech Moss from the pack of players trying to sweep in behind Sampras and Aggasi. First, he was married and had a baby daughter. Second, his big sister was in the North Tower on 9/11.

The search teams and rescue dogs never found anything, not limb nor locket, to suggest the presence, or even the existence, of Catherine Moss. She was 33, a wife, mother and Hank's only sibling. He could not accept that one day she was fine, alive and vibrant, still red and itchy from a Sunday outing to the Long Island beaches with his niece Sally, and the next, gone like the cartoon faces Sally liked to etch in the sand. Hank tortured himself wondering what Catherine thought when the building shuddered that morning. The North Tower went first. Hijacked American Airlines Flight 11 slammed in like a poisoned arrow between floors 93 and 100 at 8:46 a.m. Catherine, an early-bird who usually arrived by 7, was late that day. Sally had a fever and couldn't go to school. Catherine called her ex-husband, a history professor at St. John's who was off for the summer. He was agreeable but overslept, which ruined her schedule. Still, she got to work at 8:15, and was likely at her desk when Flight 11 struck, and somewhere on the mobbed staircase trying to flee when all 110 floors of the North Tower collapsed in a smoldering heap of steel, concrete and glass. Thousands were buried alive. Screams customary in Tel Aviv and Beirut and Baghdad rang throughout Manhattan. Network anchors began preparing for marathon coverage. Catherine worked for a telecommunications company on the 89th floor. There was nothing to retrieve, no body to mourn, no ashes to scatter. Hundreds of questions, no answers. No one knew for certain if she was killed on impact, leapt from the burning building or was crushed by the rubble. They wound up placing a few mementoes in her casket — a childhood Bible, a family photo, her diary and a lock of her daughter's hair. At the wake, five-year-old Sally gestured toward the casket and tugged his sleeve. *Is she in there, Uncle Hank?* That was when Hank decided to put his career and family on hold and go fight in Afghanistan. "Hitting tennis balls seems ridiculous right now," he told *Sports Illustrated* the day he enlisted. "I don't want publicity. I don't want special treatment from the Army. I just want to go." Outwardly, the tennis world and everyone else hailed Hank as a selfless patriot. Privately, they said he was nuts. The night before he left, Isabel Moss begged her husband to reconsider. He continued stuffing his duffle bag. His father had fought in Vietnam and returned intact. Isabel reminded him that his grandfather had also gone, and was cut down by a Nazi machine gunner less than 15 minutes into the attack at Normandy. He didn't even get off the beach, she said. It made no difference. After boot camp, Hank spent some time at Fort Benning in Georgia. Within six months, he was among the 9,000 U.S. military personnel fighting the Taliban in Afghanistan. On Independence Day that year, a resolute President Bush told the troops and the nation that, *In liberating oppressed peoples and demonstrating honor and bravery in battle, the members of the armed forces reflect the best of our nation.* One day the nation would pay them back. Hank never heard the President's inspiring words. On May 16, he was killed, one of 52 American servicemen and women to die early on in *Operation Enduring Freedom.* A homemade grenade apparently blew his beautiful body to bits. The bits and pieces that could be collected — and there were but a scant few — were flown home, placed in satin, and buried in a hero's casket at Arlington.

That was two months ago.

Chapter 4

"I'm sorry, Mrs. Moss. What kind of help are you looking for from Congress?"

She looked up and didn't tell me to call her "Isabel." This was a different woman than the one who walked in showing off her legs. This was a nimble, cold-eyed warrior widow dug in on two pointy heels. I pictured her in metal breastplate and goatskin (mini) skirt carving up the Washington bureaucracy and anyone who dared block her way. This, I figured, was how she looked the day she called the newsroom and snitched to the boss about his asshole Washington reporter.

"I don't believe he died the way they said, Danny. I don't think any terrorist made the grenade that killed my husband. I think it was made right here in America."

Sly. She knew she was putting me on the team — *her* team — when she stuck my name in the middle of those provocative sentences. It wasn't anything formal; ethics and editors precluded any formal arrangement. It was more like being summoned to pinch hit at a key moment. *Bases loaded, Danny, boy, all's we need is a single.* It's not that I wouldn't have gotten involved anyway. No matter what you've heard, there's a link between reporters and underdogs. They're always seeking out one another. Sometimes they hook up, mess around a little in the dark, and investigative journalism is born. Other times it just doesn't work out. I counted backward. She was 23 when she married Hank Moss. Twenty-three is barely out of college, the grunt work of a first job, constant scraping to pay the rent, buy decent clothes, catch a movie, and maybe, because everyone's nagging you to do it, save a little in the 401K. Or, if you happen to go into the county school system, 23 means having some cranky, overworked father look at you like you should still be babysitting around the neighborhood instead of teaching his kid.

Back when I was 23, I was thrilled just to get three of the five W's into the leads of stories I turned in to my first editor, an inky old-timer who banged out copy on a typewriter until he walked in one morning and, to his extreme outrage, found a computer in place of the old *Royal.* I was no more equipped to handle the death of a young wife and life as a single parent than I was to show up at a rodeo and wrestle a steer.

Ellie and I hadn't joined forces yet. I learned later that she, too, was pretty green at 23, struggling to figure out the political order at her first school in palm-ringed Fort Myers, trying to get kids to shut off their Nintendos and pick up Steinbeck or Hemingway, and dealing with pushy parents and the varied money and boyfriend problems of her roommate Bree, a psych major who wound up working at the county health clinic. I tried to imagine Ellie, on top of all of this, as a widow with a kid. A disaster, though she would have done better than me.

And so I could have objected, protested, made it eminently clear to Isabel Moss that all she could expect was fair and objective reporting. No slant, no favors, great legs and peachy scent not withstanding. Instead, I said:

"You have any proof?"

And she answered:

"You think I'd get you down here on women's intuition?"

Bella

Chapter 5

One of my boy's first moves was to wave bye-bye and blow kisses. Later, he learned to clasp hands to say hello, goodbye, to pray (though we are not religious), and to show affection. Once when he was nine, Robin got mad at Ellie, turned his back, squeezed his eyes shut and gave her the middle finger. I saw it and we had a talk. My hand did not meet his bottom, though I was tempted. He never did it again. He *did* learn to high five to celebrate winning baskets, put palm to palm to begin arm-wrestling contests, and lock pinkies to affirm the bet was on. He learned secret handshakes, how to shuffle cards, and the basics of playing the piano. He learned to plant tomatoes and use what he grew to create a decent spaghetti sauce. Perhaps one day he will hire a fortuneteller to read his love and life lines. All of it made me wonder, who was the first to lay those incongruous words side by side? *Hand grenade.* Great minds have always been fascinated with the hand. Da Vinci said, *Where the spirit does not work with the hand, there is no art.* Romeo pined, *See, how she leans her cheek upon her hand! O that I were a glove upon that hand.* Jerry and Elaine jousted about having *hand* in a relationship, meaning the upper hand. Wild-haired funnyman Steven Wright challenged a crowd, *All those who believe in telekinesis, raise my hand.* And yet someone's hands created the first grenade. Certainly it was intended as a weapon. Grenades don't enhance or beautify. Did it all begin with firecrackers, the kid-sized grenade? Isabel Moss had done some homework. She said the use of grenades indeed began with *the advent of black powder, followed by Chinese firecrackers, Roman Candles and Greek Fire Bombs.* By the time the Spanish decided to clear Native Americans out of the New World, their soldiers came armed with grenades.

"What does any of this matter?" I asked her.

She assessed the question, decided it wasn't worth answering. From then on, she said, through the American Revolution, the Civil War and the World Wars, Korea, Vietnam, you name it, grenades were common as corpses in war. The more corpses the better. Technology improved some over the decades — they figured out how to launch a grenade from a rifle, for instance — but the intent remained constant. Sometimes the technology went backward. Crudely equipped enemies learned to improvise, creating booby traps out of everything from soda cans to suicide vests. The experts came up with a term, Improvised Explosive Devices — IEDs — to cover package, vehicle and suicide bombs. According to the Army, it was a Taliban IED that killed Specialist Hank Moss, the tennis playing soldier, husband and father from Tampa, Florida.

I sabel Moss said it was warm and rainy the afternoon her husband died. Specialist Moss was on patrol in eastern Afghanistan on the outskirts of Jalalabad. "He liked that name," she said. "He thought it was romantic. He made up a story." *Gather round, little ones ... One dark night in the time of our wisest elders, an evil sorcerer named Zarka tricked Princess Aryana into drinking a potion that made her an old, ugly woman with a humped back. He thirsted not for Aryana's love, but to rule the kingdom. Khalid, a humble goatherd, rescued Aryana, fed Zarkar his own evil brew, and the sorcerer spent the rest of his days breaking his humped back hauling horse dung from the castle stables. Khalid and Aryana married and Jalalabad enjoyed a golden period of great prosperity.*

These days, the city had a university and a medical school, as well as summer weather all year long. Oranges, rice and sugarcane grew in abundance ...

Isabel used the Army's jargon-laden official report as an outline, filling in details of the tragedy as I guess she imagined them. Most of it was probably close to the truth. The way she told it was certainly plausible.

Hank's radio reported that American soldiers had been ambushed three blocks north of his position by what they believed was a nest of Taliban sniping from a vacant two-story building. He was ordered to move in from the south. "They told me he ordered his men to stay put. He would lead them into the building," she said. Rainwater hit and splashed off his helmet as he crept forward. Some earlier battle had torn the roof from the building. There was no more gunfire and he could not hear anyone within. Anxious moments passed; sweat and dirt streaked his face. "A stray dog growled and he pointed his weapon without firing."

I considered asking how she could possibly know about the dog or the rain splashing against his helmet, but she had her eyes closed and it wasn't worth breaking in.

She sighed and said Hank came to a corner and peered around and up into the darkness of a short stairwell. Nothing. Satisfied, he inched forward a few yards until he reached a cypress tree. He turned to signal his team to move forward. Three GIs crouched and began to follow. They moved as they had been trained, smoothly and efficiently. In another moment, the Americans would lay claim to a few more yards of valuable turf. In normal times, the same sad corner of land would go unnoticed, she said, or perhaps be claimed by junkies or novice gamblers. "I'll bet they rolled dice against those stairs," she said, eyes still closed.

"Hank must have heard the clank before he saw the weapon." She put her hand to her mouth, then let it fall to her waist. The sound was dull, she said, a hunk of metal bouncing and skidding along the hard ground. It burped gray smoke. There was a flash like white lightning and a horrible explosion. Concrete, metal, and a man's flesh and bones were blown high and fell back to Earth in a gentle red rain. "No one else from his unit was injured; the other soldiers dashed back and behind the corner when the bomb bounced into view. A two-man American team from the north arrived moments later. Communication was difficult because Hank's men were temporarily deafened by the explosion." Not that there was much to say. There was no more gunfire and no enemy soldiers were spotted. The wind was still and the air stank of gunpowder. "The Army told me he didn't suffer," Isabel said. "May 16, 2002. That's when he died — the afternoon of May 16. It was raining."

Chapter 6

The strapping left-hander had been guaranteed free passage into the next major tournament once he was discharged by the Army. If all went according to plan, he would come home the following spring, after Wimbledon and eight weeks or so ahead of the U.S. Open. She showed me one of his last letters. *I'd have two solid months to get ready. I'm in good shape; I'll just have to get my timing back. If I could win a round or two, Bella, I'd be right back where I was. I think the crowd would be with me. New Yorkers always root for an underdog. Especially one who fought for his country. What do you think, honey? Kisses to you and Katie. Always, forever, Hank.*

"Bella?"

"He's the only one who called me that."

All that came home of Hank Moss was a handful of bone chips small enough to fit into a marble sack. Isabel Moss passed me the predictable stories that appeared in the daily press and sports magazines. The Secretary of Defense posthumously promoted Hank to corporal and awarded him a Silver Star for gallantry, valor and heroism. "A hero and a patriot who made the ultimate sacrifice," the Secretary said. One of Hank's best friends gave a TV interview. "Rock solid, never had a bad thing to say about anyone. He loved Isabel and their little girl. Katie ... " The friend could not go on, the cameraman could not stop recording. The station aired six seconds of a man sobbing and apologizing for his lack of control. The newspapers wrote it up detail for detail.

"You don't seem to get upset when you talk about all this. Is it because you've told it so many times?"

She leaned back in that big-ass chair. We studied each other. She seemed to be weighing pros and cons. She bit her lip and a fleck of red came off on her tooth. She wiped it clean. How she knew it was there I don't know. "I'm going to tell you about the last time I cried. This isn't for publication. This is for you only, and it's the last thing I want to talk about today."

I took the damned tie off altogether. Off the record is a touchy subject that means different things to different people. Sometimes it means information can be printed, but not attributed to the source. Other times material delivered off the record is strictly an arrow that directs the reporter in a particular direction. The facts have to be found and confirmed elsewhere. Smart reporters establish ground rules before they start an interview. Anyone who offers me something juicy off the record better have a good reason to stay anonymous. Fear of retribution is an acceptable answer if the source seems credible. Watergate would have remained a fancy Washington hotel and nothing more if anonymous sources hadn't fed key facts to Woodward and Bernstein. On the other hand, if someone just wants to snipe without being held accountable, I pass. Grow some gonads or shut up. And don't try the old business of spilling your guts, then announcing it was all off the record. Negotiate first, or everything is fair game. I'll print your name *and* your picture. When Isabel Moss said her story was for me only, she meant it could not appear in print. I folded my tie twice and laid it flat in my briefcase. She wasn't afraid of retribution. She just didn't want the world in on this particular secret. It seemed reasonable. It seemed she had something private to tell that wouldn't add any new substantive facts. I clicked my pen closed and set it on the table.

"There was a wake at a funeral home in Virginia. They did it up here instead of Tampa because the burial was next day at Arlington. I always thought you needed a body to have a wake. You don't, did you know that? A few bones are enough, even a few chips of bone ... Everything smelled like formaldehyde. Harsh. Antiseptic. It made my eyes sting. Flowers, candles, and chemicals. I remember the priest started: *Friends, is there ever a greater sorrow?* I was nauseous ... Why would they need so much formaldehyde for such a pathetic little bag of bones? I asked the funeral home people. I asked them why it was so musty in there. They circled around me. They were afraid the priest would hear. Their voices hurt my skin. *It'll be okay, honey. Poor woman. Her little girl is so precious. Katie. She looks like Hank, same smart eyes. And left-handed, like him.* One guy touched my shoulder. He had a black suit and a white face. Dracula. I swear he had on make-up. I threw off his hand. I said, *Get the hell off me, bloodsucker.* People stared like I was holding up a liquor store. Even the priest shook his head. I couldn't help it. I don't like people touching me, I never did. Just Hank."

Her voice and shoulders sagged. She was gone from the Capitol and back in the dank, stinking funeral home with her little girl Katie, Hank's parents, a startled priest, and God knows who else. I felt and fought an urge to comfort her. *Not your job, Danny.* The silence lengthened. We'd been in the conference room nearly two hours without a break. I'd learned many intimate details and still knew nothing. Her hand was on the table. She wore her gold wedding band and her nails were the same pearl color as her shoes. I touched her fingers lightly and she didn't withdraw, a small thing that seemed to mean a lot. I'd like to think I would have done the same for anyone hurting that bad. When she spoke again, she was gazing vacantly upon a portrait of Senator Patrick Montrose Dennison, one-time chairman of the Senate Finance Committee from the great state of Wisconsin. Fine, square-jawed Midwesterner, solid stock, a pay-as-you go, answer-his-own-messages kind of guy. Family made a fortune in low-fat dairy products. She pulled her hand back and crossed arms over her chest. "I lost it. I made them all leave. A lot of those people came all the way from Florida; I didn't care. I told them I wanted to be alone with my husband. Didn't I have that right? Hadn't I gone through enough? Thirty people give or take. At first they wouldn't go. I screamed for them to get out. *Let me be alone with my husband. Please!* Hank's mom took Katie. Everyone left; the priest was the last one. He took a step toward me and must have seen it was a bad idea. Then we were alone, me and my sad collection of body parts. This was all that was left of him, my big, strong man, my husband … my professional athlete. I dropped down to my knees. I wasn't praying; I just didn't have any strength, and my legs gave out. I don't know how long I stayed there; it might have been five minutes, it could have been 20. When I could focus, I saw the pictures. Someone had pasted dozens of them on three poster boards. *Baby Hank in his stroller. Hank in a Little League uniform. Wildcats. Hank on the roller coaster. Hank at the beach, wearing a Batman suit, winning a tennis trophy, driving for the first time. Our wedding. Our baby. Our first apartment down in Tampa.* I looked at each picture stuck up there on those easels in front of the casket. There should have been 60 more years worth of pictures. Anniversaries and graduations, birthdays, family picnics, pictures of the other kids we were going to have one day … Then it hit me, Danny. Hank wasn't an extravagant man. He came from a modest family; I used to make fun of him for going to the same barber his whole life. His haircuts cost eight dollars, including tip. Even when he started winning on the tour, he never went out and bought a Ferrari or anything. He didn't want a mansion for us or private school for Katie or anything like that. How ridiculous to have that giant gleaming casket for a few miserable limbs and bones. I knew how much it cost — nearly $6,000 — one of the most expensive they make. *Solid nickel, safe from air, water, rust, corrosion, and all outside elements,* they'd told me, as if it made a difference, as if the damage weren't already done. I made a note to ask Dracula if it was safe from grenades and IED's. There was a casket for Catherine, too, you know, after 9/11. Two caskets, nothing to bury. The waste made me furious. Use the damn money to buy better armor for the soldiers."

She stopped. The black of her eyes moved to the corners, as if she were done and thinking about something new. I began carefully, "Did you happen to —

She cut me off. Whatever I had to say or ask wasn't important. "Next to the casket and the pictures there was a three-foot statue of Jesus. It was pretty, polished gray marble. One hand held a long wooden cross; the other was raised to the sky, palm outward. He looked very serene. I think it was supposed to be Jesus rising, because somehow it seemed he was slightly off the ground."

Here she paused again. The word *Jesus* echoed in my ears. I wasn't sure she'd finish, or maybe that was it. Done, end of story. I glanced up; Chairman Dennison of Wisconsin was waiting with me. In his time, he would have circled two impatient fingers around the rim of his filmy water glass, whispered something to an aide and ordered the witness to go on. *This committee is quite busy, m'am; please complete your testimony.*

She said softly, randomly, "Sunday School. I tried. It seemed so insincere, so out of touch. Jesus said, *As I have loved you, love one another.* What was that? Advice? A plea? An order?" Her voice rose and with the rise came bitterness that edged toward hatred. "Love one another or else. Or else what? No one's obeyed, no one's been held accountable, not since the 12 of them sat around that table in their long robes. And I … I was alone except for words. More words, words that rang empty: *Do not fear, for I am with you; do not be dismayed, for I am your God. I will strengthen you and help you.*" She breathed deeply. "I felt no strength; I felt no help, none at all."

Her hands balled into small, white fists. She saw me watching and flexed her fingers as she returned to the story. She took my elbow and then the other. Her eyes were dry, yet seemed to plead for understanding. She said, "I got up from my knees, Danny. I got up and ran to the statue and, so help me … I spit in the face of Jesus Christ."

She watched me closely as she said it. My mouth was open slightly, though it was all I could do to swallow. When several moments passed and it was clear I would not voice a reaction, she dropped her chin and looked at her lap. "That," she said, "was the last time I cried."

Bella

Chapter 7

Some would have had follow-up questions. I had nothing. It was like an abrupt end to a sad movie. The credits roll, the lights go on and you're still sitting there digesting. So she ignored me and went on, speaking in a new, matter-of-fact voice, about how she happened to get her earlier meeting with Senator Newlin. Most people think senators and congressmen are accessible to average citizens. Show up, announce you'd like to discuss Supreme Court nominees or the long-term solvency of Social Security, and out pops the senator with a pad and pencil. That's what they'd like you to think, especially around election time, when they come around knocking and smiling and your mailbox is always full of partisan slop with the incumbent's mug and message. Truth is, you don't get five minutes of quality time with a senator in off years unless you're a CEO, a union leader, or unless your name is high on his list of big-time campaign contributors.

"What I told you before about all that came home of Hank wasn't entirely true," she said. "The Army also sent me what was left of his uniform."

I thought it bizarre and ghoulish, and, again, couldn't think of a question that wouldn't sound ignorant or insensitive. I tried to begin thinking of how to frame a lead or at least a headline for a story and realized I didn't even know what the story was yet. She barely paused.

"Obviously it was in pretty bad shape. They tried to clean the blood stains. Only a fraction of his shirt was left, a square, partly burned, all in tatters. I washed and ironed it and started keeping it in my briefcase. One day I went to see my local congressman, Mr. Dwoark. I wanted to tell him about a phone call I got. I went to his office in the Federal Building in Tampa and they said no problem, he'd be with me in a few minutes." She let loose a wild chuckle that made me wonder if she was as composed as she was making out. "He's kind of goofy, you know. Tall and goofy; he didn't know how to handle me at all. He ran around his desk like Rhett Butler in *Gone with the Wind*. Held out my chair, offered me iced tea, went on and on like a nervous woman. Don't forget this is a few weeks after the funeral. I settled down a little. He kept saying how sorry he was, that Hank was a hero, he died for the cause of freedom, blah, blah and yada-yada. He was so jumpy he didn't give me a chance to say anything after hello. Finally he got to the part about, *If there's ever anything I or my office can ever do* … I stopped him. I told him there *was* something. I'd received a call, anonymous, unlisted number … I could see him tense up. Dwoark isn't known for taking chances. More Henry Winkler than Henry Clay, right? You know I'm right; I read your columns every Sunday morning at a little diner that I go to with Katie. She likes *Sugar Pops* and silver dollar pancakes ... Anyway, I told him that a few days earlier, my phone rang. I answered and a man whispered, *Isabel Moss?* I said it was me and he said, *I can only talk a second. It's about Hank. He didn't die the way they said.*" I think someone came then because he hung up.

She cackled again. "You never saw a guy's expression change so fast. Suddenly the congressman didn't want anything to do with me. He said I needed to report it to the Army, follow the chain of command. I told him that wouldn't do. If the caller really knew something, the Army would know too. They're the ones who told me how Hank died. Dwoark said there was nothing he could do; he wasn't even on the Armed Services Committee. I said, *But you're a congressman. My congressman.* He took off his suit jacket and said I didn't understand how it worked in Washington. You have to be on the committees, he said. You have to be a chairman or a subcommittee chairman. You can't just start making waves, especially without something concrete. I said, *Concrete?* Yes, that's right, he said. You need solid, concrete facts. You can't just come out with wild rumors or half-truths passed on by anonymous sources. I said again, *Concrete?* Those generals, he went on, the Army Chief of Staff, they'd laugh in your face. And the press … They'd be all over me. We've got a lot of military people among my constituents. I've got McDill Air Force Base, CENTCOM, the Special Ops Command … I can't get those people mad … "

" — Concrete?"

" — Mrs. Moss, please, I … "

"I put the briefcase on my lap. I opened it and took out my small piece of Hank's uniform. I slapped it on Dwoark's desk. His eyes got all big; he looked like he was going to hit the button that calls the cops. They all have one of those buttons, don't they? I said, *This is all that came back of my husband. Is this concrete enough? I need to know what happened to him, congressman. I need to know if the military was honest with me. I need you to help me however you can. I don't care about your other constituents. I'm your constituent too. So's my little girl. Hank Moss' daughter.* He stared at the shirt and rubbed his hands together. He wanted to know if the caller said anything else. I told him there was nothing else, and he hadn't called back since. But what else could he have meant? *He didn't die the way they said.* Then, with me sitting there, he called Senator Newlin. He had his home number in his cell. *Derrick,* he said, *Ed in Florida. Something's come up and I could sure use your help.* Turned out that while Dwoark wasn't on the right committees, he and Newlin are old college buddies. I didn't know Dwoark went to Princeton, did you?"

What I didn't know could apparently fill the Sunday paper. "How did you leave it today with Newlin?"

"Two minutes into the story he stopped me. He told his aide — a kid named Ed who looks like he's a year away from ordering his own beer — to get me in tomorrow afternoon. Ed said the day was booked. Newlin cut him a look and Ed said he'd make room at two."

Isabel and I were both drained and I needed recovery time, to say nothing of food and water. We planned to meet in the morning for breakfast at her hotel, the Marriott next door to the Press Building. She hugged me goodbye, holding it a second longer than necessary, and telling me, by the way, that Mrs. Moss was her mother-in-law. "I'm Isabel. God's promise."

I slid back; she uttered a derisive little laugh. "That's what my name means. Isabel, God's promise."

She touched my cheek as she said it. Given how much she'd revealed, the display of intimacy didn't strike me as odd.

Chapter 8

"Robin's teacher wants to see us."

Just what I felt like hearing after that sweaty subway ride to the Maryland burbs. Our split level in Silver Spring, rented for $745 a month plus utilities, had three bedrooms, a decent family room with a broken fireplace, and a brick patio out back with rusty wrought iron furniture. It was to the patio I headed, a cold one in hand. Ellie followed. I considered running ahead and hiding between the houses. Ellie was the youngest and smallest of three sisters; the two ahead were six and eight years older. They did not share and the family was far from wealthy, so Ellie brought a lifetime of cagey fighting skills to each of our little quarrels.

One of the neighbors cranked up a mower that sputtered, caught and began its work. I plopped into a cushioned lounge and breathed in a not unpleasant scent of gasoline and fresh-cut grass. She sat opposite and started in about Robin and the other first-grade felons. I cut her off.

"Listen to what happened on the Metro." Interrupting was a bad play that I knew wouldn't distract her. She glared and tapped on the table, dislodging a flake of orange rust that floated to the ground. "Guy in a suit's sitting there reading the Post. Guy behind him in a Hawaiian tank top starts clipping his nails. A skanky nail lands on the first guy's paper. He lets it slide. It happens again and he stands up, moves in on the other guy, and snatches the nail clipper as we pull into Union Station. He smiles and says very calmly, like the old monk lecturing *Grasshopper,* that, *Nail-clipping is a bathroom activity.* He studies the clipper a second and chucks it out the door as we're pulling away. Tank top is stunned; I mean his mouth was open. People start laughing, then they give the second guy a big ovation. It was really — "

" — Robin, Joey and Steven Gillman wrote fuck all over the black-board at recess."

I considered and said, "As a noun or verb?"

"You think it's funny?"

"I'm serious. Was their intent to insult or bang Miss Lipinski? Because if it's the first, it's one thing; if it's the second, that's pretty advanced and the three of them might need to skip ahead to middle school."

"Asshole." She fired up off her seat. Cardinals screeched and a black squirrel tip-toed across the back fence. Why I do these things is a mystery even to me. It seemed early for a mid-life crisis, though true, I'd been thinking about how to come up with the down payment for a jazzy convertible. "Hold on, I'm sorry." She stopped without turning. "It was a shitty day; I'm working something new. I didn't mean to make fun. Send him down. I'll talk to him and we can go see Miss Lipinski whenever she wants."

"She wants us tomorrow morning."

Naturally — right when I was supposed to meet again with Isabel Moss. "That's the only time I can't make it." She pressed again toward the house, calf muscles popping like small beer cans. "I'm good any other day, even tomorrow afternoon." The *crack* of the screen door ended our backyard retreat. No romance tonight. I pressed the cool bottle to my fore-head. Too many evenings were ending this way lately. I couldn't account for it. I was starting to think the differences that make opposites attract undercut the same relationships after kids come along. It floored her the first time I suggested we make love in my old Pinto wagon. A little pot, persistence and, don't gag — I had my moments — Patragno persuasion, brought her around. *Way* around. Soon we were doing it in the car, on the car and against the car. *She* was the one who started keeping a blanket handy because the back of the old Pinto wasn't built for comfort. I loved — make that *love* — everything about the way Ellie's put together. Her sisters were ordinary. She, though, has high cheekbones, quick blue eyes and brown feline lashes, all set off by waves of chestnut hair that smells like forest wildflowers. Her neck, too, is special. Answers a kiss like a fuse answers a match. I know her face turns heads, and take pride in knowing that it looks as good the morning after as the night before. She's changed hairstyles four times since I've known her. Right now it touches the tip of her bare shoulders. Very sexy, and yet there's been no car sex for about a decade. Now she's a grown-up. Adults have to act like adults. I could hear her and the guy on the train lecturing me and Grasshopper as we sat cross-legged on the temple floor: *Intercourse, gentlemen, is a bedroom activity.* Parents who once did reefer and screwed on the hood of a Pinto now had to lay down household laws and punish their little transgressors. Why, I'd ask, can't we have the same fun as before, and she'd answer, *You've got nothing to complain about, Danny.* It was true, and yet James Taylor's warning to *Never Die Young* had begun nagging me. Ellie was more concerned about practical matters such as the boy's safety, the importance of which, by the way, could not be overstated. Were it up to her, he'd go through childhood in helmet, mouth guard and shoulder pads. Indeed, when five-year-old Robin was finally able to navigate the slide at the park a few years back, Ellie insisted he wear a bike helmet. Poor kid could barely see and fell off the ladder. His head was fine; the main bone in his elbow, the ulna, split in two. They had to pin the bone together. He spent July and August that summer in a cast. Maybe that was when he learned to toast ants with a magnifying glass.

I sank deeper in the chair, thinking about how to explain to the editors why the Hank Moss story was worth so much of my time and their money. Several routine stories would go uncovered and my weekly production would drop off. The payoff could be big, or we could come up empty. My gut said to work it a week and see where things led. The mowing next door stopped and I begin to drift off. When I awoke, the last sherbet streaks of sunlight were visible through the oaks that ringed the backyard. "Mom said you want me." I yawned. There before me was Robin Louis Patragno, a gangly, barefoot boy in red shorts and a white T-shirt with fuzzy hair and teeth way too big for the current size of his potty mouth. He was already stuffing himself into eight-and-a-half sneakers; it wouldn't surprise me if he ended up six-five like Ellie's dad. "Why'd you write that on the blackboard?" He shrugged. "Do you know what it means?" He stood with hands on hips and pawed dirt with his big toe. If he'd have said, 'Verb or noun?' I might have kissed his cheek and laughed the whole thing off. He didn't say anything. I waited. I still might be waiting because he wasn't about to say a damned thing. "You know it's not a word to be used by a first-grade boy? You know you made your mother upset? That your teacher wants to see us?" He shrugged and pawed and kept his hands hidden. I had an idea he might be giving me the finger behind his back. "Put your hands where I can see them." He did, giving me the finger with his eyes. "You have anything to say?" He had *nada*. "Ok, to your room. Shut the door. No computer, no TV, 8:30 bedtime. And tomorrow you apologize — to Miss Lipinski and your classmates. Start right now with your mom. I'm going to check up to make sure you did it." He turned and skulked away. I looked at the ground and saw that he'd pawed a crude "F-U" in the dirt. Ballsy kid, no? Maybe he'd grow up and be a reporter.

Chapter 9

I've mentioned my mid-section (soft) and height (average). The rest is similarly unspectacular. I am what women call not bad, with no inflection. Not bad with inflection, as in, *Not bad!* is something altogether different, but that is not I. Five-eleven give or take, with enough full brown hair to warrant a $12 visit every three weeks to *Clips* in the neighborhood shopping center, wedged between the chain cell phone and grocery stores, decent enough dresser to invest in tailored slacks (albeit at a discount men's store), confident enough to call a congressman by his first name and wink at his secretary after he's yelled at me about an unflattering story. I choose not to skip shaving, bungee jump, or get tattooed, though I find a dreamy little butterfly or water lily just below a girl's belt line, front or back, strangely erotic, like the next clue on a treasure map. I had reasonable success before Ellie; several Lady Seminoles at Florida State seemed to like that I knew what I wanted (to be a newspaperman), that I was good at connecting with people on paper and in bars, and that I wouldn't let any bullshit go by, not from professors, the student government, or even from them. Amazing how far decent communication skills can take you. But sheer head-turning quotient? Maybe a seven, which is why it surprised me that Isabel Moss sat close enough next morning at breakfast to make sure our knees — hers, naked below plaid shorts, mine in tailored navy slacks — accidentally brushed as we shared French toast and fresh fruit and talked over the game plan. Or was I wrong? Maybe the contact was accidental. Maybe she was just thankful for an ally, even though I had yet to declare any allegiance or written the first word about the late Hank "Screech" Moss or his Army bosses. No doubt she was lonely. *And lovely, in that maroon sweater. No jewelry today, save for a pair of small jade-crusted gold hoops. Hair pulled back into a tight black ponytail ...* What if she invited me to her room at eight in the morning? What if I went? What if we did it and I couldn't do it? Or if she got pregnant? *Jesus, Danny, stop! Quit being a puss. Keep it about the story.* Our young Latin waiter was also indulging in lewd thoughts, I saw as he refreshed the water goblets and checked out all that filled her summer sweater. It was not cut low, and she was not a heavy-breasted woman. I think the waiter and I might have agreed she was perfectly proportioned. The quick smiles she shot at him, me, the slim blond hostess, and the old guy in the beret who borrowed our creamer got me thinking again about how quickly she'd recovered from her loss. Wife one day, widow and single parent the next. Or was it that simply that daytime was show time? Maybe she was bawling herself to sleep each night. Maybe she dreamed that she was calling to him in those last moments and he couldn't hear. *Don't go around that corner, Hank. Back away. You have to listen, darling. Back away!* Maybe I'd ask sometime. For now, building, writing and selling a story I could get into the paper was enough challenge. The explosion in the roofless Afghan stairwell hadn't left enough for an autopsy, not that any medical report would have revealed who threw the bomb. She had an American flag, pictures from the funeral, a death certificate and a letter of commendation that went with Hank's medal. I saw myself storming the Pentagon and confronting the Army Public Information Officer. *I demand to know who killed Hank Moss. And he would say, He was killed by enemy fire, just like we told you.* I would tell about the anonymous call, and he would nod, indicating the widow needed professional help, and it might be a good idea for me to tag along as well. Now I knew why *Dorkman* nearly pissed his pants when Isabel Moss insisted on help from her congressman.

"Have you made any friends in the military, officers, someone high up, maybe the wife of a general?"

"I don't get along well with women, so no. And Hank wasn't in that long, so I didn't get to know many people anyway."

The news about no girlfriends didn't surprise me. Women who think and look like Isabel Moss prefer men, and other women immediately sense and resent it. "So we have no witnesses, no documentation, no corroborating sources, no leads. We have one 10-second call that could have been from a guy who knows something or who gets off torturing new widows."

"You think I'm crazy."

"I don't." I looked at her evenly. "I think you may be after answers that don't exist. Nothing changes, you know, even if you prove all you're trying to prove."

"That's my problem and I'll deal with it."

"Yes."

"So you don't think I'm crazy."

"I've known crazier." That won half a smile. "Really," I pressed, anxious to lighten the mood, "I wrote once about a small-town mayor who opened a strip club out in Hillsborough County. He called it *Triple X-tacy* and kept it filled with watered-down booze and hookers just this side of Social Security. His wife didn't know. We only found out because he missed some tax payments the tax collector fined him and the documents became public record. I went out there with a photographer one night and we got a great shot of the mayor with a shot of bourbon in one hand and a girl named Boom-Boom in the other. Another time I covered a city council race where the two lunatics running got so mad, one guy went to the other's house and axed up a bed of prize-winning roses. I remember … *Sussman!*"

"Sussman? Was he the guy with the ax or the roses?"

"Neither." I picked up two wet grapes and ran them inside my fist like dice. Why hadn't I thought of Sussman right off? I rolled the grapes and Isabel caught them before they flew off the table. Her eyes brightened. "What's with you?" I plucked more grapes and she put her hands up like a soccer goalie. "Gavin Sussman was a Washington reporter who lost his job, which ended up costing him his marriage and his house. It started with the fondling of a secretary who didn't care to be fondled. Sussman was a good reporter, broke great stories about a Kansas congressman who wheedled some tax breaks for a big contributor. He swore he didn't do anything to the girl. She said he did it, and more than once. Rumor was they were sleeping together and she got pissed when he broke it off. Sussman's bosses decided the secretary was more credible. They gave him three months severance and told him to get lost."

"So?"

"So he wound up buried in some GS 11 press job at the Pentagon."

"How would a low-level bureaucrat know anything about Hank?"

"I'm not saying he does."

"But it's worth talking to him, right?"

"I'll talk to Sussman; you meet with Newlin and keep your cell phone on every second. If your friend *Deep Throat* calls, let me know right away."

"Got it. When will I see you again?"

Her tone was slightly ambiguous and it stopped me. It's not that she purred the question, or that I was hunting for words that weren't on the page. Tenor is like mercury in a thermometer; it moves with the temperature. The way a cop says, *License and registration*, tells if a ticket is coming. The way a boss says, *Got a minute, Roy?* could mean promotion or pink slip, depending on tenor. *When will I see you again* wasn't as obvious, more like accidental knee touching. All through breakfast I'd wondered whether the contact was innocent. Now I wondered if her send-off hinted at something more than business. The mixed signals were starting to make me dizzy. Was she doing it on purpose? "I'll call you, Isabel," I said and dropped $30 on the table.

"Danny — "

"— It's okay, the paper will pay me back."

"I didn't mean that. What I was going to say, *Woodward,* is that you don't have my number." She laughed and took my reporter's pad and wrote her cell number on the inside cover.

Bella

Chapter 10

Four *Starbucks* and the same half-dozen street bums marred the six-minute trail Gavin Sussman humped each morning from his D.C. apartment to the Metro, where he caught the Red Line and switched to the Yellow to get to the Pentagon. His feet knew the way; his bored brown eyes rarely ventured more than a foot beyond the toes of his commuting sneakers. He was aware of the cookie cutter cafes and the bums, knew there were many hundreds of people, thousands, probably, who reached deep and donated each morning to the homeless and to the pretentious coffee chain. Not him. Not at a buck, ninety-eight for a large, plus the ignominy of having to speak their snotty jargon: *Grrrahn-day Drip, No Room, Please.* Then a creepy smile from the clerk that said, *Great job ordering,* but which really meant, *Gracias, Potsy, you just paid two bucks for a ten-cent cup of Joe.* Gavin didn't like the Asian business-men with their soft black leather briefcases that he passed each day, or the grizzled Armenian who sold fruit off a wooden cart from May until mid-November. He ignored the stores he passed, like *Dickey's Frozen Custard, the Unique Boutique and Gallery Office Supplies,* and he disliked the drifters. Each day he walked by holding his breath because, really, who could stand the smell of those people and their carpet pad blankets, especially during the sweaty Washington spring and summer? Some of the beggars tried to play for their pay — trumpet, sax, flute, guitar, even a shabby violin. Gavin saw them as shiftless and dirty, and the supposed musicianship, with Manilow-esque singing added in the bizarre case of the Jamaican guitarist with corn rows thick as egg rolls out by the K Street entrance to Farragut North, as unwanted, unsolicited noise. What gave them the right? Disturbing the peace is what it was. If the losers could be out panhandling by seven, why couldn't they strap on clean pants and a shirt and get work hauling, lifting, sweeping, painting, *any* damn thing, for Christ's sake? Anything, that is, except hosing the sidewalk. *Those guys* … It made him furious. Hired by building management to spray the front sidewalk, God only knew why; there were water shortages everywhere! *Samuel, Bruno, Ricardo, Gino.* The names stitched in bright cursive over the heart pockets of their starchy blue shirts. Every half block, another one, out early, hair greased, hoses coiled, bronze nozzles spurting and soaking long slabs of concrete so everyone's damned shoes got wet — all to shoot a few cigarette butts, leaves, hunks of dried gum and pigeon crap into the street, onto turf that was someone else's responsibility. It was all of Washington in one muddy puddle: cover your ass and let the next guy beware. The hose men pretended to let up when people went by, but Gavin knew accidents happened on purpose. They feigned sub-servience — *Morning, sir, Hot one, sir, Yeah, those Orioles tanked again, sir, how about the Nationals?* Everyone knew the hose men went for the cuffs of a nice pair of dress trousers now and then, all the while letting the unwashed homeless crash in any doorway they wanted. *God, the stench.* Gavin Sussman believed Good Samaritans who plunked coins or even bills into the bums' scummy *Big Gulp* cups were suckers. Come noon, probably earlier, the cups would be brimming with *Thunderbird* from *Capitol Wine and Liquor* at 18th and I.

Bella

No, it didn't take long to see that my old colleague Gavin Sussman was bitter about being forced from the newspaper game. When I called to set up lunch, he was glad to hear from one of the old crew and readily agreed. After clearing me through security, he led us to a cafeteria, which was still crowded at half past one.

"And work, Danny, you wouldn't believe it. I research speeches for the *ASA (ALT) AAE* — the Assistant Secretary of the Army for Acquisition, Logistics and Technology *slash* Army Acquisition Executive. You should see his business card — not a speck of white." Gavin folded a paper napkin and blew his nose without facing away from the table. "I never knew how much I'd miss being a reporter, writing hard-hitting stuff that got people sending letters to the paper. Didn't matter if they liked the work or called me scum. I had their *attention*. My work wasn't going down some black hole like now. It sounds like bullshit, but when I rode Metro each morning, man, I felt like that Up escalator was launching me into a new day. I know. Goofy, right?" I tried to smile. "Thing is that now ... *Now* what I do is — listen to *this* — I help *execute the acquisition function and the acquisition management system* of the Department of the Army." He said it as if telling how he picks up after his dog. "Makes me miss my press pass," he said. "Makes me wanna' puke."

Given his gaunt face and slender frame, it wouldn't have surprised me if there was something working on his insides besides past mistakes. He looked sickly. What he needed at the moment — what he clearly hadn't had in a long time — was someone who would listen. I listened.

"I work at a gray cubicle near a fax machine and a little kitchen area — the *coffee mess*. I have a black laptop that they make me chain to my modular desk. Like I'm going to walk out of the Pentagon with a stolen computer. You see the size of those gorillas back there at security?" He mashed the plastic wrap from his sandwich into a ball. "Up on my floor, there's always a line at the microwave. I don't know when people work; they're always eating. All day I smell popcorn and leftovers. Know how you put sounds with places? My sounds at work are the microwave dinging and the fax squawking. Everything I write goes through four bureaucrats who think Steinbeck is a piano and Chekhov is what you do to boxes on a federal form. Simple doesn't work for these goons. Jargon is their porn; the more, the better. They don't buy tanks; they *acquire vehicles that will provide mobile firepower for armored formations.* Jeez. Everything we put out reads like a dishwasher repair manual. And the material … I work on things like *performance-based logistics* and Army policy on the *proper use of non-Defense Department contracts.*" He cracked all 10 of his bony knuckles. "I swear they better never let me get my hands on a weapon …"

I didn't worry about any rampage. He was exasperated, not dangerous. I asked about quitting for another newspaper job and he said no editor wanted him after his alleged sexual misconduct. "I was bangin' her Danny, but had a relationship. She wanted me to get a divorce, which is what I wound up getting. I got divorced from my wife and my career, and then she didn't want anything to do with me. She was a nut job anyway. I'm better off." He said he answered dozens of reporting ads in *Editor and Publisher,* called newsroom after newswroom. Albuquerque. Kansas City. Buffalo. Miami. Philly. Nothing. He even showed up unannounced at papers large and small in Maryland, D.C. and Virginia. "Only one guy was honest. He said they loved my clips but couldn't take a chance. He said the women on staff would have revolted. So I took this dumb-ass public affairs job with the Army. I complain but I'm glad to be working. At least I'm writing. I could be wearing a green apron and serving *Caramel Macchiatos,* if not for the be-all-you-can-be Army." Gavin Sussman sank his teeth in a homemade tuna on cold toast and a piece of tomato gushed out the side. "So how's by you? What's new in Florida? Any hurricanes coming?"

I began talking about Hank and Isabel Moss. He stopped eating. He wiped his mouth with another napkin from his brown bag and didn't take another bite. "You're kidding, right?" Mind you, I hadn't asked for a thing. He wiped again. Three quarters of the sandwich remained. "I don't hear from you all this time, then you show up and ask me to be your bitch and spy around and maybe rat out the U.S. Fucking Department of Defense." I didn't think our previous conversation could turn more one-sided. It did. He tore off another hunk of sandwich, chewed some and pushed what was left to a wet corner of his mouth. "And what do I get if you're right and it turns out that some American kid out of Iowa slipped up and mowed down your soldier boy from Tampa, and the media go nuts and senators start hauling generals up to the Hill? I don't get any credit; I don't get any money. I sure as hell don't get a promotion. What I *do* get is to worry my ass off about getting caught, or cut loose again, or maybe put in front of a firing squad. Your paper run a witness protection program? They going to get me a new identity and a job in Tucson?" He shifted as if someone might be listening and swallowed. I waited, thinking that calling Gavin Sussman was a bad idea after all, and wondering vaguely if he'd learned any nasty soldier tricks since taking a job at the Pentagon, like how to murder a man in three seconds with a plastic fork. We sat and regarded each other. A short-haired woman who clearly knew and disliked Gavin walked by with a salad and a bag of microwave popcorn that she lifted and shook at him. "For later," she taunted, obviously aware of his distaste for the pungent snack. My guess is he'd complained, and a superior had ruled that popcorn — fresh from the bag or microwaved until you could smell it a block away — was acceptable in the workplace. He frowned. I thought he might even go after her. But he fooled me. Instead, he took a drink of bottled water, also brought from home, judging by the sweaty, half-peeled label, and said, almost casually, as if we were making plans to take in a ballgame, "Fine, I'll poke around. Happy?"

Bella

Chapter 11

Tennis, reporting and plenty of disciplines are alike in that no one can teach anyone else to play. A good pro can explain how to whack a serve and hit ground strokes and the difference between slice and topspin, just like a good journalism prof can lecture on what makes a story newsworthy, and how action verbs liven up routine copy. The only way to become a player, though, is to play. This is especially true in learning tennis as an adult. To become decent, you need 10 private lessons to flush whatever notions you had about striking the ball and to learn proper technique. Go by any courts and you'll see a startling assortment of unorthodox strokes. Even a four-year-old with a racket can figure a way to get the ball over the net. That doesn't mean it's the smartest way. Anyone who's been around public courts or even the local country club has witnessed a petite woman with good strokes punish her hulking, flailing boyfriend, who, instead of offering congratulations, ends up red with anger and bashing his racket into one of the end poles that hold up the net. It's a curious move, as the poles are often forest green, made of steel and don't give much. At least he has closure, in that he will never again play with that racket. As an adult novice, you'll be interested in saving energy, avoiding tendonitis, and hitting an occasional shot that gets your opponent to heave his racket out to the adjacent softball diamond. Lessons are the way to start. Consider it adult education, and take care to pick a good teacher. Great players sometimes make lousy teachers. After the lessons, it's up to you. Take your thimble of talent, find a few skilled partners and drill until you run through about 15 pairs of tennis shoes. Join leagues and clinics, play in the city tournament, and take on anyone banging balls on the practice wall at the park. Watch the wonder kids play on TV and study strategy and technique tips in the tennis magazines. Expect to lose a lot more than you win. After about five years, you'll begin to understand the game and start developing one of your own.

I learned all this at my first job in Southwest Florida, where I was one half of a two-man sports desk at a small paper that hated to upset local advertisers and hometown heroes. Tennis was played at the high school, college, professional, and recreational levels. Of course the well-off recreational crowd was hardest to satisfy. Any player who won a local tournament expected Wimbledon-like coverage from the Naples *Repository*. The heart of my beat, though, was the Naples High football team, coached at the time by a 51-year-old retired Marine and hometown hero whose idea of funny was calling my newspaper the *Maple Suppository*. When we met, Coach Billy Gooch was still agitated after reaming out his 12-year-old son the night before for "screaming like a little girl" when he stubbed his toe against a table leg. "Gonna' bring him a nice yeller sundress tonight," he said, interrupting his own treatise on next season's offensive line, average weight, 202 pounds. "By God," he said, "we're going to open holes big enough for Granny Gooch to wheel through in her 'lectric scooter." Though I would write about Coach Gooch and his Golden Cyclones for nearly two years, our relationship was defined in the first two weeks. Flush with the skills and enthusiasm infused by my J-school professors, I covered the team like the media would later cover

O.J. and *Enron*. I went to each practice and talked with players in the locker room. I interviewed opposing coaches. I was tough on the Cyclones when they lost. Even when they won, I made sure to include a few lines on fumbles, interceptions and missed chances. And when a star receiver drove his pick-up into a pet store one Saturday night up on the Tamiami Trail and was charged with driving under the influence, my story led our Sunday sports section. The store was called *Pete's Pet Palace*. Seven parakeets and a finch perished in the collision. A King snake escaped when his cage was shattered, and a pair of Siamese kittens required treatment from a vet. I found the arresting officer and used his smartass quote about adding *cruelty to animals* to the long list of charges facing this particular Golden Cyclone. One day not long after, Gooch called me in. His voice was even, so I thought he wanted to preview some strategy or trick play he was plotting for the next game, a big one against cross-town rival Lely High. I should have known by the way his secretary pulled her sweater around her shoulders that something was up. Sure enough, the first thing I saw when I entered his office was a stack of my recent stories fanned out on his desk, the parts he found offensive highlighted in Cyclone gold. Gooch sat me down like a kid caught smoking reefer in the boys' room. "The hometown reporter has to be a cheerleader," he said. The office was crammed with statuettes, championship pendants, game balls and autographed photos, all trophies celebrating a local conqueror whose career spanned more than two decades. "We're not the freakin' *Miami Dolphins*, Danny Boy. You can't hold us to that high a standard. We're a goddam high school football team. And a good one at that." Gooch had a knack for making a demand sound like a plea. I was two weeks on the job, a month past graduation. I don't know if I was more scared or offended. I ran a quick scan and located enough testosterone to object. I said everything I'd reported was accurate, and reminded him how much he hated whiners.

"I'm just being objective, Coach, reporting the bad with the good." Gooch was a guy who got softer the angrier he became. Right then he got very soft. "What's objective? You pick what game you're going to cover, right?" I nodded. He rubbed his crew cut front to back like he was talking to the latest in a long line of imbeciles hired by the *Repository*. I noticed for the first time that his cheeks were slightly marked, as if he'd once had acne. Voice barely above a whisper now, he said, "So you come and watch and decide what to write in your little reporter's notebook. Then you go back to your newsroom and pick what notes you're going to use. Some day I'd like to know what gets left in the notebook. You decide how you should lead your story and what you think fits in lower down. You pick which players and coaches to interview, what questions to ask, and which quotes to use. At small papers like the *Suppository*, you even write the headlines and pick what pictures go with the story. Christ, you take the pictures. All that's *subjective*, ain't it?" He was right on each count, except the part about being a cheerleader. "Objective," he said as a Jew might say *Holocaust*. "Objective my ass." I left his office red-faced and overwhelmed by the realization that college had not taught me to be a reporter. I needed more time on the practice court.

Which is not to say I didn't have professors back in school with real reporting backgrounds who could see beyond the classroom, who knew what it was like to cover a 20-car pile-up, or interview the loser of a tight congressional race, or confront the County Commission Chairman on why his brother-in-law got the contract to put in the new sewer line. I did — two terrific teachers in four mediocre years. One was now dead. The other was Dr. Wendy Hearn, my next call after I left Gavin Sussman at the Pentagon cafeteria.

Bella

Chapter 12

My cell rang twice before I could dial Professor Hearn. First on the line was Isabel Moss, who had something new she didn't want to share over the phone. I said I'd meet her at four at the hotel. She started to suggest the restaurant, then said, "Oh, heck, I'm tired, just come to my room: 321." As I fidgeted and pondered a reply (*What if she answered the door only wearing a Redskins jersey? What if there were scented candles burning inside?*) The phone flashed and Ellie's number appeared in the ID box. I told Isabel okay to get off the line quickly and said hello to Ellie, who was calling to report that blackboard graffiti was only one of many crimes committed lately by the young outlaw Robin Patragno, my blessed son and lone heir (so far) to the Patragno name. Miss Lipinski wanted his parents' butts in her first grade mini-chairs at Forest Glen Elementary directly after school. I'd have to push Isabel back until after dinner. Great, now we were going to be alone in a hotel room after dark. No way. I hunted down her number and nearly dropped the cell when it rang yet again. "Dan Patragno," I said.

"Patragno, delightful to hear your voice." Editors and sarcasm are another inevitable part of a reporter's life. "Canton," I said with exuberance phony as a campaign pledge, "I was about to call you."

Though half a dozen bosses in Tampa had enough juice to call me up and order a story, Canton Spivey was chief slave-driver as well as my newsroom advocate and link to front-page play. I needed him enthusiastic when he went to the afternoon budget meeting and pushed to get my Washington stories on A-1, hopefully above the fold. There was also pressure the other way — from management, to ensure that the D.C. reporter kept producing stories worthy of leading the paper. "Know that woman you made me talk to the other day?" Silence, and in the awkward quiet, a reminder of another inevitable fact about editors. They light fuses and then act like Alzheimer's patients when you call in a progress report. "Isabel Moss," I said, trying to jog his memory. "The one whose husband was killed in Afghanistan. She called you to complain I wouldn't talk to her. You told me it might be a good story."

"Yeah, so?"

"So you were right; might be something decent here." Though Canton was not the ideal boss, I observed the same commandment that governed bureau reporters worldwide: *Honor thy editor.*

"Talk to me."

"It's a long story, Canton. Lots of holes. She thinks her soldier husband, the tennis pro from Tampa, Hank Moss, was killed by friendly U.S. fire, not by the Taliban."

"Any proof?"

"That's what I'm working on."

"What about everything else you're supposed to be doing? What's going on in the delegation? What hearings you covering? What's our Congressman Dwoark up to?"

"He might have a part in this story."

Another still moment. I daydreamed about Ellie hiring a private detective to follow me, her conniving husband. The hotel door opens. A camera flashes. *Wait, I cry. Nothing's going on. We're working. The next I hear is from her lawyer. Half the assets. Weekend visits with the kid. No joint custody. Robin and his step-dad.* Canton Spivey's voice brought me back. "You telling me you're dropping everything else to work this?"

"Unless you tell me otherwise." I could sense him weighing everything I'd already laid on the scale. Minor stories missed to the competition — the *St. Pete Times, Miami Herald, Tallahassee Democrat* and *Orlando Sentinel* — balanced against the slim chance of a major national scoop that would provoke public outrage and congressional hearings, to say nothing of terrific newspaper sales and perhaps some nice journalism prize.

"I'll give you a week. Update me every day. One of the copy kids will e-mail you everything we have on the guy. What's the wife like?"

"Determined, quick, quirky, kind of hot."

"Alright, Danny, one week. I'll tell everyone here so no one hassles you with other work. You bring me a story, and for the love of God, be damned careful how you handle a widow who's determined, quick, quirky and kind of hot."

Chapter 13

I had Wendy Hearn for two classes at FSU, Feature Writing and Advanced Reporting. A former *Wall Street Journal* correspondent, she was also assigned to the student paper as faculty advisor. Professor Hearn was an inch taller than me, a model thin blonde generally ranked among the best-looking profs on campus. She seemed aware and slightly embarrassed by her unofficial standing. We never saw her in anything but jeans, faded Tees, and low-cut canvas sneakers with fat silver eyelets. She looked young enough to be one of us and was in fact an entirely different breed. Wendy Hearn knew her shit and saved our aggressive but inexperienced scribes from looking stupid more times than we deserved. She taught us to write with balance, precision and, when the opportunity arose, with flair. She made us keep our opinions on the editorial page and out of the news copy. A strict ethicist, she argued for the student paper to pay its own way when our reviewers covered plays and concerts, and goaded us into adopting a rigid policy when it came to using anonymous sources. Any piece that quoted an unnamed source had to explain why the person wasn't being identified. She gave me a C on my *Advanced Reporting* final because I turned in a piece on homelessness near the state Capitol that was one-sided and larded up with every cliché you'd expect from an outraged college junior exposed to the first elderly woman he'd ever seen living under a freeway. I wrote: *Miss Rebecca resides in an asphalt garden littered with broken glass, trash and aluminum cans. She sleeps on a flattened dishwasher box and eats grass, bugs and whatever she can find in a nearby metal trash can for breakfast. Dinner, at least on good days, looks suspiciously like road-kill.* Professor Hearn began her critique by demanding to know if I'd ever seen Miss Rebecca eat grass or bugs, let alone road-kill. I hadn't. "She could have told you she was aboard the first space shuttle and you'd have used that, too." I begged for a second shot. She said if I swallowed the C, I'd never again make such naïve mistakes. If she gave a second chance, I'd go around thinking good enough was good enough. I hated her all summer, though I admit I glanced with something other than anger when the lissome Dr. Hearn passed and I was lounging on the quad with friends that torpid July. When we clashed again senior year over a story for the student paper on campus security, I thought I might give up journalism and pick something less torturous, like bridge repair. We were in her office and she was scribbling on my copy with a black marker. "Where's the response to these accusations, Daniel? You've only got one side." She was the only one besides my grandmother who regularly called me Daniel. I told her to keep reading, the school's view was lower. She said if she had to burrow that far down, it was too late. "Balance includes presenting both sides fairly. That means this has to come up …" She glanced at a sunflower wall clock. The longer of two stems was inching toward four o'clock. "I have to go. If you want to keep talking about this, come over tonight. I'll make some tea and we'll hash it out." She wrote down her address; it was maybe two miles away. I told her I hated tea. "Me too," she said.

Like all men, I thought I knew a few things. Wendy Hearn let me think what I wanted, though I'm sure she was amused by the colossal gaps in my knowledge and technique. Headline: *Casanova Returned to Minors*. She never made fun or let on, and eventually I improved. My progress pleased both of us, especially me. Her precious lessons lasted four months, until I landed that first job in Naples. I told her I loved her and she even edited that simple sentence. She stroked my cheek and then playfully slapped it. "You don't. You love what we've been doing. Two different things." A light kiss on the lips. "I also loved our time together. It was fun and very precious. Now it's over. It's time you get started. You're going to have a wonderful career because you're smart and you care about things that matter, and you're fair."

"And discreet," I said, grinning like a baboon. She answered, "Yes, Daniel, and discreet. Know that you can always call me about your work."

And so I called. We hadn't spoken since my problems years earlier with *crazy* Coach Gooch. She answered and her husky voice whisked me back to Tharpe Street and the lovers' swing on her backyard porch and the second-floor bed with the Americana quilt and her old-fashioned circle shower with the brass head, all markers of the second education I received in college. "You need at least two independent sources," she said after I relayed the story of Hank and Isabel Moss. "You've got plenty of work ahead. You're going to be tempted to confront people at the Pentagon. That would be a mistake. Don't take it to any military officials until you've got the accidental death part nailed down. And I mean nailed solid." I felt like it was 15 years earlier and she was threatening another C. "What else,

Bella

Wendy?" She told me to find out all I could about Hank Moss because as compelling as his accidental death was the upbringing and character that led him to join up in the first place. "This wasn't an ordinary kid, Daniel. His personal history will add critical depth to your story." I thanked her and she said to call again if I wanted to talk through any parts of the story. "How you doing otherwise?" I said. "Having a good semester? Taken an interest in anyone special at the student paper?" I said. She ignored the bait and repeated Canton Spivey's advice about watching myself around Isabel Moss. "That woman doesn't sound right," she said.

Chapter 14

Wendy, who knew me better than most, was one of the first to say I should have been born earlier and peaked around the time Frank was king. Sure, why not? I love those boxy, chromed-up old gas guzzlers with the ferocious V-8s and bench seats big enough to get into all kinds of trouble. Given a choice, my laptop would be a portable typewriter. I like it when pressing harder makes a difference. And I prefer piano, bass and drums to anything that's pumped up with hi-tech gizmos that turn Charlie Brown into Charlie Parker. I vote for keeping science off the bandstand and in the shuttle program. I remember not minding that TV was black and white, and I loved when pro ballplayers stayed on the same team year after year and you knew their numbers and spot in the line-up. To me, nothing was sexier than women in nylons, and no one before or since has come close to the stars of my adolescence, Sophia, Ingrid, and young Lauren Bacall. Why these things occurred to me that night wasn't clear. Probably because of the earlier encounter with Miss Lipinski, whose rap sheet on Robin forced me to realize we had an official situation in the Patragno home. Our little *Beaver*, it seemed, was a liar and vandal who, in one wild spree, snapped the antenna off the principal's sports car, abused not only schoolyard ants but also a stray cat (something about white paste and masking tape), and whose latest work — chalk on brick this time — declared that anyone in the Cub Scouts is a "punk'd up bitch." Where does he get this stuff? Not from me. I've got nothing against the Scouts and, honestly, couldn't even explain what is meant by "punk'd up bitch." I know it is not a compliment. The fact that it was communicated so nastily by my offspring made me sigh and think how wonderful it would be to return to yesteryear, when the toughest challenges were keeping the diapers and bedtime stories fresh, when Ellie smiled more and when dear Miss Alana Lipinski was still years from her own classroom at Forest Glen Elementary.

I felt like sharing my anguish with someone, and the someone opposite me at the moment was an awful choice, Isabel Moss. I was upset, she was alone and lonely. It added up to trouble, and yet I went anyway, though with one caveat. Rather than meet in her room, I pushed for my office in the Press Building next door to the hotel. It was already past eight and we were alone. There was no difference from her room, I realized, except that the office didn't have a bed, shower, or fruit basket. It was just as private. She sat by my desk, smelling and looking good as I took notes on the computer. It felt like a cheesy cop show. *Appreciate you coming in, ma'm. Can you remember anything else at all that might help us? I could get the sketch artist ...* Her news was that Senator Newlin had quietly opened an investigation into the death of Sgt. Hank Moss. I thought fleetingly that Newlin's move could be used as a vehicle to get the story into the paper. Such a story would ruin the investigation, though, because it would alert the generals and anyone else involved in the alleged cover-up. That would dry up any potential sources who might be willing to talk about what really happened.

"You're sure Newlin's guy won't leak it to any other reporters?"

"Newlin told him no leaks. He was very firm. How about your friend at the Pentagon?"

"He agreed to look around. He's a little strange. Obsessed with street cleaners and outdoor musicians. His elbows don't bend when he walks. I'm not counting on much."

So that was that. We could have exchanged this meager information on the phone. Why did she insist we meet? And, was the meeting now over? I thought, in the sudden quiet, of the warnings from Wendy and Canton. I leaned back and rocked forward, making my old chair creak. It was time to speak frankly.

"I'm sorry I asked you to come into town," she said before I could begin. "I could have told you on the phone."

And I found myself saying, "No, it's okay. Things were kind of rough at home today. I needed to get out."

"Really?"

I thought, not for the first time, that it was funny how bad news energizes some people. They say misery loves company, but company also doesn't mind a little misery. Makes one's problems seem a little less daunting. Isabel said, "I thought you had the storybook marriage. Wife, son, home in the suburbs, big-time reporter with your own column every Sunday. What's it like being married a long time, Danny? We didn't get three years in before Hank died. I saw us playing shuffleboard in Boca one day. Sorry, that's so corny." She wet her lips and my pulse spiked a little. I reminded myself she was a young widow talking about her dead husband. *Get a grip.* She didn't notice. She said, "All these weeks and I still keep his shirt in my bed. It smells like him. I wake up, my eyes are bloodshot like I haven't slept at all."

I thought about being married, how problems bubble up you never expect that sweet day you shove the cake in each other's kisser. The crappy wedding band butchers your favorite love song, uncles you barely remember get sloppy drunk and press pastel envelopes to your chest, and none of it seems quite real because all you can think of is that after all those years of fruitless, unsatisfying dating and one-night stands and maybe a real girlfriend or two along the way, you've found someone to love and to bear your children, to help mow down whatever devils are waiting around the bend. Your eyes mist with greeting card emotion and of course it's hard to see it may not always be this way. Now, if one of you dies in the early years, there's no chance for fights, affairs, long-term illness or seedy lawyers. You delude yourself, thinking it *was* perfect. Ever wonder what JFK might look like if he hadn't been gunned down so young? Take a look at how Ted wound up. An early death means never learning the band kicked off a life-long marathon when it botched the opening love song. Absent a freak tragedy, the first hard turn of the race comes and you're still glad to lick frosting off your darling's nose. You're happy and hungry for each other, even though you're running faster and the temperature's rising. Then suddenly — sometimes it's gradually — the markers vanish and you're in the woods. One gets a little ahead and takes a fork the other never sees. Maybe there's a cute little wood nymph off to the side. Maybe you do, maybe you don't. Maybe you do and get caught and learn your lesson. Or not. The trees get thicker, the trail, wilder. Sometimes you catch up to each other at a clearing. Some couples share a grown-up martini and press on; some argue about bills, religion, getting fat, braces for the kid's crooked teeth (inherited from *her* side), mom's visits, and whether the lazy-ass garbage man comes Thursday or Friday, and who the hell you call — the city or the county or maybe it's the contractor — when the trash guy spills egg shells and gristle on the driveway and it smells and the ants and squirrels and raccoons come and no one wants to clean it up. You pound down dinner and grocery store dessert and demand to no one in particular, *Worthless son-of-a-bitch garbage man! Where's the county? What the hell do we pay taxes for?* And she looks at you hard and says with blazing fury, *For Christ's sake, wipe the damned frosting off your face!*

Either way, the race resumes and on you go. It's not even clear what you're running for — 3,000 square feet of house, 2.5 children, a promotion that means seven grand more a year and six more headaches a month. You want your boy to learn a two-wheeler and watch before he crosses and one day catch a free ride to Yale. You never think he might wind up spitting curses at his first-grade teacher.

Isabel's image of her marriage would remain as flawless as the handsome young president slain in his prime. Hank got himself killed before anything could go wrong, years before one hair on his head would go gray. There was still romance and excitement in his climb up the pro ladder and in Isabel's struggles when he was on the road. Still, I remembered the way she asked about a couple being together a long time, as an eight-year-old might ask of *Pegasus*.

"Some things are good and some are awful," I said.

"How did you meet your wife?"

"*I* ask the questions, lady. How'd you meet Hank?"

Her eyebrows lifted a little. She rose and walked toward the couch in the outer office. I followed the sway of her dark gray skirt. Except for the sandals, she looked ready to close a deal, straight black hair perched softly on a buttoned-down, pink silk shirt. When she spoke, I thought she might be crying. I nearly asked her, a la *Old Blue Eyes* in his charming *Rat Pack* days, to tell me where it hurts, baby. I joined her on the couch and saw she wasn't upset at all. Rather, she was almost bemused, as if telling an amiable story about someone else. What a saucy girl.

Bella

Chapter 15

I drove back to Silver Spring thinking about Hank. Photos told me what he looked like — ropey muscle jutted from the Florida-ripened tan, yet the placid green eyes that caught Isabel and his slightly furrowed brow suggested deep thinker. Few deep thinkers make good tennis players — success depends too much on raw intuition — yet there were plenty of stats affirming his athletic prowess. Now I also knew he was a guy who could be moved — at least once in his short life — to put himself between a pretty girl and a guy trying to hustle her out of a club. I chuckled at Isabel's account as I headed up 16th Street toward Silver Spring.

"Seems like so long ago ... I was out with this other guy. Lawyer. Cute. Blue-striped shirt, white collar and cuffs, fancy chess board cuff links. He was laying his smooth lawyer BS on me and I was trying to concentrate and off in the corner this other guy is watching. Hank. Each time our eyes hooked, he smiled and I smiled back. I think I was on my third Champagne Fizz. The lawyer was too wrapped up in his stories to notice. Finally Hank over in the corner rolls his eyes at the guy and I start laughing. The lawyer thinks I'm laughing at him and gets pissed. You'd think with all the lawyer jokes, they wouldn't be so sensitive. He grabs my arm. Remember, this is our first date. Before I could say anything, Hank has his hand on the lawyer's arm. The lawyer was cute. Hank was cute *and* extra large. *Johnnie Cochran* lets me loose right away and backs out, looking at Hank like he just broke out of the crazy jail. So now Hank and I are sitting there and it's a little awkward. He apologizes and says he never goes to bars or gets in fights; he just reacted when the guy grabbed me. He had these eyes ... jade-colored, intense, passionate — I couldn't help it. I told him thank you so much and kissed him on the cheek. He said I was welcome and kissed me back much better."

Eight months later, she said, they married.

It was after 10 when I pulled in the driveway. The house was dark except for a fluorescent counter light in the kitchen. Ellie and I hadn't spoken much after the meeting. I think we were both jarred by Miss Lipinski's list of grievances, and how bad we must have looked to the young teacher. Funny how you think you control your kids. You set bedtimes, rules for the TV and computer, how much candy and soda they can put into themselves ... The truth is you're only in charge until the first play group away from home. That's the start of outside influences diluting your message, to borrow some political speak. Your kids do well, you're golden; they screw up, people mutter about *what's going on in that house*. I had new ideas on how to rein in the little terror and figured it was a good time to sound out Ellie. I walked in and was surprised to find Lucy the sitter working on her math homework at the breakfast table. I enjoyed Lucy because she didn't toss five "likes" into each sentence, and because she knew — thanks to two younger brothers of her own — precisely how to handle Robin. She lived four houses down, another bonus, since there was no drive home. "Mr. P," she said, pencil poised, eyes riveted on her calculator. "Mrs. P had to go somewhere. Said she'd be back around 11. Since you're home, I guess I'll take off. You any good at calculus?"

"The word gives me a headache, Lucy." I dropped my briefcase on the sofa. "Robin asleep?" She said he watched TV and went up around 10. "How'd he seem tonight?"

"Fine and dandy. I heard about the trouble at school. I wouldn't worry. He's just acting out a little."

Great, now I was getting parenting advice from a 16-year-old. Which isn't to say I disagreed. Between me working late and Ellie hustling around day and night to work the lard off her lazy-ass clients (*didn't they ever hear of jogging and push-ups?*), Robin was probably getting and feeling short-changed. My own parents ran a small cleaner's in Florida when I was growing up. Fourteen-hour days common, and I remember getting into a few scrapes myself.

I folded a ten that Lucy accepted with a little curtsey and then watched from the porch until she reached her front door and shot me a thumbs-up. Five minutes later, Ellie walked in, gym bag slung over a shoulder. She walked into the kitchen and stood so still, I knew something was up. The bag slipped off her shoulder and dropped to the floor. I figured it was about Robin. I hugged her and she burst into tears. Ellie looked like a little girl when she cried or came up from underwater, eyes puffy, hair matted back off her face. I told her we were all going to be fine, absurdly repeating Lucy the sitter's line about pre-teen rebellion. She pushed back. "It's not that. It is — I *am* worried about him, but … " I suddenly felt sure she was going to tell me she had cancer. My mother died of cancer, as did old Uncle Robin, Robin's namesake. Ellie looked fine. I could see all the working out in her arms and legs, had felt the strength in her triceps when she pushed away. Tears aside, she looked young as a Maryland coed. "I … I've …" My mind raced as she stammered. Maybe she *did* have cancer. A tiny scowling tumor, buried deep below her scalp or in a corner of her breast. The doctor must have discovered it during a routine exam. Six months and she'd be gone. I'd be alone with Robin, struggling and failing to do the job of both parents. Cooking, cleaning, helping with homework, trying to work full time. I started to sweat and opened my shirt. This was my punishment for flirting with Isabel Moss. Each year on the day she died we would go to the cemetery and pay our respects, Robin hugging the pathetic little gravestone and me placing fresh-cut marigolds on the crusty earth. Until then, there would be chemo and vomiting and a wig to hide the baldness. "Tell me," I insisted. "It can't be that bad. Is it a tumor?"

She looked at me cock-eyed through her tears and gathered herself. "A tumor? No, Danny, I'm not sick. I've been, I've … "

"What, for Christ's sake? *Finish*."

She whispered it. "I've been seeing someone."

I repeated the words to myself. It didn't make sense. At first I thought she meant she signed up a new client. I thought, she doesn't have cancer, but the way she said this new, undecipherable thing seemed like it was worse, diabetes and heart disease rolled into one, horrid death sentence. "It's over now. I saw him tonight and ended it." I fell back into a chair in the family room and thought, how odd to discuss a spouse's lover in your own family room. "I think … " She hugged herself hard enough to leave red finger stripes on her bare arms. "Robin's problems … they're my fault. I haven't been here for him. That's going to change. I swear."

I didn't know what to say. I felt thrown from the roof, breathless, crushed, wide-eyed. Another guy? We'd been together since forever. She'd never given me any reason … The quiet stretched. A floorboard creaked, the ghost, perhaps, of cheaters past. I wiped my forehead and my hand came away wet. She said, "If you want me to go for awhile, I'll leave. I understand. I can stay at a motel or a friend's."

A friend's. Sure, great. "No," I said, somehow reasoning through the fog that I'd rather she be home than possibly back with her boyfriend. *Her boyfriend! The guy who's been doing my wife.* My reporter's mind produced dozens of questions, yet I couldn't summon the words. I was hurt, angry, embarrassed. My cozy cave was crumbling; I could run out or be buried alive. "I'll go. I'll stay at Clay's."

"I don't want you to go, Danny."

My life was about words. Usually I chose with great care. Words have such power. They can hurt and wound, inform and enlighten, engross and amuse. The words I used to answer were words I never thought I'd say to Ellie Patragno. They surprised me as I heard them come from my mouth. "I don't think I care what you want anymore."

I felt her eyes on my back as I left without as much as a toothbrush.

Chapter 16

I met Clay Ohrbach six years earlier in a pick-up basketball game, quickly learning he was a guy whose mind designed brilliant moves that his body would not and could not execute, not ever, not if Michael Jordan himself moved in and drilled him until the rubber wore off his sneakers. Sir Mike's knowledge of *Aero-Astro*, on the other hand, probably did not exceed how long he could hang in the air on a fadeaway jumper. We called Clay *Double A* for three reasons: he was expert in aeronautics and astronautics, his batteries never wore out, and because it was great fun to pin a rapper nickname on the whitest of white men. Brainiac Clay couldn't slam dunk; he could barely jump high enough to catch a finger in the bottom of the net. His touch was considered lethal. That didn't mean a high shooting percentage. It meant when he took a shot and missed, the rebound clanked off the rim or backboard so hard, it could break someone's pinky. Clay wore silly spaceman goggles, flesh-colored knee braces, and his *Freedom's Sentinel in Space* T-shirt, with a radiating star shining high above the blue and green globe. What the guys came to learn was that Clay knew everything about the game — plays, zones, angles, stats — except what counted most — how to get the damned ball into the basket. Seeing the prize and not being able to touch it might

Bella

frustrate some, but Clay, 6-3 and near skinny enough to squeeze through prison bars, was good-natured about his coordination issues. He didn't call cheap fouls and was a stickler about giving up the ball if he judged himself guilty of some infraction. He was also a relentless and effective defender, possibly because of his scientific approach to the game, and was loved by the shooters, myself included, because he was always quick to pass. He understood picks and percentages and was never the last chosen when we made teams. You almost expected to see him show up for hoops with matching pens in a plastic pocket protector. Yet *Double A* was usually on the winning side. We played every Sunday morning from nine to eleven at Jonathan Matty Middle School in Bethesda.

Clay let me in and, after seeing my distraught face, nearly bear-hugged me into a waist high Asian vase. "It'll work out, buddy. I set you up in the room next to the kids." We slugged back a few shots of a tangy vodka that he pulled from the kitchen freezer. Funny that though we'd sweated together for two hours each Sunday for half a dozen years, I didn't know much about what he did off the court. His was one of those worlds that no one cares about except those in the field, like, say, zoologists who can't get enough of the desert-dwelling, banner-tailed kangaroo rat. I twirled a wooden napkin ring around two fingers while he peppered me with small talk about the *Maryland Terps* and *Washington Wizards*. I had no heart for it. After the third shot, I thanked him again and slipped off to my room. That was when the questions started popping. Who was the guy screwing my wife? Where did they meet? Was he a client? She was a private trainer. Sordid one-liners came to me about building new muscle, working out on the apparatus, *feeling the burn* ... How long was it going on? What was she going to tell Robin about me not being home?

Did they do it at the *house*? And why, more than anything, was I obsessed with talking to Isabel Moss? It made no sense. I got my cell and sat on the edge of Clay's guest bed. The mattress barely gave. She answered on the second ring.

"Sorry," I said, "I know it's late."

"I'm up. I don't sleep so much most nights."

We spoke over an hour, until nearly 1 a.m., about everything but Ellie and Hank. It helped, getting involved in Isabel's story, imagining her as a little girl. She told me she grew up among the newly rich in north Tampa, the only child of a Brazilian-born and American naturalized architect named Martin Urso who was gone a lot on projects in South America. She took ballet and classical piano, got good grades, and was cautious — thanks no doubt to lessons inadvertently passed along by her dallying father — about the boys who came around. She said her mother died young, and her father married twice more before Isabel was 16. She stayed Isabel Urso until the day she married Hank and became Isabel Moss. Both stepmothers were stunning; neither was maternal. "Before my prom, Stepmom number two looked me up and down and said I'd get noticed, though not by any modeling agencies." I was lying on the bed, still coming to grips with the night's events, my head cushioned by two of Clay's guest room pillows. "Harsh," I said. Isabel said no, "She was honest. I liked that about her. It was the *only* thing I liked. Well, she also taught me how to dress, as she put it, to accent my assets." I yawned and Isabel said she was getting tired too. "Come over," she said, surprising me. "There's a few mini-bottles of tequila. We can be tired and awake together."

New strength surged. I glanced at the dresser clock and dismissed the cautionary red numerals that read 1:13 a.m. I wanted to go. My life was unraveling and, unaccountably, I yearned to be with this woman I barely knew. Between my ears, I heard, *Go for it*. And the counter: *What?*

Bella

You'd swap one woman for another the way we traded the station wagon for the minivan? Not to mention she's an important source for an on-going story. Where'd she get the power to make you dump everything you believe in so easily? And how would you explain it to Robin? Mom and dad had a fight, buddy, so I spent the night with another woman. You understand, right son? I flashed suddenly on how Isabel Moss tried to manipulate our first meeting, though that yellow flag swiftly fell to the memory of her flesh against mine at breakfast. Then there was Ellie's cheating. I was considering it; she'd already committed the ancient sin. Did I want Isabel or did I want revenge? I looked in the mirror expecting to see smoke hissing from my ears. Actually the debate wasn't much of a contest. What I wanted, needed, was to fill my hands with Isabel Moss.

"I'd like to come ..."

"So come."

I left Clay a note.

W hen we were together, locked like scissors, nicely buzzed on mini-bar tequila, she reached down and closed her small fingers around me, controlling pace and penetration. Half in, half out, I pressed harder, trying to mash her fingers so she'd let go. She dug a warning nail into my flesh. I shot a hand between us and she grabbed it, pulling me up and sucking two fingers into her mouth. Her tongue, wet and fast, paralyzed like a weapon. She asked me if it was nice, and I said yes, unbelievable, and she said yes, yes it was, and then she came, moaning, quivering, her controlling hand still working frantically between us. I struggled a moment more, then wrenched her fingers loose and plunged wildly to a place so good, I knew then that whatever the risk, I would do anything to return.

My breath was still ragged when she flicked on a lamp and drew a blanket around her shoulders. In the low light, without make-up or jewelry and even without the clothes that accented her assets, she was still beautiful. I ran a finger lightly from neck to hip, causing the blanket to fall away. Her flesh was smooth and moist; I enjoyed the touching, smiled to myself at the goose bumps that rose under my finger. I was angry at the nasty step-mother, who, by any objective measure, had been dead wrong. I felt a rush of empathy; nothing I'd ever done as a kid was good enough for my old man. "Come lay back down, Isabel." She stayed where she was. I thought somehow that it might all work out, that Ellie and I would reach an amicable settlement and I would not spend one day alone. *No one would.* Ellie had already proven *she* could find someone new. Once Isabel and I broke the story of how American GIs accidentally killed Hank Moss, we'd become famous. I saw a movie. A screenplay. I'd never written a screenplay; how hard could it be? What was dialogue but quotes? I'd been quoting different characters for 15 years — politicians, athletes, businessmen, fans, voters, you name it. I knew voices and even a little about dialect. Any of the current pretty boy actors able to handle a racket could play Hank. Danny and Isabel would be a power couple in Washington *and* Hollywood. *What a team! And the sex!* Sure, it would be okay. Couples broke up all the time. Ellie and Robin could stay in the house. He would learn to live with divorced parents; and I could be a decent father for Isabel's kid, Katie. One day she might even think of me in that way, as a dad. *Katherine Moss-Patragno.* It had a ring; it was possible. There might even be a time when we all could get together. Katie and Robbie could be like brother and sister. We could have sleepovers and pizza parties. These days there were a lot of blended ...

"— You need to go," Isabel said, cold as a cop ordering a bum off the corner. I tried to stroke her neck and pull her back to me. She hurried off, sweeping up two little tequila bottles from the night table as she repeated, "Please go." I longed to tell her we hadn't done anything wrong, well maybe a little, but that it was beautiful and sensuous and by God, we should do it again, right then, right there. I never got the chance. She dropped the bottles in the trash and disappeared into the bathroom. It was the last I saw of her, and she did not answer when I pulled on my clothes, called out good night and slipped out of Room 321 and onto dark, lifeless F Street at 3:40 a.m. For some reason, I remembered Gavin Sussman would be getting up in a few hours for another day at the Pentagon. The slick-haired hose guys were probably getting ready to accidentally wet him down.

Chapter 17

By eight the next morning, I was at my desk, poring through more than 30 stories about Hank Moss emailed by the copy kids in Tampa. My stomach was so acidy, my eyes burned. I hadn't shaved, had barely been able to throw on yesterday's rumpled shirt and pants and drag myself to the office. My tie was missing, a good thing, as wrapping it around my neck would have made me gag up the cheese bagel I snatched bolting out of Clay's. I could not think about Robin, Ellie or even Isabel. Okay, not true. As I read about Hank "Screech" Moss and stared at his pictures, some in training at Fort Benning, some blasting tennis balls on courts around the world, all I *could* think of was the woman he'd rescued from the craven D.C. lawyer and later married. I imagined him alone with Isabel, wondered if she'd acted as lewdly with Hank as me. I guessed no and, though disgusted with myself, reveled in every detail I could remember from the night before. She must have tossed me out because she was confused, or maybe feeling disloyal to Hank, or guilty about banging a married guy. No matter. I would talk her through any misgivings, if only she'd call. I put my head on the desk, smelled lemon and breathed dust. My behavior had been far worse than Isabel's. My decisions were flawed, my actions, immoral and unethical. No punishment would be too severe.

Bella

I felt like crap and deserved it. I could not bear to think what Wendy Hearn would say, or Robin, when the kids at school began asking why his parents lived apart. Yet when Linette the English office receptionist brought me coffee and some mail, I couldn't stand without revealing that, while sorry I may have been, the thoughts careening around my pounding head that morning were not remotely related to newspaper work. Did I regret it? Sure. Would I have regretted it more if I'd stayed all night at Clay's? Get serious.

So I stayed seated, the tenting evidence hidden from Linette's unsuspecting gray eyes. By 10, I couldn't stand it and phoned the hotel. I had ideas about lunch that didn't involve food. "I'm sorry, Mrs. Moss has checked out. Yes, I'm sure. Thank you, sir. I *did* check twice." I called her cell and got the recording. After the beep, I drawled, "If the headache came first, I'd never drink tequila. Call me. I'm at the office all morning." Morning passed. I read more about Hank. Together, the stories added up to a smart kid who worked hard and was unfazed by success. His mother told one reporter that what separated Hank from so many players was that he could laugh when he played poorly. "He'd step into traffic on Bayshore Boulevard before he'd throw his racket," she said. "He was like that about everything. Hank and his sister, two great kids, all any parents could ask for, both of them gone." I would have to talk with her about why he enlisted. And delicately ask for a comment if the story panned out. *What do you think of the fact that American troops accidentally killed your son, m'am?* I'd learned not to hate asking such things. Early in my career, once I'd left Naples and crazy Coach Gooch behind, I thought obvious questions would enrage people. *Oh, I'm pleased he was blown up by a friend instead of a stranger, asshole.* Most of the time that didn't happen. Most of the time, they weren't offended; they used the opening to get things off their chest. Hank's mother might say, *He's dead. What does it matter who killed him?* Or she could say, *They killed him; then they covered it up. I didn't think that could happen in this country."* If I handled it right, she'd probably say plenty.

Lunch went by. My stomach was still a mess and I didn't eat. Canton Spivey called for a progress report. I briefed him on everything but how close I'd gotten to my foremost source. "You okay, Patragno? Sounds like all your tires are flat." Christ. I told him my tires were fine. "Then get a hump on. They're already breathing down my neck … I need a story." Editors ought to get the hell out of the newsroom once a year and start writing again. After newsmen get behind a desk, they turn into businessmen. They dwell on production and *outcomes.* They take a bunch of bullshit ideas and call it vision. Readers become *stakeholders.* Good work turns into *best practices.* A smack is what they need, one good smack and a week back on the night cop beat. "Me, too, Canton," I said. "I need a story too. I'm working on it."

I laid the clips aside and thought about my next move with Ellie. I could sneak home when she wasn't there and get more clothes or stop by around dinner. Did I need to confess? *Now we're even, dear. What's next?* I didn't want that; more hurt would prolong the anguish. When had it become anguish? All those years … the vows … our son … his friends … old Uncle Robin and all the relatives … the holidays … the neighbors … all the things that brought us closer and made us a family. I picked up the 5x7 on my desk. Robin came into the world loud and demanding as a rock star. Then we took him home and his booming cry shrank to a whimper. The doctor suspected meningitis. My son was recalled like a life jacket that wouldn't inflate. That night, Ellie slept with Robin in the hospital room. She tried to feed him and he wouldn't nurse. They loaded him with antibiotics. I paced at home until I couldn't stand it and raced to Suburban General. They wouldn't let me near my new son. I waited

12 hours in the lounge. I read newspapers and watched game shows. I talked to strangers and prayed, wondering if God ever answered desperate men who only called on the hotline. *Don't let him have meningitis. Please. Make him better. He hasn't even started yet.* I tried making promises that He would like and that I knew would be impossible to keep. In the end, it was a routine virus. Baby Robin was fine in 48 hours. That first Christmas was special. I bought him a tricycle with black and gold streamers that he wouldn't be able to ride for years. Ellie laughed and we held hands by the fire, Frank's version of the holiday songs swinging in the background. What would the holidays be like now? Or birthdays, Little League games, band concerts and graduations? Isabel, I knew, would have given any-thing to have Hank for half the time Ellie and I'd been together. What a slug I was for not feeling worse. I fit my forehead into my hand, as if the answer might be divined by massaging my own temples. The morning sickness had worn off. I felt strong, primitive, alive with the caveman high that follows a fresh conquest. I knew the euphoria was sex-induced and temporary, that all the questions and self-doubt would soon return to kick my ass. *Oh yeah, you're going to pay for this one, Danny boy. Guilt. Sleepless nights. Lies and deception. It's all coming.* I also felt sure that my wreck of a marriage was over; we'd both visited the lot and tested new models. The uncertainty of what lay ahead was almost exciting. Maybe everyone could wind up happy. Linette stuck her head in around five. "Need anything else, Danny?" Before I could answer, the phone rang. I shook my head at Linette and answered.

"Know who this is?" All I knew is that it was a man and not Isabel. And who the hell starts a conversation that way? The voice was familiar. I rubbed my burning eyes. It was no time for people pestering me with stupid story ideas. I started to say so and he interrupted. "It's Gavin, dip-shit." I grabbed a pen and zig-zagged some lines on a legal pad to get the ink flowing. He wanted to talk in person. "This thing's red hot. Meet me. Lafayette Park. Seven. H Street end, by the U.S. Chamber."

Bella

Chapter 18

I knew the spot. The official name is the *U.S. Chamber of Commerce of the United States of America*. Tourists probably mistake it for the Treasury Department. Treasury's *Bureau of Engraving and Printing*, over on 14th between C and D, is where the feds make paper money. The Chamber does the same thing. That is, it helps 3 million member businesses make reams of paper money. Its promise to America is *to advance human progress through an economic, political and social system based on individual freedom, incentive, opportunity, and responsibility*. Fine. When you put the cat out each night, it's still about making money. True, the Chamber doesn't get to print the stuff, though, from the street, it looks like it might. Three-story Corinthian columns circle the massive exterior, solid and steadfast as the American Heartland, which is where they trekked back in the Twenties to gather the requisite Indiana limestone. The building hogs a chunk of historic real estate across the street from Lafayette Park, in plain view of the White House, on land once owned by Daniel Webster, the lawyer, politician and one-time secretary of state, who, by the way, was a farmer's son born in New Hampshire. Webster sold it in 1849 to Washingtonian W.W. Corcoran, a name known even to popsicle-licking artists who work in *Crayolas* and construction paper. The Chamber bought the land in 1922 and opened shop in 1925, fashioning itself as the place "where America gets down to business." Fitting, I thought, as I waited to get down to business with Gavin Sussman.

At 7:08, he still wasn't there. I scanned the park and saw the usual. Kids trying to coax squirrels close enough to get a dose of rabies. Grinning vacationers snapping away at Andrew Jackson atop his horse, doffing his hat, four Spanish cannons aligned around the base of the park's signature statue. It was a breezy, tolerable night, a brief vacation from the sweaty Washington summer. I wondered if Bush ever heard of Hank Moss, the budding pro athlete who gave his career and life for his country. Or if he or Laura looked out a window now and then to see what was going on across the street. Tonight they would have seen it all: their neighbors were protestors, bums, artists, businessmen, chess players, lovers and one guy in a black suit with a 1950's crew cut. He was cradling a *Washington Times* and kept glancing my way. I was beginning to get self-conscious when someone tapped my shoulder. "Walk with me."

I got up and fell in beside Gavin Sussman on the neatly laid red brick sidewalk. "Why all the drama?" He peered ahead and kept walking down H Street, away from the Chamber, at a fast clip. His pants were too short. I could see the tops of his navy blue socks drooping like dying flowers and a nest of prickly black hairs matted against his white skin. Middle of the summer and the guy needed a tanning booth. It was still light, but clouds had darkened a swath of southern sky that was lit suddenly by a flash of lightning out toward the Smithsonian. When we hit Madison, he stopped and looked in toward the park. "Did you know all of this was once part of the White House grounds?" I didn't, and couldn't have cared less. "They sold slaves here, and once used the park for a cemetery," he said, his eyes drawn to a few kids messing with the squirrels. "For Christ's sake, Gavin. What do you have?"

He leaned against a tree and looked at me over his shoulder. "My name never gets tied to this in any way."

"The newspaper and the public aren't too crazy about reporters using unnamed sources these days, Gavin."

"That's it — I'm outta' here." He started to move off. I stepped in front of him. "Okay, okay, I had to try."

"No fucking around with this, Danny. Nothing, *nothing* that ties me to the story." I agreed. He thrust a finger in my chest. "*Say it.*" I said it. He took the finger away and ran it along the craggy tree bark. "Bet people have traded secrets around this tree for two hundred years."

"Everyone says shit like that. Trees get sick and die too. There are diseases and insects that attack the roots and the bark. There's rot and blight and cankers. It's not all lovers carving — "

" — She's right, Danny. They killed him. Another American unit. One unit coming north, the other going south. Both looking for the enemy. One guy heard something, got jumpy, and threw a grenade. A Southern kid; I couldn't get the name. That was it. Moss went up in a hundred pieces. An accident. Took maybe five seconds." He looked over my shoulder, then left and right. I thought of the man in the black suit. We should have picked a more private place.

"Okay, where's the paper?"

"What paper?"

"The report. The document. The proof."

"No such thing, least not that I've been able to find."

I wanted to slap him. "You know how it works, Sussman. No paper, no story. What am I supposed to do, quote an anonymous source quoting an unnamed official?" Another streak of lightning and a loud crack. No drops yet, but the air now felt thick and wet. "Who's your source?"

"Can't tell you. Someone who works for someone who knows."

"Can you be more specific?" He lit a cigarette and looked at me like I'd requested a kidney. "No, Danny, I can't be any more fucking specific." I'd already learned it was a good play to let Gavin Sussman stew in long silences. The quiet pricked his conscience. He said, "I know it isn't enough to write a story. I was a reporter too." I waited and let him think about what he'd just said. He couldn't stand the quiet. He popped a mint and bit it so hard, I heard the crunch. "Look, I confirmed your theory. What do you want from me? Those fuckers might be watching us *right now*." I remembered Robin in the yard, drawing curse words in the dirt with his toe, and said *nada*. "I'm not breaking into offices looking for a report that maybe doesn't even exist." He sighed and grimaced at a scruffy protester with a poster declaring America an international terrorist. "We go too far with the freedom of expression thing." He kicked a fat acorn into the street. It ricocheted off a curb and nearly shot down the sewer. Gavin wagged his head. "Close but no cigar, story of my life. I hear more, I'll let you know. That's it. And quit lookin' at me. This isn't my crime to solve. I work for the government now."

"I thought that meant you worked for the people."

"The *people*," he shot back, "happen to hate the media. The *people* happen to trust auto mechanics and nursing home operators more than they trust reporters. Don't you know anyone else on the inside besides me?"

Twenty yards off, a little boy screamed and started pulling at his hand. No surprise. Scratched by a squirrel because he got too close. We watched as his mother tried to tend to the hand. The boy, wailing now and afraid to be touched, ran around a concrete bench. She gave chase. He was too quick and wiry. She put her hands on her hips and waited until he stopped crying and trudged into her arms. "Bad squirrel," she yelled at the rodent as she kissed the boy's fingertip. Another flash of lightning and I tightened in anticipation of the crack that came moments later. Gavin, unmoved by the gathering storm, snickered, "Little fucker got what he deserved." I looked at the boy and thought, scratched because he got *too close*. Was it a hint? I thought, my own boy Robin in trouble for roasting insects ... for using a magnifying glass to bring the sun's power closer to Earth. I wondered ... Clay ... Satellites ... His goofy government T-shirt: *Freedom's Sentinel in Space*. Was it possible some satellite gathering intelligence had accidentally captured the evidence I needed?

"Thanks, Gavin. Call me if you get anything else." Torrents of rain began to fall as I ran to the car.

Chapter 19

I eased into the outbound traffic on 16th Street. Until 24 hours ago, I lived like I drove, 12 notches over the speed limit, eager to stay ahead of the pack, disciplined enough to resist reckless impulses. The mistake a lot of people make is thinking that speed alone is the answer. It isn't. Reckless speed is no shortcut. Getting someplace faster requires staying a step ahead, and that's more about strategy than speed. Football coaches talk about controlled aggression; politicians, strategic thinking; and piano instructors teach reading a few bars ahead of the notes actually being played. I didn't tailgate or run yellows. I signaled on lane changes, never rolled through stop signs and usually waved people into my lane. I liked a stick shift for the same reason as everyone else: the illusion of control. No car's going to tell *me* when to change gears. So careful, so pragmatic, and yet still I'd been blindsided. *Danny makes plans and God sends Isabel.* I had no more illusions. I was now naked in the far left, needle in the red, chassis trembling, unable to slow down, begging to be pulled over. I glanced at the mirror and sure enough, a white D.C. cruiser was behind me, lights blinking. Christ, it was supposed to be a metaphor. "Know why I stopped you?" the cop said after we'd pulled alongside a curb reserved for Metrobus. Thick drops were still falling. I shut my wipers and watched the windshield quickly flood before turning to the cop. He was a big kid with a face that had barely sprouted whiskers. I knew a half dozen reasons why he was right to stop me and kept them all to myself. Soggy commuters crammed into the bus shelter seemed happy for a diversion. "He was flyin' through here, officer," said an elderly woman wearing a plastic lawn bag for a raincoat. "He's been drinkin'. Make him walk the line." The cop gave her a stare and said to me, "Right brake light's out. This here's your warning." He made a note in his leather pad. I told him I'd drive straight to a gas station. Another lie.

I hit a long red light and checked voice mail. I called the office and listened for messages there as well. Nothing. I passed the tennis stadium at 16th and Kennedy, all lit up like the World Series. Anyone could use the courts all year long except for two weeks each summer reserved for a pro tournament. I'd checked and Hank had never played the D.C. tourney. Why they had the lights on in a driving rainstorm was beyond me. *How could she not call after that great night? How cold is that?* I wondered if something happened to her. Somehow I hoped we'd be spending another night together, the whole night this time. I looked over and saw another cop car. Woman cop driving, plain-clothes cop beside her. The guy pointed angrily at the curb and I pulled over. He approached and flashed a badge. I looked up and sank low in the seat. I knew him. The suit, the crew cut. *The businessman from the park.* Chills and a taste of bile. I fought an urge to slam the car into first and tear away. I stepped on the clutch — an experiment just in case — and let it back out. He tapped with an expression that said he was annoyed that I would make him tap. He was older than the kiddie cop who stopped me 10 minutes earlier. The rain, lighter now, dripped from his short, gray-flecked hair. He motioned for me to open up. "I know about the brake light," I said weakly. "Another officer just … " He held up a hand. "You really should learn when to be quiet. It's a good quality not many of you reporters seem to possess. May I see your license and registration, Mr. Patragno?"

He didn't say a word about us both being at Layette Park. Or how he knew me. He said he was writing me up for talking on the cell while I was driving. No warning. A hundred bucks. "I wasn't talking on the phone, you know; I was just checking messages. And I was stopped at the light. I wasn't driving." He smiled and walked back to his car. When he returned, he leaned on the door with both hands and said, "You look like the kind of guy who loves his country. Am I right? You *do* love your country?" His hands were rough, with large bony knuckles that pushed up and made the skin look white. His fingers twitched as if anxious for violence. Our eyes locked. I forced myself to think of Hank Moss ordering his troops to stay put while he checked for danger, and Isabel crouched before the Jesus statue. My fear ebbed; who was this fuck to be giving me lectures on patriotism? "Yes, sir, I sure do." I kept my eyes on his as I accepted the ticket and mashed it into a yellow ball. So much for resisting reckless impulses. He wagged his head and smiled again. "Guess I'll have a look at that brake light now."

After they drove off, I looked at the cop's name on my two tickets. *Reese Wehrman.* It wasn't until the following morning that I would call and learn they were phonies, props, and that the D.C. Police Department did not have an officer named Reese Wehrman. I told a polite desk sergeant that I'd been stopped and given two tickets by an Officer Reese Wehrman. "Did he ask you for money?" I told her no. "Did you get the other officer's ID number, or the number of the police car?" No and no. "Did he ask you to get out of your vehicle?" Nope. "May I ask your age, sir, or how long you've had your license?" Those were too embarrassing to answer. In the silence, I heard her wondering what kind of dickwad she was talking to, and what he did for a living, that he could be stopped and suckered so easily. *I'm a newspaper reporter, a good one, really, except when I get scared. Then I wet my diapies and forget to ask questions.* She thought a second and said, "What color are the tickets?" I told her yellow and she said, yes, someone had definitely fooled me. "D.C. tickets are white. You're lucky you weren't hurt. Didn't you ask to see his badge?" When I hesitated, she cleared her throat and asked if I wanted her to send a detective. I did not.

After two apparent encounters with the law in less than a half-hour, I drove home, irritable, wallet already feeling lighter. It was nearly 9. Robin and Ellie were watching a dinosaur movie that, as usual, didn't seem to be going well for the dinosaurs. Robin, shirtless and wearing raggedy red pajama bottoms, ran to me, something he hadn't done in awhile. He had a white test paper in his hand that crinkled when he hugged my waist. I put on my best Ricardo Montalban. *Look Carlos, it eez the very rare Robin Patragno ... from the Galapagos. Maybe he weel grant us an interview.* I patted his head and he held on a second longer before letting go. When he stepped back, I saw his eyes were wet. He held out the paper. He said, "Aced my vocabulary test, Dad." Next to the *A* was a sticker of the White House, Ms. Lipinski's reward for a job well done. "Good stuff, Robbie. Keep it up. Any chocolate milk left?"

We put him to bed together like in the old, snarling nightmare days. When he was very young, Robin's busy mind whipped up a smorgasbord of especially vicious beasts willing to abandon the wild simply to come to suburban Maryland and terrorize one little boy. A wolf chased him at a band concert; a gorilla glared at him through his bedroom window; a three-legged, snaggle-toothed bear stalked him by the schoolyard. He would wake up terrified, his little pajamas soaked in sweat. "Which one?" I'd say. "The bear. He was angry. He said my trap cut off his leg. It wasn't my trap. I told him over and over. He touched me with the leg and I got all bloody." For a time, Robin wouldn't get into bed unless one of us got in with him. I believed he'd inherited the sleepless gene from me. Each night when I go to bed, a small part of me worries I won't be able to sleep, the opposite of somniphobia, the fear of sleep. The more tired I am, the more panicky the feeling. Most nights I'm fine, but Robin, I thought, may have gotten a mutant version of my occasional insomnia that took shape in vivid nightmares. The one object that comforted him, oddly enough, was a stuffed, surly tiger. After a time, the dreams stopped and he didn't want to be tucked in anymore. The last flare-up was so long ago, it felt new to be putting him to bed again. I pulled up his covers; Ellie kissed his forehead. It was hard to think that one day Robbie would be shaving, going off to college, marrying a nice girl and having his own marriage problems. "Goodnight, parental units," he giggled. We said goodnight, closed his door and went to the family room.

Ellie flicked my arm. "You should sleep here. You look awful."

"I need to get with Clay about this story. I'm running out of time and there's a lot happening I can't get my hands around … This is the biggest story — "

" — Every story's the biggest story. It can wait. Stay here; call him in the morning."

"I need to tell you something."

Any wife who hears those words knows what they mean. Ellie's eyes narrowed as if to say, *Ah, big story my ass.*

Bella

"What did you do, Danny, go out and sleep with someone last night to get back at me?"

I looked away, which answered her question. "Oh," she said. She went to the kitchen and began loading the dishwasher. I stood there, the brilliant journalist again with no words. Was it too late to reconsider bridge repair? The house was still until she said, "Maybe you're right. Take some things and go to Clay's. I think a few weeks apart might — "

My cell rang. A traditional ring, not a chime or Chopin or three bars of an angry millionaire rapper ranting against *The Man*. I preferred a normal ring. Right then I preferred silence. I glanced at the clock as I answered. Half past 10. Ellie stood with her arms crossed. I turned away and put the phone to my ear. "Hi," she said, "I'm finally returning my calls. Bad timing?" So casual, I thought. She might as well have been ordering cashew chicken. I told her I'd call back and flipped the phone closed without saying goodbye. Ellie walked in carrying a metal spatula. "Don't tell me; your new girlfriend."

"Listen, it's complicated — "

" — No it's not, Danny; get your stuff, go to Clay's and call your little friend. I'll tell Robin ... " She slapped her palm with the spatula. " ... I don't know what the fuck I'll tell Robin. I'll think of something."

"Ellie." But she'd already slipped into the first floor bathroom. I heard the click of the lock and a spurt of water from the old pedestal sink. What was it about me that kept sending women scurrying to the bathroom? Why was the friend always a *little* friend? And why did my life seem to shoot off in a new direction with every call from Isabel Moss?

Chapter 20

ou're back."

"I'm back." Clay appraised my gym bag. "Should I make you a key?"

"Couple of days, tops. If it's still okay … "

He laughed and let me in and led us to the kitchen. His wife Mary, slim and brunette with a round, unlined face that could fit a woman of 24 or 44, was tidying up in a light yellow housecoat. Mary Nielson-Ohrbach was 47 and one of the top civil rights lawyers at the Justice Department, a liberal from the Bronx with the same passion for fairness I liked to think steered me into reporting. Open and outspoken, I thought her an odd match for Clay, a guy who sat locked up all day analyzing data from satellites. Get her alone at some cocktail party, and Mary would say the Patriot Act handed the government too much power to eavesdrop, that Bush was loading the judiciary with too many conservatives, and that any speech by the president stunk like rotten oysters. She stayed at Justice because she felt working toward change from within was better than complaining from outside. Mary struck me as warm enough to kiss hello, too busy to bring the car in for an oil change. It was odd to see her restocking napkins and scrubbing stains off the countertops. Sometimes we talked a few minutes when I picked up Clay for hoops. She was usually dressed for church and always shook her head at how she, a good Catholic girl, wound up with a guy who skipped services to shoot baskets on Sunday mornings. She told me that one of her proudest professional moments was busting the *American White Hammer Union*, a sorry gang of fire-loving rednecks who burned down seven black churches in Georgia, South Carolina and Florida. I covered the D.C. press conference, since one of the churches was just north of Tampa and the editors wanted a story with a local angle. I quoted Mary and sent her a copy of the piece, which she'd framed and hung in their den.

"Danny," she said, giving me a hug. She had to stand on her tiptoes to get near my ear. She whispered, "Staying all night, or are you headed out later to chase more, um, stories?" She stepped back and gave a little grin that I couldn't help but return. "It's not what you think," I said, and she answered, "It's exactly what I think. You know it, I know it, even *Double A* over here knows it."

"I need to ask Clay about something."

"Fine, I'm going." Mary waved and told me to leave more quietly this time if I decided to go out late. We watched her go. Clay chewed a fingernail. "What's up, Danny? I'm not much of a marriage counselor."

I sat at the kitchen island, under the shadows of gleaming copper pots and pans hanging above, and told him about Army Specialist Hank Moss just as Isabel had explained it to me. "And so the other night I'm standing there in the park with this source from the Pentagon. He confirmed the story, but I still have no proof. No proof, no story. That's when I flashed on you, Clay. I don't know squat about military satellites, except that they're up there. I think I heard once that they're recording stuff all the time. So I guess I'm asking if it's possible that a surveillance satellite caught Hank Moss's death, and whether there might be photos that would prove he was accidentally killed by another U.S. unit."

"Some story," Clay said. "Come with me." He took me to his study and booted up a computer with a 21-inch flat-screen monitor and the sharpest graphics I'd ever seen. He punched up a website and clicked on a photo the size of a postage stamp. The computer launched a program that enabled Clay to manipulate the size and texture of the photo. I saw that it was an aerial view of the U.S. Capitol. The familiar dome and Statue of Freedom were way below but easily recognizable — about the size you'd expect when flying home from Florida and the pilot starts to descend.

"This is a one-meter resolution image." I asked if he could zoom in. The first click got us near enough to make out the grid of streets and build-ings around the Capitol. It had to be a Sunday; there was no traffic. I knew from a feature I'd written for the newspaper that the Capitol covers about 4 acres, and that it's 288 feet from the ground to the eagle atop the statue's helmet. There are 108 windows in the dome, no doubt an escape valve for all the hot air. A few more clicks brought up specks that were parked cars and the West Front steps where newly-elected presidents gave their inaugural addresses. But you couldn't see people, let alone faces. "Go in some more." He did. The dome got bigger and the surrounding streets and buildings began to disappear. A few more clicks and the picture started pixelating into indistinguishable blocks of modern art. "This is a com-mercial image," Clay said. "Captured and made available to the public by a commercial remote sensing company rather than by the government. Military images have better resolution, but you're still not going to find what you're looking for. The imagery might show the building, nothing else. You'd never get down to individual faces. We can't even get down to the statue's head and helmet."

"You're certain?"

"The satellites are in orbit, Danny. Four hundred miles up, scooting around the Earth at 17,000 miles per hour. Even if a satellite were directly over the building at exactly the right moment — unlikely enough in itself — it's impossible that it would pick up anything like what you've described. I'm sorry."

I rubbed off a smudge Mary had missed on the marble countertop. "Plus, didn't you say it was raining when this soldier was killed?" I nodded and he said, "Well, there's another thing. Satellites see through clouds about as well as I shoot three-pointers."

Which meant they were essentially blind. I was back to the beginning. I'd poured a lot into the investigation and had precious little to show for it. What the hell was I going to tell Canton Spivey? "Vodka, Clay, and two glasses."

Less than an hour later, I again found myself calling Isabel Moss from the Ohrbachs' guest bedroom. She was back in Tampa. I was circling the drain, as was said in the rural parts of Florida where the answer to most problems is duct tape, WD-40 or sorghum syrup. The scene with Ellie, my run-in with the mystery cop, Clay's analysis of the dumb satellite theory and Isabel's unannounced trip back home had me depressed and miserable.

"How come you left without even saying good-bye?"

She laughed at me. "That's what the *woman* would say."

I reddened. Everything flooded back: the first phone call and meeting, the many red flags and how she kicked each away with those gorgeous legs; how the legs parted to let me in, and how they tightened to keep me where she wanted. I thought of waking Mary to discuss how my civil rights were being trampled. "But — "

" — But what? I've got a child who needed me. You don't expect me to check with you before — ”

“ — It would have been nice — ”

“ — I don't have time for nice. I'm trying to find out who killed my husband. And how to be a single parent. I'm juggling bills and bank accounts … Nosy neighbors keep bringing me casseroles. They think an overdone meat loaf gives them license to ask whatever they want. What I think and feel is none of their business. Katie's acting up at school. She pushed some kid off a swing and he chipped his tooth. They want me to pay the bill and Katie to start seeing a grief counselor.” She stopped at the notion of a shrink for her little girl. I thought she was going to cry. Instead, she said firmly, “This is all new, Danny. And hard. I'm going on instinct. I've got to do what I think is right. Nice isn't my top concern.”

I resented being lumped with busy-body neighbors. I'd brought more to her table than mac and cheese. And I wasn't asking inane questions; I was helping her resolve important issues so she could move on. I thought all this and said nothing. How do you argue with a 26-year-old widow clawing for a normal life for herself and her little girl? You don't, not even if she grabs your Y chromosome and dresses it up in braids and short-shorts. I fell back on the bed, phone still brushing my ear, and looked at the ceiling.

When she spoke again, her tone was upbeat. “Don't sulk. I have important news. Are you there?” I was, I muttered. “The mystery soldier called again — the one who said the Army's lying. He's in town until they ship him out again. He wants to meet, tomorrow, 1 o'clock at some hole-in-the-wall restaurant north of town. I told him about you and he said you could come, so long as his name isn't used in any stories. What do you think?”

I sat up. “You still want me there?”

“Don't be an idiot.”

Bella

Manhood repaired, if not restored, I promised to grab the first flight out. We said good night and I shut the lights. The red numbers on the dresser clock read 1:40 a.m. I prayed for sleep.

Chapter 21

The view above Tampa International reminded me of Clay's satellite photo. Somewhere down there, when I was 12 years old, I took my first job in the newspaper business. I delivered them house to house. The old *Tampa Sun* hired me and I used my dad's pristine Schwinn *Black Phantom*, fitted with chrome fenders and a metal wire basket, to toss 70 papers a day toward the homes of a station-wagon suburb called *Old Carrollwood Heights*. Inside one of those houses lived my first crush, a sweetheart named Tanya Rodriguez with maple-red curls and freckles and a knack for appearing on Oleander Court whenever I rode up with the paper. Believe me, I lifted my chin and pedaled with military precision when I hit that block each day after school. Tanya's house was on the right, connected to the road by a blacktop driveway that broke two ways — toward the house, and toward a basketball hoop with a red, white and blue net.

Tanya was shooting baskets the day I lost my first job in journalism. I looked over and saw her toss an air ball, failing to notice one of the neighborhood's many full-size wagons closing in from behind. The driver was Tanya's teen-age brother, who thought it would be hysterical to terrorize *Dan the Paperboy*. He got close and honked, causing me to side-swipe a tree and fall off. The weight of the papers in the handlebar basket kept the bike moving long enough to crash in the road, where the surprised brother, not expecting quite so much fun when he began his game, failed to stop and flattened the black *Phantom* into a pile of black garbage. My father, when he arrived, wasn't much interested in details. He looked me over, glanced at the sullen brother, and loaded the mangled *Phantom* into his van as Tanya wiped my cuts with a wet washcloth.

Dad and mom are both long gone. He died six years ago; she followed a year later. Jimmy and Maria Patragno both made it to their seventies, not bad for lifelong smokers. Dad co-owned a dry cleaners and then bought out his partner, a barrel-chested Greek named Dimitri fond of passing out squares of licorice candy to his customers. Mom worked at the store and cried when I became the first Patragno to earn a college degree. She made a scrapbook of my first three months of clips at the Naples paper; anyone who wanted a shirt or skirt cleaned and pressed had to read at least one of Dan Patragno's stories about amateur tennis or Coach Gooch's Naples High Golden Eagles.

Their *Jim Dandy Cleaners* was in a small shopping mall a few miles northwest of downtown Tampa and sat cheek to cheek with *Orchids by Olivia*. Across a side street, on the same side of Dale Mabry Highway, were a self-serve gas station and a small family-owned diner named *Mel's*, memorable as the scene of my first date. Everyone thought Mel was a man; the owner was really a blue-haired senior citizen named Melanie Brunson who'd retired to West Palm and put her son-in-law in charge of the restaurant. Tanya Rodriguez must have felt bad after her maniac brother ran me off the road and crushed dad's bike. I bought her an ice cream soda and she rewarded me with a kiss that was far sweeter than anything offered by Mel or her son-in-law.

It was at *Mel's* that I was supposed to meet Isabel Moss and the man I'd come to think of as the Unknown Soldier.

H e was Hollywood's vision of a fighting man — a square-jawed, 5-10, 190-pounder from outside Chicago accustomed to addressing everyone as *sir* or *ma'am*. Private Bart Jefferson was 23, with close-cropped black hair and a chin that looked like it needed two shaves a day.

The three of us drew little attention at *Mel's*. Tampa was home to MacDill Air Force Base, a command of 6,000 airmen and civilians that, as Congressman Dwoark intoned over and over as he trolled for votes every two years among active-duty service members and veterans, pumped over $6 billion a year into the local economy. MacDill was home base for USCENTCOM — the U.S. Central Command, one of nine joint commands that coordinate the operations of American combat forces. The Tampa-based outfit was responsible for the territory from the Horn of Africa to Central Asia. MacDill, I knew from my coverage of mind-numbing military budget matters in Washington, also housed the U.S. Special Operations Command (SOCOM), the Joint Communications Support Element, the 6th Air Mobility Wing, and more than 40 other tenants. In addition to their patriotic missions, Dwoark and the Tampa Chamber knew the facilities were also responsible for putting crowds of airmen, soldiers and other servicemen and women in Tampa's shopping malls, movie theaters and family diners.

Bart Jefferson, in Tampa on a stop-over, was hardly the unknown solider I'd imagined. For all he'd seen and been part of in Afghanistan, for all his muscle and military bearing, he was pretty much a scared kid without a hint of hype or mystery. He'd witnessed a tragedy, joined the conspiracy by keeping silent, and now needed things set straight so he could sleep nights. He told us that he'd been part of Hank's three-man team the night of the accident. On Hank's order, he and another soldier, Oscar (*Osky*) Sanchez of Laredo, Texas, had ducked behind a corner seconds before the grenade exploded. Afterwards, they raced to Hank. There was simply no one to help, not even much of a body to send home and bury. Two other soldiers arrived moments later from the north. One began sobbing when he saw the first team and learned he'd killed another American. The second soldier, Sgt. Marlin Falk, ordered everyone to resume their patrols. Falk said he'd handle the paperwork. He made sure that everyone understood Hank Moss was a hostile casualty, killed in action by enemy fire. He stood before all three men — Bart, Osky Sanchez, and the soldier who threw the grenade — and repeated, *We clear on this, soldier?* Each barked back a *yessir*.

I counted four witnesses: Bart, his teammate Sanchez, who was still overseas, the soldier who threw the grenade, and Marlin Falk. When Bart Jefferson said Hank Moss was the most selfless man he'd met in the Army, that he wouldn't ask his men to do anything he wouldn't do, and that he spoke all the time about his wife and little girl, I reached for Isabel's hand under the table. She pulled away and stared at the kid from outside Chicago until he began looking uncomfortable. I caught his eye. "Bart, I know it's a longshot, but I thought there might be satellite imagery showing what happened that night."

"Satellite photos. No sir, no way."

"I know. They don't zoom in that close, plus it was raining, and what would the odds be of — "

" — There *is* a tape, though."

"A tape."

Bart scanned the diner, looking jumpy for the first time. His burger sat untouched. I could see a small patch of grease spreading on the plate. I'd probably eaten 200 of *Mel's* burgers waiting for rides home when I was a kid or taking breaks when I helped out at our store. I took a wide angle look out the window and saw that *Jim Dandy Cleaners* was no more. The real estate company I'd sold it to when the folks died turned it into a cell phone store. Business was good; we never had a line of customers out the door, not even on Saturday mornings. Bart leaned toward us and said softly, "Streaming video shot by a drone."

A drone. I thought of *Star Wars* and tried to remember if the drone was the tall, chatty gold android or the squat, dome-topped thing with camera eyes and arms that reached to the ground. *Military drone.* I imagined a rolling, whistling, whirring, silver-plated robot with camera eyes in Army fatigues.

Isabel hadn't said a word since we'd sat down in the booth opposite Bart Jefferson. She wore jeans and a pale orange polo that looked nice against her black hair. She'd spent the last few minutes with both hands wrapped tightly around her coffee cup. Now she looked directly at Bart. "Hank told me about drones once. UAV, for *Unmanned Aerial Vehicle.*"

"Yes, ma'am. High-altitude, long-endurance. They give our field commanders near-real time streaming video of the theatre."

"Good quality?"

"Yes sir, very high resolution."

So the video — the embodiment of modern warfare, more precise and conclusive than DNA — would clearly show Hank and the events leading to his death. "How big are these drones, like a kid's radio-controlled plane?"

Bart looked at Isabel to see if I was kidding. She rolled her eyes, he chuckled, and the tension eased.

"I know the specs," he said. "I'm studying integrated and unmanned systems. Top to bottom, it's about 14-and-a-half feet; wingspan, 116 feet; length, about 45 feet. Gross weight at take off: 26,000 pounds; maximum altitude, 65,000 feet or so. Not a kid's toy, sir."

"How long can they stay in the air?"

Bella

"About 35 hours."

"So what we have is like a guy robbing a convenience store getting caught by the surveillance camera."

Again his eyes went to Isabel. "Something like that, sir. Like I said, our drones fly at up to 65,000 feet. They send surveillance, intelligence and reconnaissance info to our commanders on an area that measures 40,000 square miles. That's a little bigger than your average 7-11. And it's not a static camera." Isabel smiled. "But you're right," he added quickly, "drones don't pick and choose what they record. Everything that goes in gets sent back to command for analysis."

"And you're saying a drone caught what happened to Hank, and that a tape of it exists."

"That's what I was told, sir."

I slid forward. "*Told?* What are you saying? Either you know or you don't. Have you seen it or not?" He hesitated.

"Bart?" Isabel said.

"I was told they have it. I haven't seen it myself. I'm sure it exists, that it shows conclusively that — "

" — You *think* you're sure. Are you kidding?" I took his wrist, not realizing that under the hairy cover, it was the size of an average man's ankle. He looked at my hand. Both of us knew he could crumble my five fingers like almond biscotti before I uttered another syllable. I was too far in to stop. "You're sure someone told you it exists, but you haven't seen the tape. Therefore you're not sure about anything. Unless you have a copy, that is. Do you have a copy of this alleged tape?"

He brushed away my hand. "No," he said. "I didn't see the tape and I don't have a copy. What I have is *this* — a name and an address." He passed me a torn square of loose leaf paper. I looked at the name, written in a precise, steady hand with a black, fine-point. It meant nothing. The address was in Charleston, South Carolina.

"That's the guy who threw the grenade. Marcus Ravoli. Went to the military college in Charleston." Bart closed his eyes and moved a fork from thumb to pinky the way a cheerleader transfers a baton across her fingers. "*Ravioli*. We called him *Ravioli*. They cut him loose. Honorable discharge. Find him and he might tell you the truth. Do it fast; I hear Marcus' not doing so great. None of us who were there are doing so great. *That* much I'm sure about, Mr. Patragno."

Isabel took the paper and stared at the name for long seconds. I knew what she must be thinking. *Marcus Ravoli, barely out of college. A scared kid who tossed a grenade at the enemy and killed my husband.* "I gotta' go," said Bart Jefferson. "Please don't try to contact me."

"Hold on." I read back through my notes. "What about this Sgt. Falk? What's he about? Where is he now?"

"Falk's still in-country, somewhere near Kabul, I think. He's a lifer — never married, served in the first Gulf War, a hard-ass, but loves his Army."

We stood and shook hands like businessmen. "Something might come up where I need to get to you, Bart." I gave him my cell number and he said he'd get in touch in a week. Isabel stayed seated, her eyes wet, the paper still in her hand. "Good luck, Mrs. Moss," he said, gently squeezing her shoulder. "I loved your husband. We all did."

When he was gone, I said, "Quit crying on the paper; you'll smudge the address."

She laughed and turned into me. She hugged me hard, arms slung around my neck, and I brought her closer and she started crying again, big, heaving sobs, and my damned shoulder started getting soggy and then we *were* drawing attention, so I whispered we should leave. Jesus she felt good. It was better than the sex. Warmer. More intimate. She kissed me quick as we pulled apart and her lips were sad and sweet and I thought, how staggering that so much life would, could, start, end and begin again between the two kisses I received from such different girls at *Mel's Diner*. I wondered whatever happened to Tanya Rodriguez. When I tried to tell Isabel what I was thinking and how small and inconsequential it all made me feel, I found she was amazingly composed. She pressed two fingers to my lips and said, "Shh. Wait. See what happens." What was that? I remembered a bit of Kafka from college philosophy: *Don't even listen, just wait. Don't even wait, be completely quiet and alone. The world will offer itself to you to be unmasked …*" I remembered and still had no idea what she meant. Nothing about this story was going to be revealed without a lot of digging. Kafka — great philosopher, but he would have made a lousy reporter. Isabel needed someone new to quote. Brokaw, maybe.

STEVE PIACENTE

Chapter 22

I dropped her home and stared a moment from the driveway. 726 Laurel Canyon Drive. This was where Hank and Isabel had begun building family and future. It was strikingly common: beige stucco exterior, beige fence missing a few slats, beige curtains in the windows; a few skimpy palm trees and a rusty tricycle in the yard beside a beige and chocolate shed that housed the lawnmower. I wanted to go in and poke around — I was certain the ordinary house would yield vivid details for my coming stories — but had to whip down to the News and report to Canton Spivey. Isabel read my thoughts. It was probably the first time we'd been together that I was staring at something other than her. "Come back later. I'll make dinner; you'll meet Katie."

I thanked her for letting me borrow the car, an old, pumpkin-colored ragtop Mustang that she now mentioned had been Hank's since his senior year in high school. I yanked my hands off the wheel and she laughed. "The car's not haunted, Daniel." She kissed the inside of her first two fingers, touched my cheek, tilted her head to the side and pressed her lips together, looking like she'd decided I was a decent guy after all. "Come back hungry, mister." I leaned across the console and kissed her mouth. Only a few seconds in, she uttered a tiny, exquisite moan that made me want to take her right there in the driveway. She shifted a little and began dragging her nails lazily up and down my thigh as we kissed. Her mouth was perfect. We fit like lost puzzle pieces finally found and connected. Anyone watching would have ordered us inside. *And pull the shades, you two. There's kids around here.* No one was around. I made sure our embrace lasted long enough to bust down the wall that went up after the night at the hotel. She seemed in no hurry, and I honestly thought then that she was beginning to love me.

Newspapers these days are hurtling toward something called *convergence.* It's a bullshit word that means to media types what synergy means to federal bureaucrats, who stole it off the private sector. All it means is working smarter, but "working smarter" doesn't have the flair of convergence, especially in the irreverent, ink-stained newsrooms of America. What it means is that newspapers, desperate to increase their appeal, especially among the instant satisfaction addicts of the *click-and-get* generation, have thrown up online editions and, in some cases, begun teaching print reporters to gel their hair and repackage stories for TV. Convergence means using different media to draw bigger audiences, a three-ring circus instead of one lame showcase. The *News* was one of the forward-looking papers, going so far as to build a small hi-tech TV studio off the newsroom and hiring a slick speaking coach who also worked with politicians, athletic coaches, comedians and anyone else who could cover his outrageous rate of $2,500 for half a day. Convergence advocates spoke wondrously of the continuing evolution of the daily newspaper. Newsroom traditionalists welcomed the TV studio the way Arabs welcome Jewish delis to the Gaza.

I put myself among the purists. TV reporters were overpaid actors and entertainers. The worst were shameless, smarmy thieves. Christ, I could count a dozen times when one of the local anchors stole a story I'd written and presented it on air as original reporting. Still, I was curious to mess around in the new studio. The paper was only a few miles away from Isabel's, on Parker, over a small drawbridge that carried cars and pedestrians over the Hillsborough River near the minaret-capped University of Tampa. I hadn't been to the office since my last half-year review five months earlier. I parked and headed for the double-glass doors, only to be intercepted by Canton Spivey, who was sitting cross-legged on a bench usually claimed by the building's few remaining smokers. I looked at him and saw trouble. "You don't wanna' go in there right now, Danny," he said, shaking my hand. "Few of 'em want your hide, including me." He pulled out the morning's *St. Pete Times*, our main competitor. I hadn't seen any papers since getting on the plane to meet with Isabel and Bart Jefferson. Canton let the front page fall open. I saw why the bosses were upset. *The Times* had a *holy shit* story about one of Florida's U.S. senators, Kirk Lawton. Holy shit stories are the ones that make retired husbands call to their wives at breakfast, Holy shit, *honey, listen to this …* Lawton was a pompous, four-term incumbent in his sixties with a 40-inch belly and no hair except for two rogue white tufts that grew fast and furiously above his ears. I took the paper and started reading. Sweat began oozing along my lower back. It seemed the senator was robbed while walking home alone from a late committee hearing. When stopped by two men in their twenties, he protested, "Do you know I am a United States Senator?" They were so impressed, they took his wallet for money and his pants for a souvenir. Kirk Lawton was so outraged, he marched *sans* pants to the nearest police station, where, I would later learn, the *St. Pete Times* Washington correspondent happened to be waiting for his girlfriend, a rookie detective. Before questioning the senator, the reporter called a freelance photographer, who lived nearby and showed up 10 minutes later. Which was how the story of Kirk Lawton's mugging and a picture of the senator's fat, hairy legs wound up on the front page of the *St. Pete Times*.

"I wouldn't have had this story even if I was up there covering my beat," I told Spivey. "It was a fluke. The *Times* guy had a source or happened to be at the police station when Lawton walked in."

"No one wants to hear that, Danny. When the star hitter strikes out, his team doesn't want to hear about the other pitcher's lucky day." He nodded toward the *News* building. "All they know on the third floor is we missed a big one. This is all anyone's talking about today — Fucking Kirk Lawton tramping down to the cop station with his ass hanging out. Crazy bastard. Probably get reelected with 60 percent next time."

Canton was right about one thing. No once cared that I'd been working my own behind off. Missing a big story to St. Pete was horrible. "What should I do?"

"I'm hoping you're going to give me something I can go in there with to explain why you weren't around. Otherwise you might be moving back here to cover City Hall again."

I gazed beyond the bridge toward downtown Tampa and the shops, restaurants and cigar factories of Ybor City. Those weren't such bad days, watch-dogging the mayor and city council, seeing Tampa grow from a sleepy town to … No, wait, that was crap. The way I covered City Hall won a few regional journalism prizes and got me to Washington. I wasn't coming back, especially as punishment for missing the Kirk Lawton story.

"Let's walk," Canton said. We left the parking lot, crossed the bridge and headed toward town. It wasn't New York, or even New Haven, but a fair number of buildings shimmered in the distance, some new since I'd last been to Tampa. It was a typical late August Florida afternoon. Everything at high boil. The river hot and still, too sleepy even to lap the shore. Between the heat and getting whipped by St. Pete, I felt like one of the ants trapped under Robin's notorious magnifying glass. Canton kicked a stone that bounded off the clawed foot of a red and blue mailbox. "Goddamn, Danny, where are we on the dead Army guy and his nutty wife?"

I thought a second about all that was in play. The senator's investigation, Bart Jefferson's first-hand account, the alleged tape, the South Carolina ex-soldier who threw the grenade, the phony cop who stopped me in D.C., a few more pieces I'm sure I didn't even know about yet ... I knew Canton Spivey wasn't interested in how we butchered the cow; he wanted a juicy burger to feed management, one we could plop down on the front page with a big greasy splash. I explained where we were, that I was working closely with Moss's widow, that we had to go to Charleston, South Carolina to find *Rigatoni* or whatever the hell his name was, but that, above all, we had to find the video shot by the unmanned aerial vehicle, the UAV.

"UAV," he said, stone-faced, as if I'd told him there was a Spanish galleon loaded with gold *Pesetas* sunk in the Hillsborough River. "And this tape. You're going to walk into the Pentagon and just ask them to hand it over?"

Enough. I was tired of being treated like a slacker. I got four inches from his face. "First, taxpayer dollars paid for the drone. Same for the military guys who send it up and analyze all the data. They work for *us, we the people.* Same fucking thing goes for whoever decided to cover up the truth about what happened to Hank Moss, which by the way is a lot more gripping than the saga of Kirk Lawton's stolen pants. Jesus, Canton, I don't know how I'm going to get the tape, but I know the public has a right to see what's on it. So does Isabel Moss. *Especially* Isabel Moss."

A city bus whisked by, fanning us with hot, grimy air. "I've got to stay on the chase. I've got to get to South Carolina and find the kid who made this terrible mistake. Can I go?"

Canton Spivey wasn't accustomed to being yelled at by his reporters. He started to answer and sputtered to a stop. He threw a look at the river and turned back to me, his eyes dark and fuming. He shook his head and made clucking sounds. He bit the corner of his lip. He found another chunky rock and kicked it into the street. "Go," he said finally. "Go before I change my mind."

"Thank you."

"Don't you make me sorry, Patragno."

I called Ellie on the way back to Isabel's. My wife wasn't interested that I was in Florida or anything else I had to say. "Is Robin there?" I heard her cover the receiver and call him. "Dad?" he said. "Rob-O. What's going on? You still doing okay with Ms. Lipinski?"

"When you coming home, Dad?"

"I'm working, Robbie. Big story, front pager if I get it. I'll be home soon as I can."

"Okay." Kids don't even try to hide disappointment. I told him I'd bring a surprise and all I heard was his heavy kid breathing. Sounded like maybe a cold coming. "Robby, be good for mom. I'll try to be back in a few days." He promised half-heartedly and hung up, forgetting or purposely neglecting to say good-bye. I looked at the phone and considered chucking it out the window. I began calling back to yell at him and realized the ridiculous conversation that would come of it.

Say good-bye next time, son.

Okay, Dad. Bye.

Bye. I stuffed the phone in Hank Moss's glove compartment.

"**M**y specialty. Smell good?" she said, stirring the red sauce with a wooden spoon. The scent of bubbling *Roma* tomatoes and roasted garlic was heaven.

"Delicious." Whatever she was serving didn't matter. She wore a simple black dress and very little makeup. She didn't need much. We sipped a nutty chardonnay from long-stemmed crystal glasses. I liked her small white gold earrings and matching necklace and said so. "Thanks," she smiled. "They're from Italy. Presents from Hank." I moved behind her, intending to circle her waist with my hands. She turned suddenly and put the spoon to my lips. "Taste." I did and told her I was too hungry to wait much longer. She smiled and told me I'd be waiting until Katie was safely asleep. Neither of us knew the night was about to twist in a different direction.

The little girl, too somber for a child of four, had a creamy angel face topped with delicate eyebrows and framed by brown ringlets that flowed in gentle waves to the middle of her back. Wherever she went, a beige cotton blanket that matched the house went with her. Her *Hanky*, named for Hank, her dead dad. Wherever she stopped, she stroked the blanket as if it were a Persian kitty. When I spoke to her, she looked at her nails, which were sunk in the beige cotton. "Your mom's a great cook, Katie. Do you help her?" She shrugged, bending her neck so far, her cheek brushed her shoulder. She twirled and abruptly left the room without a word, the blanket trailing behind.

Isabel didn't even glance up. She began making rapid circles in the sauce, which did not need any more stirring. She went too fast and a crimson splash shot from the pot and splattered on the floor. She stopped suddenly and stepped back from the stove, hands on her thighs and listing forward as if gripped by a stomach cramp. I touched her arm and she recoiled. I wasn't sure what to do, so I cleaned. I ripped a paper towel off the roll and wiped the floor. "What is it?" She turned down the flame, said she'd be fine in a minute. I remembered that the last time a woman wanted to tell me something painful, it turned out my wife was having an affair. Isabel let me guide her to the kitchen table. We sat and she put her cheek near mine. I felt tears and smelled her peachy perfume. "We were at the P.X. the other day — I'm allowed to shop there because of Hank; it's like 30 percent cheaper than regular stores," she said softly, the earlier playfulness gone. "I had so many things to buy: groceries, a lamp for the dining room ... Katie needed a new coat; she's growing so fast ... I had two lists. We walked in and got a cart and I started to look at one of the lists ... " Isabel pulled back, laying elbows on knees, chin on her palms. I could almost see the life being sucked out of her by this latest unforeseen chapter in the story of Hank, Isabel and Katie Moss. "She seemed like any other kid that morning. She even left her *Hanky* in the cart while she was skipping around the store. I looked away a second and when I looked back she was gone." Isabel began to rock slowly. She seemed dazed. "I started down this massive aisle. Then I saw Katie — and *beyond* her — and I realized where she was going. A guy who looked like Hank, thirty yards away, in fatigues. Looked so much like Hank, *I* did a double take. I called her. 'Katie, Katie.' She kept running the other way, yelling, 'Daddy, Daddy.'"

Isabel toyed with a silver salt shaker. I took it from her and held her hand. Her fingers were cool even though the house was warm. She said, "By the time I got to her, she had herself wrapped around the poor guy's legs. I tried to get her off and she wouldn't let go. She was screaming and I was crying and trying to explain at the same time. *Daddy's gone; we talked about it so many times; you know he's gone.* The poor boy — he looked like he was 19, fresh from the farm in Sioux Falls or someplace — you better believe they never taught him how to deal with something like this in basic training. He thought he was going to do some shopping at the base exchange and look what he got instead. A crazy little girl clinging to his boots. Her crazy, frantic mother crying and trying to tell him how much he looked like the dead husband. Everyone watching us like a terrible car wreck, waiting for an ambulance that wasn't coming. You should have seen his face. The pity. Like he'd trade being there for being trapped behind enemy lines in a second." She put her head on the table and wept. "How am I ever going to forget something like that, Danny? How is Katie going to forget? How can we ever go back there? What's going to happen to us?" Her despair was so profound, tears came to my own eyes. When I caressed her neck, she looked at me, laughed ruefully and said, "There's more. While all this was going on, someone got on the loudspeaker. He must have thought there were broken bottles or something. He sounded so bored. He said: *Clean-up, Aisle 16.*"

D inner was uneventful. We discussed plans to get to Charleston in the morning. Katie didn't say a word. She ate with her right hand and stroked the blanket with her left. That night I slept in a guest room and Isabel did not visit.

Chapter 23

They already had a live-in sitter on call to cover Isabel's quick trips out of town. Mrs. Rachel Kingsford arrived at 9 and, after some instructions about meals, bedtimes and emergency numbers, drove Katie to pre-school. Two hours later, Isabel and I were on the 11:13 to Atlanta. We switched planes and landed around three in Charleston, the *Holy City*, so named for its many church steeples, the city streets all trimmed out with gas-lit lamps, horse-drawn carriages and other nostalgic whiffs of the Civil War. All through the ride up from Tampa, I'd thought about my sleepless night, how I waffled between slipping into Isabel's bed uninvited and hoping she'd join me in the guest room. It wasn't until nearly sunrise that I'd realized neither would happen. I fell asleep on my back and was jostled awake maybe an hour later by a Florida sun that yawned and stretched and fired a scorching band of light across my face. I groaned and pulled down the shades and laid there wide awake until I heard the little girl Katie get out of bed and hurry to the bathroom. I pictured her with the Hanky dragging behind.

Hours later, at the Tampa Airport, I picked up the morning *St. Pete Times*. Their Washington reporter had a follow-up on Kirk Lawton. Turned out the good senator was legally intoxicated when he was robbed and reported the mugging. So there'd been a stop between hearing and mugging. The cops must have tested him as a matter of course. Since he wasn't driving and never became abusive or a nuisance, he wasn't in any trouble, at least not with the police. What voters thought might be a different matter. *That old dog Kirk Lawton ... You say he walked into a police station all liquored up? With no pants? You serious?* Lawton filed his report, gave every detail his booze-addled brain could summon up, and left the station. All I knew was that my bosses would view it as another good story missed. I shut my cell.

"Were you okay in there last night?" Isabel said as we grabbed our overnights and headed for the rental cars. "You look like you didn't sleep at all."

I didn't tell her anything near the truth. Or that I'd gotten up around 3 and snooped around a little, examining family photos, tennis trophies and other Hank Moss memorabilia. Maybe after we'd gotten Private Marcus Ravoli's story on the record, I'd take her to dinner and we'd hire a horse and driver. As we clip-clopped along the cobblestone streets of Old Charleston, perhaps sipping red wine from clunky goblets forged by long-dead Confederate artisans, I'd tell her about my bumbling late-night adventure and we'd have a good laugh. Or maybe not, depending on how forthcoming Ravoli was about throwing the grenade that killed Hank Moss.

"I know you were up prowling around in the middle of the night," she said. I spun around. She poked my belly before I could utter a word. "It's okay. I expected it. Find anything interesting? I would have been happy to give you the official tour, you know." I plunked 35 cents in a newspaper rack and pulled out a *Post & Courier*, Charleston's local paper. Big headlines, lots of color photos and mostly local stories. All of it even more parochial than the Florida papers. "I was a little restless, that's all.

I didn't want to wake you." She cut in front, dropped her bag and faced me, that finger again in my stomach. It occurred to me that her favorite position was eye to eye. Irritated travelers were forced to walk around us, but she remained planted and stared me down until I had to look away. "Such bullshit," she laughed. We continued toward the rentals and I threw my arm with the newspaper around her shoulder. "Tough broad. Ever consider a career in journalism? I work alone, but there might be an opening somewhere ..." She sniffed and said, "More BS. And by the way, I know you changed the subject."

Still, we were getting along well and I felt good.

According to Bart Jefferson's neatly written note, Marcus Ravoli lived near the Citadel, Charleston's 160-year old military college known in the early 1990s for its adherence to a stubborn 11th Commandment that prohibited female cadets. In 1996, The all-male policy fell faster than a gay plebe when the sensible men and women of the U.S. Supreme Court ruled on Virginia Military Institute's all-male policy. The final decree: *Admit Girls or Forfeit All Federal Funds.* In the end, VMI and its Charleston cousin went with the money. A feeble Citadel news release announced the school was dropping its gender requirement, and that, *Effective immediately, the Citadel will enthusiastically accept qualified female applicants into the Corps of Cadets.*

Think of the surrender etched on Lee's face at Appomattox as he handed his sword to Grant. That's how enthusiastic they were to accept women cadets.

I threw our bags in the trunk; Isabel climbed in front and unfolded a map of the city. Ravoli lived near Huger and Kenilworth Streets, about two blocks from one of the main gates at the Citadel, his alma mater. I found the airport exit and hopped on I-26 east toward the city. It was a straight shot and there was no traffic, either on the highway or once we hit the Rutledge Avenue exit. Isabel told me where to turn and soon we were passing clean-shaven young men in gray uniforms or joggers in Citadel shorts and T-shirts, all in tip-top shape. It felt hotter than Florida; papery Spanish moss that looked ready to burst into flame hung from trees older than John Calhoun. Isabel fed me directions that would have delivered us to the university's Lesesne Gate. I wanted the Hagood Gate, closer to Ravoli's house. I turned right on Congress and Kenilworth, intending go left on Huger. Isabel tossed the map in back and picked up the newspaper. "Fine," she said, "you're on your own." She was done giving directions if I was going to take my own route. I was about to explain when, a half-block before Huger, I saw the street ahead blocked by a city police car, front door open, lights flashing. An enormous cop stood in the road talking into his radio and writing on a clipboard. Beyond the cop, the street was blocked in both directions. Official-looking investigative types were milling around one house that had been cordoned off with yellow tape and orange police bumpers. The tape said, *Police Line, Do Not Cross*. I looked at Isabel. "Oh, God. Danny." She glanced anxiously from the street view to the Charleston paper. She thrust the local section at me and pointed to the lead story in the Metro section. I read:

Young U.S. Vet Takes Own Life
By William L. Corbin
Post-Courier Staff Writer

A 24-year-old U.S. Army veteran and Citadel graduate said to be despondent since returning from duty in Afghanistan committed suicide Sunday, according to Charleston police.

Bella

Private Marcus Ravoli, who received a medical discharge from the military, shot himself through the head with a U.S. Army pistol. Though Ravoli worked as a waiter, friends said he planned to return to graduate school shortly to study business and marketing.

"This was a smart kid. I don't believe it," said Art Browner, owner of the Boathouse Café, where Ravoli worked as a waiter. "He was just marking time here. This boy could have been anything he wanted."

The story ran another eight inches. No mention of anything unusual during his stint in Afghanistan, or about any combat-related medical conditions. It didn't matter. We were a day late. Ravoli must have killed himself sometime before 11 the previous night. That was the only way the *Post and Courier* could have gotten it into the morning edition.

"Now what?" Isabel said.

"I wish I knew." The big cop was walking toward our car. I waved and started to back up, showing him I was turning around.

I drove without a plan and wound up in downtown traffic inching along a maze of one-way streets near a famous Charleston landmark, Institute Hall. The building before us at 134 Meeting Street was actually a clever copy, according to an engraved street placard that I read to clear my head. The real place burned down a year after the event that made it famous. On December 20, 1860, delegates gathered at the original hall and ratified the Ordinance of Secession, making South Carolina the first state to quit the Union. Local residents partied in the streets and invited Lincoln's Washington to kiss their Southern-fried asses.

How incredible to think that Marcus Ravoli was whisked a world away to fight for American ideals and wound up killing himself because he accidentally took the life of an Army brother. Back in the days of Lee and Grant, Southerners accustomed to giving instead of taking orders decided they'd shed the blood of anyone from New York, New Jersey or anywhere else who came between them and their plantations. And they did. Talk about Americans killing Americans. Ravoli's misdeed was nothing. When the U.S. Civil War ended in the Virginia countryside about five years after the fiesta outside Institute Hall, more than half a million Union and Confederate soldiers were dead. *Half a million!* And there was nothing accidental about it.

Doubtful any of that occurred to Marcus Ravoli as he loaded the bullets in his pistol.

"It's rush hour. Everyone's headed home from work." I wasn't sure if I said it to myself or out loud. I glanced at Isabel. Her face was white and stricken, as if she'd seen the body face down in a pool of blood. I turned a corner and there was a parking spot. I pulled in and we started toward a nearby café on the same side of the street. Isabel fell in on my right. We both walked faster than necessary. The time to rush was yesterday, not today. I assumed she was thinking the same as me. That poor kid, so racked with guilt he decided to put a slug in his brain rather than live another day with his secret. The newspaper story said he used an *ASP* pistol, small, powerful and made especially for close-range assignments. Isabel faltered. I put my arm around her waist and kept us moving. What agony had Marcus Ravoli endured, and for how long? How often had he thought about pulling the pin on the grenade that killed Hank Moss? What was he thinking as he reached for his pistol and turned it on himself? He used violence to achieve peace, a lesson he'd learned from his government. The newspaper story had a color photo. Ravoli was smiling. He was a husky kid with short black hair and a mouth full of white teeth. He didn't look like the sort who could kill himself. He looked like a guy who goes to a college basketball game with his face painted the school colors and is first in line to high-five the school mascot.

The story said he didn't leave a note, and that there was only one survivor, his mother, who declined comment.

"Wait here." Isabel nodded and sat in a booth. The café was empty; no one stops for a coffee at dinnertime. I wondered if Marcus Ravoli ate a last meal before taking his life. What did he eat? Or did he check out on an empty stomach?

A bored high school girl with a pierced lip and acne handed me two coffees that gave off an almond aroma. Her nametag said *Agnes*. I pushed a five at her and she said, "That's $5.85." As I gave her the extra bill, we both whirled toward an awful sound from the restroom, where Isabel had apparently rushed to throw up. Agnes looked back at me and said, "What's with your friend?"

"I've got to find the mother and make her talk to me. I was getting myself ready to interview Hank's mom; now there are two mothers with dead sons."

We'd checked in to the Harbor Inn (separate rooms on the second floor, at her request), cleaned up and landed at a nice seafood restaurant on King Street. Isabel, master of the quick recovery, seemed her old self. She wore a pale green dress and black-beaded necklace, and ate like she was determined to replace whatever she'd lost in the café bathroom.

"Why would Mrs. Ravoli talk to you if she wouldn't talk to the local reporter?"

"She probably wouldn't. I'm betting she'll open up once she sees you and hears your story."

She began to protest and stopped short. Both of us needed the mother to cooperate. Isabel would ride shotgun without complaining. "You're always a step ahead, Danny."

"Not always."

We agreed to put aside business until morning. Isabel called home and seemed more relaxed after she spoke to Katie and heard from Mrs. Kingsford that everything was fine. Katie even had a friend sleeping over.

The grilled shrimp were fresh and we emptied two bottles of wine. It was nice being in a town where no one knew either of us and everyone smiled, busboys and waiters included. We talked about frivolous things, her favorite movie (*Sabrina*, the original, with Audrey Hepburn), clothes (ironed T-shirts), cars (any convertible), celebrities (she said for her, privacy trumped fame and money) and sports (anything but soccer and hockey). She said she was a big tennis fan even before she met Hank. She liked the more fiery Russian players on the tour and thought most American pros were boring. We shared a decadent hunk of Parisian Cream Cheesecake for dessert. Playful Isabel wanted to feed me. She carved off a piece with her fork. When I closed in, she pulled it away. Twice more she played the game, giggling more wildly each time. The fourth time, I grabbed her hand. "Don't tease," I said, eating the cake and noticing to myself that the wait made it taste better. I resolved not to let her know, though she probably had it figured out. After dinner, I walked her back to the hotel.

We took the side entrance stairway to our rooms. Isabel climbed the first wooden step, turned and faced me. The extra inches made us the same height. I put my hands on her waist and we kissed very gently, our bodies barely touching, as if we hadn't already been together. "I'm not sleeping with you tonight," she murmured, her lips still brushing mine. I said it was alright. All that mattered was the moment, the feel of her flesh beneath my mouth and fingers, the salty breeze blowing off Charleston

Harbor, the thrill of playing out a private moment in public. We might have stayed that way for two minutes or twenty; I couldn't tell. When I stroked the back of her thighs and dared a caress under her dress, I discovered she was naked underneath. She uttered the soft moan that I remembered from Hank's pumpkin-colored Mustang, and I knew I'd lost more than my sense of time. I pulled her to me and, for the first time, she resisted. I kissed her neck. "Come to my room. Your heart's so loud I can hear it. And this ... " I said, reaching between her legs. She laughed and broke away. I kept a hand on her waist. "Don't you want to feel our bodies touching without clothes?" She smiled naughtily and spun around. When she turned back, her blouse was open and her bra was in her hand. She undid my shirt one button at a time, not even bothering to check the courtyard for spies. When the shirt fell open, she hugged me and kissed my chest. "Nice," she murmured. "You were right." I assumed the teasing was over and tried to lead her to my room. Again she pulled back, drawing her blouse closed and climbing two more steps. "Not tonight. I can't after what happened today. Don't be mad."

Mad wasn't quite the word.

T wo hours later I was still awake. My head ached from too much wine. There were other problems as well. I considered an erotic movie, but they wanted $14.95 and it seemed like a lot. Plus I'd have to explain the itemized charge for *My First Master* to the newspaper and Canton Spivey, which wouldn't have been easy. I could hear him shouting across the newsroom, *Jesus, Patragno, is this what you mean by 'working hard'?* I turned from back to stomach and side to side. I moved the pillows and put my feet at the head of the bed. I made the room colder and, 10 minutes later, found myself shivering. As I rose again to adjust the thermostat, there was a scratch at the door.

The pace was not as frantic as the first time, though there were still struggles. I left on a small lamp; she shut it. "But I want to see you." She answered, "Feel me instead." Who would argue? I wanted to go slow, massage her feet, rub oil into her neck and shoulders, build the tension. She was tense enough and wanted it faster. When I complied, she rolled me over and got on top. Once she guided me inside, I stopped analyzing. She positioned my hands — one curved around her breast, the other between our waists. She put my thumb on the fleshy nub that gave her the most pleasure and showed me how she liked to be touched. "Yes, that, not too fast," she said, moving above, grinding down. Somewhere I worried about how much control she seemed to need and insisted upon. All I said was, "You're amazing." When she came and I tried to switch positions, she kissed me and whispered in my ear, "No, let me. Please. Something different." She slid down and took me into her mouth. In my limited experience, oral had always been prelude. This was different; it was new and filthy and thrilling. My hands went to her hair and very soon I was bucking so hard, I thought she would surely choke. She didn't and I forced myself deeper, not knowing or caring if she could breathe. "This is what you wanted, right?" I hissed. She groaned and clutched the backs of my thighs, pulling me in so far, her nose pressed into the bottom of my stomach. When I reached the end, she didn't pull away. And a few moments later, when we finally caught our breath, she laughed wildly — as if our smoke-filled plane had touched down safely after losing an engine, all passengers shaken but unharmed. I laughed too, and then realized I had no idea what was so funny. She kissed me without warning. I was repulsed. She climbed back on top and forced me and next thing I knew we were on to round two.

We didn't speak again until morning, when it was time to get Isabel up for breakfast. I didn't know when or why she left my room, and tried my best not to think about it.

Chapter 24

Louisa Ravoli, listed in the local phonebook, lived 20 minutes north of Charleston in Mount Pleasant. The towns were connected by a pair of old, three-mile erector set bridges frequently splashed on the face of postcards from Charleston. The hotel matre d' told us a move was on to replace the bridges, which spanned the Cooper River, the famed waterway that once served area plantations made rich off the sweat and muscles of slaves from Africa. "Traffic will be headed into town. This is a good time to go." Isabel said Mrs. Ravoli might be at the funeral. I pointed to a second-day story in the Charleston paper that said the service was still a day off. We took showers in our own rooms, packed up and left for Mount Pleasant and — with some luck — a meeting with Marcus Ravoli's mother.

Several cars were parked in front of her white-sided home in the modest subdivision off bustling U.S. 17. Isabel and I watched as men in ties and women in summer dresses went in and out. Some of the women brought food, some were crying as they left. I tap-tapped the dash. "We can wait all day. There's never going to be a good time to do this." Isabel was fighting with herself. "I don't know if I can go in there. When Hank was killed, reporters tried to talk to me. They put those cameras in my face. I hated them. I hated everyone. Someone got the priest to talk to the press. I was too upset."

"This is different. She may have information we need."

"I know. It's just hard. I lost a husband; she lost a son."

"Try and remember you two are connected in a way no one can understand. It might be a relief for her to meet you."

We got out of the car and approached the house on a stone path ringed by gold trumpet daffodils. There was a one-step walk-up. I went first and rapped once on the screen door. A man in shirt, tie and blue jeans answered. "Were you Marcus' friends?" he said, smiling solemnly. I told him not exactly, that I was a journalist from Florida and that Isabel was … He cut me off with a harsh whisper. "Fucking reporters. You know what this woman's been through?" I told him of course, and we didn't mean to intrude, but there was something important to discuss with Mrs. Ravoli, and could he please ask her to step outside for just a few minutes … "Let the woman alone. Her kid just blew his brains out. Her only kid." Isabel hadn't said a word. Tears were streaming. The man seemed surprised. He shrugged as if he were dealing with a rookie. *Fine, let the rookie reporter learn not to barge in on someone's personal tragedy.* He was ready to walk off when a petite, gray-haired woman joined him. "Who is it, Fred?" He told her. She looked at me as if it were a shame I'd never learned any manners. She said, "The two of you ought to think a little about … " That's when Isabel put her palm on the screen door. "Mrs. Ravoli," she said, "we're so sorry to come at your time of sorrow. My name is Isabel Moss." The woman crossed her arms and was about to spin around and walk off, leaving Fred to deal with the mess at her front door. Then she stopped. Her arms dropped to her sides. "Moss?" she said. Isabel nodded. "Oh, god. Fred, walk these two around back."

They comforted each other for long moments in the still heat of Louisa Ravoli's backyard before either said a word. Then Fred, who turned out to be the live-in boyfriend, brought a pitcher of lemonade and the four of us sat at a picnic table. "Listen, Mrs. Ravoli, I ... "

" — No, you listen, Mr. Reporter. I was a journalist 25 years in Shelby, North Carolina before we moved here. I know how the game's played, and I'm telling you plain as rain — you may *not* use anything I say here without my prior approval. You agree to that, you can stay. If not, Fred here will show you out."

I thought, I could stay and listen, and possibly negotiate the use of some information later, or sit in the hot car and watch the mourners come and go. I agreed to her terms. She made me repeat my vow and then, satisfied, though not a hundred percent, turned to Isabel, clasping both her hands. "Marcus was very sad." Isabel was barely holding it together. Mrs. Ravoli said, "I begged him to get help. It was hard 'cause he couldn't tell anyone why he was so hurt. The Army made him promise to keep it secret and they held him to it. They said they'd take care of him, that everything would be alright."

"Mrs. Ravoli — "

She shut me up with angry eyes and returned to Isabel. "He didn't mean it. You've got to know that. He was torn up about killing another American boy, accident or not. He didn't tell me right away. Took him a long time to get it out. I thought once he did, he'd feel better. He didn't, no ma'm. He started staying alone a lot. Went hunting alone. Saw movies alone. That scared me. Him alone in the woods with a weapon. Ate by himself. He used to come up here for dinner every Sunday. He stopped coming. I called and he wouldn't answer." She finally let Isabel's hands loose, but held her eyes. "Mrs. Moss, my boy Marcus believed in what he

132

was sent over there to do. He loved the Army and he loved his country and all it stands for, same as your husband, I'm sure. Now both of them are gone. I don't know what else to say. I haven't slept; I keep thinking of him as a little boy …"

Isabel breathed deeply and began another of her amazing transformations. Grieving widow one minute, power forward the next. "I don't blame Marcus, Mrs. Ravoli. If we'd gotten here in time, I would have told him that. It was a terrible accident no one can un-do. But the Army … They made it worse. Maybe if they'd allowed Marcus to accept responsibility, he'd still be here. The Army officials who made these decisions need to be held accountable. No other families should have to go through this. I didn't even get enough of Hank back to have a decent burial."

Louisa Ravoli bowed her head as if expecting divine instruction. "I don't know, Isabel. They're both gone and like you say, nothing we do will bring them back. And there's another piece worrying me — all those other soldiers over there still fighting. How would they feel if this came out?"

"I think they'd feel like their country hasn't forgotten about the ideals they're trying to bring to that part of the world." Mrs. Ravoli lifted up her head and bowed it again. Isabel took her hands. "There's something else. You don't know this. Hank was a professional athlete. He was on the verge of a breakthrough when the terrorists flew those planes into the Trade Center. Hank's sister Catherine lived in New York. She worked in one of the towers and called her mom before the building collapsed and she died with all the others. Mrs. Moss — Hank and Catherine's mom — wasn't home. Catherine had to leave a message on her answering machine. Imagine coming home from the grocery store and hearing that message. Losing his sister was a big part of the reason Hank put his career aside and joined the Army. I lost a husband, you lost a son. Hank's mother buried both her children."

"Mercy."

Everyone fell silent until a deep voice said, "Louisa, she's right." It was Fred, who hadn't said a word since pouring the lemonade. He dabbed his moist eyes with a napkin. "They did us wrong. I loved that Marcus even though he wasn't my own. I miss him already. Folks 'oughta know the truth."

"Isabel," Mrs. Ravoli said, "do you have a child?"

"A girl, Katie. She's four. She carries around a little blanket that she calls her Hanky. And Catherine had little Sally, Hank's niece."

"And you want this reporter to write a story in his Florida paper exposing what happened, this scandal about how Katie's daddy died?"

"I want him to write a story that tells the truth."

Louisa Ravoli took off her glasses and wiped them clean. She reached for Fred's hand. She said, "I don't know. I have to think on it. First thing I've got to do is bury my son." She turned to me. "You. Brown eyes. You call me in a couple of days. What's your name?"

"Dan, Daniel Patragno, ma'am."

"Fred, give Daniel Patragno the number."

Bella

Chapter 25

By 4, I was headed back to Washington and Isabel was on a one-way to Tampa. It was the first moment I'd had to think about the last two days — the meeting at *Mel's* with Bart Jefferson, Marcus Ravoli's suicide, and sitting with Louisa Ravoli, who confirmed — even though it was off the record — that her son killed Hank Moss, the rising tennis star who joined the Army and went to Afghanistan to avenge his sister's murder on 9/11.

We were about to get busier still. Isabel and I had to check in on the Senate investigation ordered by Sen. Newlin, keep digging for the UAV video, and double back and talk again to Mrs. Ravoli. I knew the progress we'd made would fuel the work that remained. I could feel the momentum. I also knew I'd fallen so hard for Isabel Moss, I wasn't even thinking about unethical behavior anymore. Who needed to be objective? Two solid sources already confirmed the story was accurate. It wasn't necessary to keep any professional distance between us. We wanted to be together, and together we would be. I had allowed and even encouraged a source on the biggest story of my career to become a partner and, worse, a lover. I shifted and closed my eyes as we descended toward Washington. Somewhere deep down a voice was speaking to me. *Moron*, it said.

I wasn't sure whether to go to home, to Clay's, or to a hotel. I picked home and headed for the Metro, switching from yellow to red at Gallery Place for the train to Silver Spring. The train was jammed as usual and I wound up belt to butt with a woman linebacker with a nose ring and sideburns who smelled like she'd been hauling something heavy since morning. I cursed myself for not driving to the airport in the first place. And I still had to take a bus after the subway.

Ellie's car was in the driveway next to mine. Maybe it wasn't such a good idea to come home after all. I had my keys. I could get the car and drive to Clay's. Before my next move, the front door flew open. "Dad's home," Robbie shouted as he bolted toward me. I lifted and hugged him and was glad he caught me before I could sneak away. "How you doing, champ?" He didn't ask for the present I'd promised. He asked if we could throw the ball around. Ellie appeared in the doorway. She'd been in the kitchen and still had a dish towel and wet frying pan in her hands. Several strands of hair had broken loose and were dangling down her forehead. She looked terrific. "You hungry?" she said. "Come eat. We had breakfast for dinner, eggs and pancakes." I told Robbie to get the gloves and ball and I'd be out after I had some breakfast for dinner. Then I walked in my house as if I were a guest.

It wasn't until after I ate, played catch with Robbie and sent him off to bed that we talked. I told Ellie the whole Hank Moss story as a reporter would explain it to an editor. Then I added the personal part, sparing details, but making plain that I had feelings for Isabel and would keep seeing her. "I'm sorry. It's out of control. There's nothing I can do."

Ellie surprised me. She didn't cry. She took my hand and kissed it, right above my wedding band. "You're going to get hurt, Danny. This woman — I'm sure she's lovely." Eyes brimming with pity, my wife added, "She doesn't care about you. She's probably nuts. Who can blame her after what she's been through? But you … You should be smarter. Her life was taken from her. You're giving yours away. Career, family, everything. That poor boy from South Carolina blew up Hank Moss. Nobody's blowing up your life but you, Danny."

She was so right I winced. She waited for me to answer. When I didn't, she said, "There's something else. I need to finish telling you about … "

My cell rang. The display said *Ohrbachs*. I told Ellie to give me a second to get rid of Clay. But it wasn't Clay; it was Mary Ohrbach, and her voice was trembling. "Dan, we need to meet, soon as you can." I'd never heard unflappable Mary so upset. I knew her as one of those smart, passionate lawyers able to stay objective no matter what gets flung their way. Funny, too. One Saturday night the four of us went for Indian food. When talk turned to the Sunday pick-up basketball game, she stroked her husband's neck and said, in loving reference to his crummy shot, "You be sure to pass and rebound, honey." Mary asked to meet at the playground near their house. We hung up and I told Ellie. "I don't know what it is. You know Mary. She doesn't screw around like this. I don't know why we couldn't meet at the house. I've practically been living there. I'll go and be back soon as I can."

"Sit down a minute, Danny. I know what it's about." I was surprised and did as told, mind racing. Ellie sipped from her water bottle. She put it on the table, seemed to read and analyze the nutrition facts, and said, "Mary knows what I was about to tell you." I hadn't a clue until that moment, but now I knew too. The air rushed from my chest and my heart got tight. Of all people. *Don't say it, Ellie. Please don't say it.*

"I'm sorry. We didn't plan it. We knew it was wrong. You, Mary, Robin, their girls — we felt so shitty after. We cut it off before anyone found out. Maybe that's worth a few points." All I could do was wag my head and pray that I hadn't heard correctly. Ellie read my face and decided there should be no confusion. She said, "It was Clay, Danny. The man I was seeing was Clay Ohrbach."

She was sitting on a swing and barely swaying when I got to the park. She didn't look up. I took the next swing and matched her pace. They were little kid swings; our feet scuffed the ground and made uneven lines in the dirt.

"You know why I called?" she said, staring ahead. I did now, I told her, and asked, "How'd you find out?" Her eyes were a dam about to blow. "My brilliant scientist husband charged a room at the Marriott in D.C. on our VISA card." *Christ, the same hotel where I slept with Isabel. We could have run into each other, passed a message from home. Make sure to pick up milk and Cheerios; we ran out.* Mary said, "I pay the bills. How could he think I wouldn't notice? The weasel didn't even try to lie. I showed him the bill and he confessed. Clay and Ellie. Shacking up for weeks. *Months*, for all we know. I didn't even think they liked each other."

I reached across and touched her cheek. "Did he tell you they broke it off?"

"He did; I'm not sure I believe him. I'm not sure it matters. If he needed a girlfriend, he's not satisfied at home. Fine. Let him go start a new life. The girls and I will be just fine." She stopped swinging. "Right now I'm so angry, I don't trust my judgment. I'm going to wait. If I still feel this way in a few weeks, I'll divorce him." She kicked a mound of dirt under her swing. "What about you? How are you handling things?"

"Not sure; I'm not really one to pass judgment." She dug a foot in the loose dirt and grabbed my swing. "What do you mean, *not one to pass judgment?*" I told her it was a god-awful long story. She said she had plenty of time and wouldn't mind a long story that had nothing to do with her scummy husband. Besides, she'd thrown Clay out. "He wanted to be in a hotel so bad, that's where I sent him." I grasped the chains of my swing, leaned way back and gazed at the sky upside down. The shimmering orange sun promised jungle heat tomorrow.

W hen I was all talked out, she returned to being a lawyer. "There are two things going on, one private, one public. I'm not judging you on the first. You and Ellie work it out. The second — shit, Danny, that's atrocious. Tell me again about the space camera thing."

"Unmanned aerial vehicle," I corrected, and told her.

"I'm sorry. It sounds like utter bullshit. An *unmanned aerial vehicle* on routine patrol — 50,000 feet up in the sky, no less — shoots streaming video of an American soldier on the ground in Afghanistan getting blown up by another U.S. GI? And there's a tape made from the video, and apparently a conspiracy somewhere in the Army to keep it secret? C'mon, Danny."

I heard the way she said it and the whole thing *did* sound like an old *Star Trek.* "I haven't seen the tape. A credible source told me it exists. And I'm 99.9 percent sure Hank Moss was killed by friendly fire."

"That doesn't mean — "

" — I know. It doesn't mean I can prove it."

She pulled out a pack of spearmint gum. I took a piece and used the quiet to process all we'd discussed. We didn't speak for several minutes, though I was sure she felt the same as me, that we were now linked forever by our spouses' infidelity. She stopped chewing and spit out her gum like a little kid. "This UAV stuff — Is that what you asked Clay about a few nights ago?" I told her I'd asked about satellite photos, not UAV surveillance tapes. "Clay set me straight about the images. The satellites can't get that close and they don't penetrate clouds. He didn't say anything about UAV's."

She planted her feet, halting the swing. "And you didn't ask?" I told her I didn't ask because I was a political reporter and never heard of them until I went to Florida and met Bart Jefferson.

"But Clay didn't offer anything about UAVs?"

"Nope."

The thought seemed to strike us at the same time. "You're acting like he could be hiding something, Mary."

"It's possible. He's capable of deception, as we've seen. I'll do some snooping. I'll let you know if I find anything."

"You'd do that?"

"I would. And it has nothing to do with anything else he's done."

I kissed her forehead and left for home.

T he couch was my bed that night. I was grateful Ellie still cared enough to put on a sheet and blanket. Maybe I was flattering myself. Maybe she made the bed because she knew I'd flop down and pull a blanket over my head, and wanted a sheet between me and the sofa.

"You okay?"

Ellie at the top of the stairs, barefoot and wearing a light pink robe. The betrayer who got betrayed, up late to make sure I was comfortable.

"Fine. Thanks for making the bed."

Bella

"How's Mary?"

"Okay. Not your biggest fan at the moment."

She walked down and got a bottle of wine and two glasses. "Of course not. I don't like myself very much either at the moment."

One problem with having an affair is that the inevitable comparisons are usually unfair. A new girlfriend won't slide into bed with vomit green exfoliating moisturizer on her face. She won't bitch about your music or how loud you make the stereo. And, because she hasn't seen all your tricks yet, she's delighted with how you play the harmonica, rollerblade backwards, and make witty cracks at her boss's cocktail parties. The same things once impressed your wife. No more. Your wife not only knows your tricks, she knows every shirt, tie and pair of pants hanging in the closet. After a few years, she doesn't even look up when you go out the door. So an adoring new girlfriend — or boyfriend for the neglected wife — is great for a flagging ego. What no one thinks about is that after a little time, once the glow fades, the adoring girlfriend learns to hide the harmonica because the same songs over and over begin triggering migraines that make her feel like her eyes are bleeding. The recycled wisecracks become as annoying as they once were funny. If you don't stop, she will loosen the wheels in those new rollerblades and deliver you to the steepest trail in the county. This is roughly the time some men start casting around for a new girlfriend.

No one thinks of such things in the early going. When Ellie spoke, I watched her mouth and thought about kissing Isabel. She probably thought some about Clay as we sat together. Two strangers inside our closed circle. How did it happen? How did the loop open so easily after we put so many years into making it tight and strong? And what of the collateral damage? "I feel worst for Mary. Of the four of us, she's the only one who didn't do anything wrong."

141

"Don't be naïve, Danny. We were wrong, Clay and me. I'm not defending a thing. Don't think they had a perfect marriage, though."

She poured the wine. We touched glasses without a toast. I said, "Whose marriage is perfect?"

"No one's. Here's to the elusive perfect marriage." We clinked again and traded sad smiles. I realized why people didn't have breakfast for dinner too often. By 10 o'clock, I was starving again. I didn't know if I had to ask for permission to raid my own fridge. I was about to, just to be safe. Instead, unaccountably, I said, "Was he good in bed, Ellie? I'm sorry for asking, I know it's dumb. He's just so clumsy on the basketball court. Was it different in the sack? I just have to know."

She drew the robe tight around her neck and made for the kitchen, taking her glass, leaving the bottle. "Goodnight, Danny. Help yourself if you want anything to eat."

Bella

Chapter 26

There were two messages from Canton Spivey when I got to work next morning. The first was short: *What the fuck, Patragno?* The second was not as diplomatic: *Call if you still like your job.* I called. I told him everything he needed to know, deleting details that were none of his business. I wasn't sure what to expect, and was nicely surprised when he said, "Good work, Danny. Now pull the last few strings and finish it." I told him it would take at least a few more days, maybe a week. The phone went dead. I figured, that's it, the era of peace and goodwill is over. Not quite. "Look, you're doing great," he said. "We're going to rip St. Pete and the *Herald* a new one with this story. Move as fast as you can. Don't compromise accuracy. Double-check your quotes and sources. I'll keep everyone here off your ass. I've got Doyle Butcher following the Kirk Lawton story. He actually came up with something new yesterday. Whoever stole the senator's credit card used it to buy $300 worth of porn and a $250 massage at *Lily's Pleasure Pagoda* in DC."

"My story should have such a happy ending."

"Funny. Okay, back to it and call in soon as you're solid."

I thanked him and threw my feet up on the desk. Spivey wasn't a bad guy. If I could keep my affair (*ugh, the word was starting to make me retch*) with Isabel quiet until after the story came out, neither of us would get burned. Once the story was published, she would no longer be a source. Then I could do as I wanted without compromising my alleged journalistic integrity.

"Where you been, Patragno? Vacation?"

It always bugged me that Dorkman — Tampa Congressman Eddie Dwoark — got so much mileage out of camping in his office and showering in the House gym instead of renting or buying on Capitol Hill like everyone else. Each year around tax time he called a press conference and returned $30,000 of his federal salary to some Treasury Department sourpuss in a wrinkled suit. Each year was the same — the Treasury guy muttered his thanks and walked off awkwardly with a poster-sized replica of Eddie Dwoark's personal check as goofy TV reporters jockeyed around like they were covering a new Mideast peace accord. Dwoark's checks were custom-made with a cartoon pelican family designed by one of the four little Dwoarks at home in Tampa. No one seemed to care that there was a tennis court attached to the congressman's home on Bayshore Boulevard or that his beach home in Sanibel once made the pages of *Architectural Digest*. His heart surgeon dad was a huge success, and Dwoark grew up in oceanfront mansions, private schools and designer labels. He was even wealthier today with the late dad's fortune piled on his own, so returning $30,000 to the Treasury was no hardship. Plus, the stunt probably earned a million bucks worth of free publicity. Dorkman was shameless. Once the TV crews were in place, he would pat his sofa and look soulfully into the cameras. "I'd rather sleep on this couch than waste taxpayer dollars on an apartment I don't need."

I had two problems with the check stunt. The first was, when he said that crap, I had a terrible urge to break the cardboard check over his stupid head. The second was that Dwoark's congressional office was the size of a bank lobby and smelled like a homeless shelter each morning before the staff — paid, incidentally, with taxpayer dollars — came in and cleaned up.

"Chasing a story, congressman, same as always."

"We going to see it in the paper anytime soon?"

He liked to bait me by saying the things he thought an editor would say. Sometimes it worked. This time it was still early and the smell of the office was a lot worse than Dwoark playing newspaperman. He thought I was there to ask about a pending gay marriage bill, and carefully set his coffee cup on the desk when I said the piece was about one of his constituents, a military widow named Isabel Moss.

"Sad situation," he shrugged, as if he knew nothing more than what he'd read in the paper, which of course was horseshit. I wasn't in the mood. "I know you've seen her, Ed," I said. He picked up his cup and sipped slowly. Only family and other members of Congress called him Ed. "I know about her laying the shred of Hank's uniform on your desk. I know you got a little freaked and called your friend Senator Newlin to help get an investigation started."

"All you know is what she told you."

"You're denying it?"

"What do you really want to know, Danny?"

"Well, to start — "

" — To start, let's agree this is all off the record."

Jeez, *that* again. "I don't think so. You don't want to be quoted, I'll use what she told me and write that you declined comment."

"Why're you being a hard-ass, Danny?"

"You don't need to be off the record on this. The Moss family lived in your district. She and the kid are still constituents. She came to you for help. You helped her. I'm writing about it."

He popped up and closed the door, telling the secretary not to interrupt. He tossed his black suit jacket on the couch to show he was done fooling around. The jacket had a nice sheen to it. I snuck a peek at the label — *Capone Uomo* — and stashed the name for possible future use. *Congressman Dwoark sleeps in his office, his $2,500 Capone Uomo suit carefully hung on a nearby coat rack.* He adjusted one of his American eagle cufflinks and tried to reason with me like a colleague. "You know how important the military is to politicians in Hillsborough County. Those generals find out I'm helping her, possibly embarrassing the Army, I'll lose a ton of support."

I reminded him we *weren't* colleagues and that his reelection wasn't my concern. "What you just said is a good quote. Give me something better or that's what you'll read in the paper."

"Damn it, you're keyed on the wrong issue. What's important here is getting justice for that woman, not my role in it."

"Sorry, you don't get to decide what's important to my readers. Jeez, where would *that* stop? Should I start checking with you before we go to print each night?"

"We're only talking about one story."

"You're trying to sidetrack me, congressman." I switched on my tape recorder and laid it on the desk. "Do you have a quote or not?"

Ed Dwoark's ears ran to pink when he was angry. They were now violet as Attila tulips. "State your question," he said. I flipped through my notes for a blank page and got ready to write, just in case the tape recorder failed. "Do you believe the Army covered up the true cause of Hank Moss' death?"

"I have no idea how he died."

"Why did you decide to help Isabel Moss?"

"Ms. Moss is a constituent. Her husband gave his life fighting for our country. He put the nation's safety and security before his own personal aspirations. I believe the only way she'll achieve closure is by getting all her questions answered."

"Achieve closure?"

"That's what I said."

I thanked him instead of calling him a douche bag, which is what he deserved. He didn't stand, shake hands, or try any more smartass editor cracks. He swung around on his chair toward a window that faced the 26,000 plants of the U.S. Botanic Garden and put the phone to one of his tulip ears.

A little rift with the local congressman wasn't bad. Dwoark couldn't afford to ignore me, or, more important, have me ignore him. I was the link to his voters back home, we both knew it, and it was healthy for him to receive an occasional reminder. I had no such leverage with a senior U.S. senator from North Dakota. Forget any interview. Derrick Newlin wouldn't trade a ring-necked pheasant for a reporter from Tampa. My second choice was the chief of staff, who likewise couldn't be bothered. I wound up late in the afternoon with the press secretary, a young Asian woman as petite as some of Robin's classmates and roughly the same age as Miss Lipinski. She assessed me with bright black eyes that seemed able and eager to focus on four projects at once. She pumped my hand. She said, "You're wondering how someone named *Gemma Uy* from the Philippines ever came to work for Derrick Newlin of Devils Lake, North Dakota." She bowed playfully. "It's this way, Mr. Patragno. We met one snowy night in a log cabin bar in Sioux Falls, started talking, one thing led to another, and now I'm carrying his little love cowboy. Please don't put that information in your newspaper."

I liked her right off, even the patched denim jacket she wore over her navy suit. "No," I said, "I just — "

" — It's fine. I get it all the time. His father and mine served together in World War II. I bugged the senator for an internship when I was at Georgetown. After school, I got a job in the press office. Three years later, I'm running it. They like young people. We work cheap, love politics, and have no lives outside the job." Before I could react, she said, "So what's up? What does the Tampa paper want with my boss?" I told her and could almost see the *no comment* coming before I finished the question. "Can't help you, Danny," she said. "All I can do is promise to call when — make that *if* — we have something to say."

"I can't wait that long."

"I'm not messing with you. We have nothing to say right now. If you decide to go with a story, call me late as possible. Ill try to get you something before deadline. Deal?"

"Deal." She slipped me a card and took off, talking to someone through a wireless headset and punching numbers in a second cell as she walked. I was thinking she couldn't weigh more than a hundred pounds when another inner office opened and Senator Newlin came out, his frontier paw on the lower back of a woman with long black hair and dark pearl heels. We saw each other at the same time and she warned me off as I was about to say hello and introduce myself to the senator. I nodded and slipped toward the hallway as Newlin and Isabel hugged and said goodbye. All I heard was his gravely voice say, "I'm sorry, I wish there was more, my dear."

Bella

"Here we go again."

"Calm down. They called late and asked if I could come up today. It was very sudden."

I waited, trying not to be petulant, angry that I couldn't help myself. Fists balled, I wouldn't even look at her. Another solo flight with me on the ground. Isabel and Danny — united in bed, united for justice, united until she decided to take off by herself. I tried to see through to the end. Once I helped her prove the Army killed Hank and covered it up, she'd slip off and I'd be wondering what happened until the movie came out on *Showtime*. I needed to get some space between myself and this woman. Ellie was right — *She doesn't care about you. She's probably nuts.* Remembering my wife's advice about my girlfriend at such a moment and knowing it was good advice should have told me something. Isabel took my elbow and tried to steer me further from Newlin's office. I wouldn't budge. She put a hand behind my head and kissed me. I resisted. I did. I resisted a little. She said, "Please stop. You're being unreasonable." Maybe she was right. Maybe I was being unreasonable. I let her lead me and soon we were outside the Hart Building, facing Constitution Avenue. A tour bus with Minnesota plates stopped and disgorged throngs of girls and boys in red T-shirts that said *Shakopee Sabers — State B-Ball Champs.* "Why didn't you call, tell me you were coming?" She took my hand and we crossed Constitution to get away from the kids. "Wrong question," she said. I glanced toward the Capitol. We were about a hundred yards away. "What do you mean, wrong question?" The usual line of visitors snaked out through the parking lot toward the Supreme Court. Wary cops were everywhere, but it was too hot for any trouble. "What you want to ask is what Newlin told me, right?" I shrugged. "Snap out of it, Danny. Don't you want to know?" I did.

"Their investigators didn't turn up a thing. No one's talking and they don't know about Bart Jefferson; they didn't connect Marcus Ravoli's suicide. And they don't know anything about the video. That's what Newlin wanted to tell me — that he was sorry."

"Did you — "

" — I didn't tell him squat."

She'd played it right. I was pleased. And yet still aggravated. Plus there was something else. "Where did all your ponderous questions go about love and marriage, Isabel? How come you never ask me anything about my wife or kid anymore? You used to ask before we slept together. Is it because you're not serious about me or you just don't want to know? Are you afraid of getting hurt?"

She answered before she could think. It was the most honest she'd ever been, or, as it turned out, would be in the future. She said, "Nothing can hurt me anymore."

I thought of challenging her and stopped. The inner voice was calling. *Get your ass outta' here, Danny.* Once again I wasn't listening.

She had a late flight back to Tampa. I wanted her to stay; she said she wanted to and would have if not for Katie. "I just got home from Charleston and they called me to come to D.C. They could have told me on the phone that they came up empty. I don't know why I had to fly in." She took my hand and walked us back toward Constitution. The cabs were moving in swarms; all she needed to do to snag one was raise a finger. I did it first, to show I was okay with her leaving. *Don't worry 'bout me, honey. I'll see you when I see you.* A checkered cab pulled over and I opened the back door. "I'll try to call tomorrow," she said, kissing me goodbye. I wanted badly to get in with her and tell the cabbie to fuck the airport, take us to the Marriott, and fast. I wanted it so badly, it scared me. A guy in a Mercedes trapped behind the cab hit his horn. "Danny," she laughed, and I realized I was still hugging her. I let go and they pulled away, the Mercedes close behind. The irritated driver shook his head at me as he whizzed by. I knew exactly what he meant.

I ran into the delirious Shakopee Sabers on the way back to my car. The novelty of being in Washington hadn't worn off; they were running wild, tossing Frisbees and chasing each other around hundred-year-old fountains and closely-cropped flower beds. Why shouldn't they be happy? They were hundreds of miles from home with two middle-aged chaperones standing between them and a week of D.C. decadence. We were all headed the same way, toward Union Station. Everyone stopped when I got to the Honda and yelled, "Shit!"

The orange boot had my front wheel in a death grip. I checked the meter. Seven minutes still remained. "Son-of-a-bitch cops." Oddly, there was no ticket on the windshield. One of the boys got on his knees by the curb. He pushed, pulled, pressed, twisted and, after repeating the procedure in reverse order, gave up. "Got a torch? That mother's on there good," he said. A squeaky girl said, "Who do you call to get it off?"

Good question. No ticket, no number to call, no sign of a tow truck or cop car. I stood there like the new panda, 30 kids and two adult Minnesotans waiting for me to roll over and lick myself. I felt their stares. I grinned at them. I almost climbed a tree. I said, "You guys will see fantastic things while you're in Washington. Then you'll probably go home and tell everyone about the dope whose car got booted near Union Station. Plato said, *Nothing in the affairs of men is worthy of great anxiety.* It's true. Learn *that* and your time in D.C. will have been well spent." One of them looked at me blandly and said, "When you saw your car, you cursed and called the cops sons of bitches. You scared us."

Well, here was a kid who wanted his Saber teeth loosened. I was about to answer the little smartass when a scrawny boy stepped up — the team manager, I learned later — and kicked gently at the boot. His appraisal: "*Black Bear* — welded steel, patented clamp and lock, state of the art, cops call it, *The Stopper* ..."

"Shut up, shop boy," one of the girls said, drawing giggles from her friends.

I stepped toward the boy. "Can you get it off without the key?"

"You mind losin' your tire?" I didn't mind, and told him it was worth a twenty if he could get it done fast.

"Cake," he said. He took my keys and got a lug wrench from the trunk. "Help me with this," he said. We got down together and he explained the strategy. Pull the *Stopper* pad back far enough to work the wrench inside. Undo the bolts, jack up the car, and slide off the wheel. Then slip on the spare. It worked perfectly. When he was done, I gave him the twenty and someone snapped a picture of us with the booted tire lying in the street, useless as roadkill.

I said goodbye to the kids and chaperones from Shakopee. (*Shakopee!* I felt an urge to learn what exotic part of Minnesota had produced my new friends and vowed to find the town on a map when I returned to my laptop. I imagined frozen lakes and ice fishing.) I was about to pull away when I caught sight of a fast-moving Ford sedan two blocks away. Sitting in the passenger seat was a guy in a suit with a familiar crew cut. Was it him? Was he smiling? I felt a chill. Was he capable of more than phony tickets and tire boots? Could the day get any worse?

My cell rang and I smiled when I saw it was Isabel. She missed me already. Maybe she reconsidered and wanted to spend the night. "Hey,"

I said.

"Danny, I just have a second; they're boarding." I told her to let 'em load the damn plane and take off without her. I'd even come pick her up from the airport. I'd get us that room. "Danny, listen. Bart Jefferson called. Oscar Sanchez is dead. Bart said Sanchez's unit was ambushed yesterday and Sanchez was one of the first killed. Machine gun. He was dead before anyone could get to him." I couldn't place the name for a second. Then I remembered. *Oscar Sanchez, the other soldier with Jefferson, Marcus Ravoli and Marlin Falk when Hank was killed.* Sanchez had stayed in Afghanistan with Marlin Falk while Ravoli was dispatched from the military with an honorable discharge. Sanchez was now the only one who died the way anyone expects when a nation sends its soldiers off to war. "Danny?"

The list of direct witnesses had shrunk to Bart Jefferson and Sgt. Marlin Falk, location unknown. I told her to have a good flight. I squeezed my eyes shut tight and closed my phone. Enough surprises for one day. Or so I thought.

Chapter 27

Waiting for me at home were Ellie and Mary Nielsen-Ohrbach, sitting quietly in the family room, two old buds sipping wine and chatting girlishly about God knew what. All friends have little fights. Someone forgets a birthday, or quibbles about the lunch check, or has a party in the yard that goes too late and loud into the night. But come on, Ellie screwed Mary's husband. And here they were — the wife and the girlfriend — lounging and getting a little blasted. What was this, Woodstock? Were they going to break out the hash pipe next? I wondered if Mary shared my obsessive curiosity about Clay. Maybe I'd walked in on the critical question.

Don't you find he's kind of a clumsy lover, Ellie?

Clumsy, yes, Mary, but hung like a polar bear.

True, that makes up for a lot.

I should've snuck around back and eavesdropped a little. Now they were on their guard, discussing lighter fare and washing it down with the same *Merlot* Ellie and I shared the night before. Way too civilized. The scene screamed for accusations, threats and maybe an outside attorney or two, not *Stepford* wife pleasantries. When I said hello, Ellie quickly excused herself, saying Mary had come to talk business with me. There was an awkward moment because Ellie didn't know how to get off stage. Mary saved her, giving a quick embrace and promising to call again soon.

All calm exited the room with my wife. "I found something," Mary said, touching my hands, grasping my fingers and then letting them loose, slightly embarrassed by her own nervousness. "Not much. A name and number. A guy at the Pentagon. I'm not sure what it means." She spoke in fragments and it was hard to follow. I knew Clay analyzed data from satellites. He probably spoke to a half-dozen guys at the Pentagon every week. I suggested as much.

"Fourteen years," she said. "Fourteen years we've been married. I take his suits and shirts to the cleaners every Friday. In all that time, I've never found a note in the pockets. No names, no numbers. Not even Ellie's."

"I'm not sure — "

" — I know his writing, Danny. It's tight, neat, precise, just what you'd expect from a scientist. This was dashed off in a rush. He was nervous when he wrote this. Look."

She passed a crumpled *Post-it.* Above the number was a name: Charles Braxton. I didn't see anything unusual. "How do you even know the guy works at the Pentagon?"

"I called the number. The woman who answered said it was the Joint Chiefs of Staff, J2. I looked it up online, Danny. It's all public information. J2 is the *Directorate for Intelligence.*" I stared at the paper and wondered if Gavin Sussman was still awake.

"Why do you want to know about the Joint Chiefs?"

"Look, the less you know the happier you'll be." Gavin thought a second. He sighed. He said, "The formal structure for the Joint Chiefs of

Staff goes back to the end of World War II. The *idea* is probably old as the Revolutionary War: no branch of the military fights wars by itself, so we need the heads of the Army, Navy, and the rest talking to each other before they advise the president. That's the Joint Chiefs. Plus, these guys have lots of people working for them. That's the joint *staff.*"

"Know someone named Charles Braxton?"

"Charlie Braxton. Yeah, I know *of* him. Master Sgt. Charles Braxton. Each service chief appoints an operations director. Charlie Braxton used to be director for the Army guy, General Stockton. Now Braxton's at J-2."

"The Intelligence Directorate," I said. Gavin confirmed and I asked precisely what they did. "It's all public information; you can look it up yourself. Get on the web and ... Nevermind. I'm at my computer. Here. J-2 is the *national focal point for crisis intelligence support to military operations, indications and warning intelligence in the Department of Defense ...* "

"That include satellite data?"

"Hmm, doesn't say, but I think yes." He added, "Let's see — J-2 *serves as the intelligence community manager for support to military operations ...* "

So Clay had — at a minimum — spoken with someone connected to the core of the nation's military intelligence community. That tidbit wasn't worth much by itself. "Gavin, would someone in Charles Braxton's position deal with the National Reconnaissance Office?"

"NRO. He might. I don't know. I'm in a different — "

" — Let me be specific. The National Reconnaissance Office" — I rummaged through my notes — "develops and operates unique and innovative space reconnaissance systems and conducts intelligence-related activities essential for U.S. national security. The NRO designs, builds and operates the nation's reconnaissance satellites (which) can warn of potential trouble spots around the world, help plan military operations, and monitor the environment. Gavin … "

"*What*, for Christ's sake?"

"Is it possible NRO had the raw streaming video of Hank Moss getting blown to bits — or maybe a tape of the original video — and Charles Braxton called someone — a scientist or mid-level guy at NRO — to order the tape delivered to him or maybe even destroyed?"

"I'm telling you, I don't — "

" — Is it *possible*?"

He paused, no doubt considering the implications of what I was suggesting. "Yeah," he said. "It's possible."

"I need Braxton's official bio."

"If it isn't online, you have to go through Pentagon Public Affairs. They get in pretty early. Just call them — "

" — Gavin — "

" — You have to go through Public Affairs because that's standard — "

" — I don't want to tip anyone — "

" — I don't give a shit. Go through — "

" — Listen, I'm not asking for the flippin' code to fire a nuke at North Korea. All I want is his bio. Where he's from, where he worked, where he went to school. Is that going to endanger the nation?"

He thought about it. I let the quiet stand. "I'll get you his fucking bio, and that's it. You can't call me anymore. I'm done. Why did I ever have lunch with you?"

"I need one more thing."

Silence. I imagined his hands snaking through the phone and closing around my throat

"I need a bio for a *Sgt. Marlin Falk.*"

"Who the hell is that?"

"He was first on the scene after Hank Moss was killed."

"And?"

"That's all I know."

"You think Braxton and Falk are tied somehow?"

"Could be."

"Spell *Falk.*" I did. He said, "I'll see what we've got. Then you better remember what I said. Don't call again."

"You're a good guy, Gavin."

"Go screw yourself."

I t was time to confront Clay. I considered driving to Bethesda and remembered he was still banished. I started to call Mary for the hotel number when Ellie and Robin walked in smiling and singing. I laid down the phone. Bubbly Robin was tip-toeing in with an ice cream cake with candles. I'd forgotten my own birthday. I was now 37, and, as Robin the jokester reminded me, a mere three years from 40. "That's over 200 in dog years, dad," he said, the little wiseass. I blew out all those candles before we barbecued the house. Both of them wanted to know my wish and of course I wouldn't tell. It would have been too hard to explain what I'd asked for — that I was wrong, and that my friend and basketball pal Clay Ohrbach wasn't involved in the cover-up. I had to be fair with Clay when I so badly wanted to crush him. The bastard slept with my wife, after all. That wasn't the worst, though. I figured I could eventually forgive the cheating. I'd done the same, though not with *his* wife. What I couldn't forgive was Clay burying evidence about Hank Moss. Did I have a double standard about betrayal? Was it acceptable to betray your wife but not your homeland? Was I playing the child's game of making up new rules as I went along?

I unwrapped my present, a nicely framed eight-by-ten of the Patragno trio on the marble steps of the Lincoln last summer. A German tourist had snapped the shot; his wife made us giggle by sticking out the longest tongue I'd ever seen. God, How Robin laughed. Good times, sweet and safe. How fast it all changed, fast as dog years.

Sometime in the night I rolled over and realized one of them was awake. I sat up on the couch, fumbled for my watch, punched the button that lit the black face. It was a little after 4 a.m. I padded into the kitchen in my underwear and found Ellie by the breakfast nook, wine glass in one hand, my new eight-by-ten in the other. I walked behind and stroked her shoulders. It wasn't easy to see her hurting. She put down the glass and said she was sorry, so sorry, about the business with Clay. Voice aching, she said, "How long are you going to punish me?" *Payback.* She thought I wanted payback. Maybe she thought I was looking for an opening to renounce *my* playmate. I wished it were so. I wasn't being cold or vindictive. I just didn't feel the same. I felt high and invincible, sick and helpless. That's how it is with new love fever. I had a bad case and, laughable as it seems today in this shitty apartment, bed always unmade, inside of the fridge crowded with leftover Thai and Chinese, and the outer door, with Robbie's crude artwork (his preference is one-on-one knife fights), that's the only way I can explain it. Weak, stupid and addicted as any junkie, each risk and every sacrifice seemed worthwhile so long as it got me closer to Isabel.

I swallowed and told Ellie change was damned hard, and at least we had nine pretty good years — well, eight and a half — and a beautiful son even if the marriage didn't last forever. "Most don't. We beat the odds, and we're both young. We can start again. The trouble with us began before Clay, love. If it wasn't him, it would have been someone else. Same for me and Isabel." I spoke with conviction, believing each word. She tapped the photo's blonde wood frame and looked down sadly at the three strangers smiling up at us. "You talk about odds. All the things in this picture — odds are you're never going to replace them. You know that, right Danny?" I did, though the information was buried in one of my many blind spots. She laid down the photo. "Do me one favor." I said sure, of course, anything, name it. I took her hand to show I was the most sincere man in Silver Spring, Montgomery County, the state of Maryland and perhaps the entire Washington metro region. She withdrew her hand. She put her wine glass in the sink and rinsed it. She dried it and tossed the dish towel on the table near the photo. As she left the kitchen, she paused and patted my chest and said, "Don't ever say that cunt's name again out loud in my house."

Bella

Chapter 28

Side by side, the resumes sketched bare bones tales of two unspectacular Americans who, despite growing up hundreds of miles from one another against backdrops as different as America has to offer, loved their country enough to wear her uniform. Marlin Falk rose without fanfare from Monroeville, Pennsylvania, one of the no-nonsense, mountain-ringed valley towns outside Pittsburgh where, when it storms, black clouds mass on the border close and low like invading troops. I could see him shoveling driveways for extra money and learning to change his own motor oil by sophomore year in high school. Two beers and he'd be ready to fight anyone who insulted the *Pirates* or *Steelers*. Marlin Falk was 34, single, and already had 16 years in the military. He held an Associate in Science Degree from the Community College of Allegheny County.

A medley of fat, brassy notes made me look up from the pair of resumes Gavin had faxed from the Pentagon. A scruffy kid with an iron cross tattoo on his bicep entered the Bethesda café, rattling a dragonfly-shaped wind chime. It wasn't Clay, so I skipped to the other bio.

Master Sgt. Charles Braxton, 39, also unmarried, grew up in the Vegas suburb of Blue Diamond, Nevada. Where Falk breathed air corrupted by grimy steel mills, the young Braxton grew up in the neon desert alongside famous and struggling singers, boxers, comedians, and strippers. He might know a few casino bosses and blackjack dealers. He surely knew how to play poker; I made a mental note never to try and bluff him. As with Falk, Braxton's background was routine as a standard issue Army jeep. An undergraduate degree from UNLV, basic training, assignments here and there, a slow moving up the ranks until — I stopped at a bulleted item about his service in *Desert Storm* and flipped back to Falk. Falk was also stationed with coalition forces in Southwestern Iraq in 1990 and 1991. I tried to remember Desert Storm — had a decade really passed since the Persian Gulf War? — and came up with hazy fragments: Iraq invading Kuwait; the first President Bush frothing to get his hands on Saddam; grainy CNN footage of the U.S.-led air assault; smart bombs; the lame Iraqi troops surrendering in droves; Iraq tossed out of Kuwait but defiant Hussein still in power.

Falk and Braxton were over there in the middle of *Desert Storm*. They were kids then — short-haired, clean-shaven patriots worlds away from the hometowns where they grew up, shot 8 ball and, I guessed, vowed never to end up like their fathers and grandfathers. They became close while kicking Taliban ass. After the brief war, they traded numbers. Maybe they spent a little time in a veterans' hospital recovering from Gulf War Syndrome. Afterward, Falk wanted to be near the action and took whatever battlefield assignment they handed him, eventually ending up at the fateful Afghan crossroad with Oscar Sanchez, Bart Jefferson, Marcus Ravoli and the bloody patch of dust that was once Hank Moss. Jefferson, ashen-faced when telling the story in our Tampa meeting, said Falk quickly and categorically decided Moss was killed by Taliban fighters, then made sure each American G.I. had the story straight. *We clear on this soldier?* Each barked back, *Yes, Sir* to affirm he was clear.

Where Falk lusted for action, Braxton, it seemed, wanted rank and status and transferred to the Pentagon. Falk was still traveling with the troops on military transports; Braxton by now probably had a high-end SUV and a coveted spot in the Pentagon lot. There were 8,800 spaces, not that many considering 25,000 people, civilian and military, worked at DOD headquarters. The two Desert Storm buddies stayed in touch after the Gulf War, which no doubt seemed like a good thing for both after Ravoli pulled the pin and threw his grenade.

It all seemed plausible.

Less plausible — impossible to believe, really — was that Ellie — my Ellie — ever slept with the next man to enter the café. My hope of a discreet meeting faded as Clay pushed the door too hard and nearly took out the wind chime. It clanged like falling cymbals until he stilled it with one of his gangly hands. That hand and its hairy mate had roamed freely and selfishly over Ellie's flesh — property I'd long considered private. I thought we were friends. We sweated together every Sunday morning for more than five years. Danny P. and *Double A*. Sure it was just pick-up basketball, but there was exceptional intimacy in the weekly struggle to be first to 11, and, once victorious, a high-five and the winners' sardonic war whoop: *Who's next?* Did he think of me even once when he was screwing her? When they changed positions? And then, later, when they kissed goodbye and made plans for next time? Clay could say, *Careful about being too indignant, Danny. You cheated too.* Let him say it. Mine started after theirs. And I didn't sleep with my friend's wife. This was the first time I'd seen him since Ellie told the secret. Clay shrugged an apology at the owner and came to my table. Several coffee drinkers watched him closely. No one suspected I might be the dangerous one.

"You're not going to do anything dumb, are you, Danny?"

I didn't realize how vicious angry I was until I saw him. I was perfectly positioned to throw an uppercut. I imagined the punch smashing his chin, just above the knot of his navy tie. His head would snap back and I'd sink another into his gut. Down he'd go. *Who's next?*

"You know how sorry — "

" — Save it, Clay. This is something else. A story I'm working on. I think you have information that would help. Please sit."

"I'm not a press guy. You're supposed to go through public affairs."

He looked confused. Good, that meant Mary hadn't said anything. "Every now and then a story comes along that's important enough to break protocol. How about you listen a few minutes, and then decide if you want me to go through public affairs?"

He sat and produced a pen and small pad. "Habit," he said. "I take notes on most everything."

"What's your relationship with Charles Braxton, Clay?"

It was if I'd thrown the uppercut. He set down the pen, click-clacked the trigger. "Braxton?" He scrunched his eyes, scanned his files. "Braxton," he said. "Charles Braxton." I waited. Such crap. Clay, it was clear, grew up in suburban Maryland, not Vegas. He didn't play poker or know the first thing about bluffing. He loosened his tie. The wind chimes announced the arrival of an elderly couple. I said, "Clay, did you know that they broke the ground for the Pentagon on 9/11?" He stared at me, relieved to get a new question, flustered by the unrelated information. "September 11, 1941. That's when they started building that place. Ironic, no?"

"I didn't know — "

" — But you know Braxton. Master Sgt. Charles Braxton. From J-2, the Intelligence Directorate, at the Pentagon."

"I … Why do you want to know about Braxton?"

"Fine, that goes down as *declined to comment.* I'll get in touch with your public affairs folks, see what *they* say. Good luck explaining to your bosses when my story gets picked up by the wires and goes into papers *around the country.*" I tossed a ten on the table and stood. "See you at hoops." His hand shot out to stop me. I pulled away, made a show of looking around like I might not stay, sat back down, leaned back on two chair legs and yawned. The waitress came and I waved her away. Clay covered his eyes with his big hand.

"I'm in trouble, Danny."

I sped back to the office, darting between cars, pushing the Honda through the yellows, daring any cop to come get me. None around. It wasn't quite time to write for publication, though I was close. I decided to call Canton Spivey anyway, right after I told Clay's story to Isabel. She didn't answer her cell, so I called the house and got the sitter, Mrs. Kingsford.

"Isabel's on a date. I'm watching Katie tonight."

I asked her to please repeat. She told me she was in charge of Katie for the evening and I said, No, the *other part.* She said Isabel was on a date with Paolo. *Paolo who?* She didn't know. "Who is this again?" she said.

"Dan Patragno from Washington."

"Oh, yes, I remember you. I'll leave a note."

I could imagine the note. *Dan P. from D.C. Had lots of questions. (Kind of rude.) Wants you to call him.* All she knew was they went to dinner and a movie, and that Isabel wouldn't be home until midnight. *A date. Paolo. No last name. Paolo. He could be a shoe salesman or an Italian designer, so famous, he didn't need a last name. Six-three, wavy brown hair, pecs out to there. A little Italian horn tattooed on his butt. What the hell was the word? Cornicello!* She'd think it was cute and sexy. I could see her picking out a slinky dress and putting on lipstick for *Paolo*. Was I jealous? Did I have a right? Isabel Moss was a young, beautiful widow; I was 37, married, a father. We had no ground rules about seeing other people. And of course I had no claim whatsoever. I could hear her — *Other people? You go home to another woman every night. You're probably still sleeping with her.* (I wasn't.) *Who are you to talk about seeing other people?* Besides, what was wrong with her going on a date? Or if Paolo came in awhile when they got home? *Jesus, Danny, get hold of yourself.*

"Please tell her to call me when she gets home, Mrs. Kingsford. I'll be up late."

"Yes, Mr. Patragno, I'm writing a note right now."

There it was, the Spivey whistle. All *Tampa Daily News* reporters knew if you could make Canton Spivey whistle, you were onto something. He didn't do it much, and when he did, it wasn't a full-out, *Yo cabbie, I'm-20-minutes-late* kind of whistle. It was more like the sound of blowing out a candle, a short, hissing burst, low and purposeful which, translated, meant, *Solid, front-page work.* All of us worked to hear that whistle. From the light-bulb moment of story conception, through the reporting, fact checks, fairness test, and final edit — never achieved without multiple rewrites — each reporter wrote hoping to earn front-page play and the moments-old Canton Spivey whistle that was still ringing in my ears.

"Where's the tape now?"

"Braxton has one copy at the Pentagon. But Clay — my source at the NRO — got curious and made another copy for himself. It's at his house. I'm going to see it later."

"Tell me again why he's showing it to you."

Canton found it hard to accept gifts of any kind, even compliments.

Bella

I could see him Christmas morning, juggling his boxes, looking from gifts to givers, wondering what strings were attached. "He's frantic, boss. He had no idea why some hard-ass sergeant at the Pentagon was ordering specific streaming video from Afghanistan. He filled the order and delivered it in person, but made himself a copy to study later. When he figured out what he was looking at, he realized he shouldn't have been so nosy. Now that he knows, he's part of the cover-up."

"Unless he comes forward."

"He didn't come forward; he got yanked." I wondered what kind of whistle I'd hear if Spivey knew the rest of the story — that Clay, my friend and source, slept with Ellie; that his wife Mary helped me connect Clay and Charles Braxton; that I was not only sleeping with my main source, but crazy jealous about her new boyfriend.

"That tape or video or whatever it is may be classified. He gives it to you, he's committing a federal offense."

"That's for him and his lawyer to work out. I guess he figures giving us the tape is better than being in the Pentagon liars' club."

"Call me after you see it. I'm going to have to take this to the lawyers. If we print classified info, we may be subject to prosecution ourselves. You could end up with a judge threatening time if you don't reveal your source."

"Would you visit me in jail, Canton?"

Chapter 29

When I got home, Ellie was pacing around the garage end of the driveway, arms tightly crossed against her chest. A cop was perched on the stoop taking notes while he talked to Robbie. I parked on the street and was barely out of the car when Ellie pounced. She shoved me against the car, pinned my shoulders to the door, shouted in my face. "What are you involved in Danny? What the hell's going on?" I slid my arms under hers and pulled her close. Ellie's solid when it comes to bad surprises. Even when Robbie tumbled off the slide and busted his elbow, she stayed calm, smiling and telling my screaming, thrashing son that he was lucky; he was going to get to skip a few days of school. Besides setting the break, there was bloody playground sand to cleanse from the wound. He didn't like that a bit. Ellie told him, very gravely, that the city was going to charge us for the sand he took, which won a pause in the hysterics and enough time for the nurse to finish mopping his cuts. Losing it here in the driveway told me something pretty bad was up. "I don't know what you're talking about, hon. What happened? Everyone *looks* okay." She fought at first, then slumped against me. Her tears wet my neck. I felt people looking at us from their windows. "He had Robbie. He had him in his car. He could have … Oh, God." I pulled away and ran to Robbie. "Danny," she shrieked. The cop stood when he saw me coming. He was linebacker big and hard to read. He seemed equally poised to shake hands or take me down, understandable, as he didn't know me from the *Unabomber*. I slowed down, tried to seem natural. Robbie stayed on the stoop, looked up from some makeshift project. "Hi, dad." He was scraping the end of a stick against the concrete to sharpen the point. "Your friend gave me a ride. I wasn't going to go with him … He said you were friends. I forget his name. He was nice. Everyone's mad. Mom's upset. I'm sorry."

A few neighbors started to press in. I thought of Isabel's experience after Hank's funeral and half-scanned the crowd for signs of casseroles. The cop assured everyone we were okay and sent them home. I cuffed Robbie gently on the back of his head. I told him not to get in anyone's car ever again, even if they seemed friendly or said they knew me. He looked from the cop to his mother and to me. "Is the policeman taking me to jail, dad?"

Inside, I gave the cop, an Officer Lansing Brannigan with outdated pork-chop sideburns, a heavily edited version of the story. Ellie listened intently. I hadn't told her about being stopped and ticketed by the phony cop with the 1950's gray-flecked crew cut. *Reese Wehrman — Guess I'll have a look at that brake light now.* Or that I'd spotted him again after my tire was booted near Union Station.

Brannigan, still writing in his police notebook, asked what my newspaper story was about. "I can't go into that." He nodded. "Well, your boy seems fine. Whoever this guy is, he knows what he's doing. This was a message — he knows where you live; he knows where Robin goes to school and when he gets out. Probably knows a bunch more." I glanced at Ellie and got back ice. The cop saw, probably figured we hadn't told him everything. "Mrs. Patragno, you should probably drop your son off and pick him up the next few weeks. Mr. Patragno, you know when this story of yours is going to be in the newspaper?"

"Not exactly."

"Right, course not." He shrugged. There was only so much he could do with limited information and semi-cooperative parents. "I'm going to ask the station to send a patrol car around the next few nights. I don't think the guy would come here. He had the boy; he didn't touch him. Why would he let him go if the idea was to do harm?" Ellie and I nodded. "Do either of you have any other enemies who might have pulled this?" Neither of us could think of anyone. "Here's my card," Brannigan said. "Call day or night if you think of something else, or if anything seems unusual."

I picked up Robbie's pointy stick and chucked it into the bushes. Nothing had seemed *usual* in weeks.

Isabel called around 11:30, all giggles. She didn't give me any chance to explain what happened to Robbie. Paolo, she said, was Paolo *Urso*, her gay gardener cousin. "Don't you remember? I told you my maiden name was Urso. Paolo's dad … My dad … They're *brothers*. He's my *cousin*. Paolo Urso. The *landscaper*. *Urso & Raposa Lawn Care and Landscape*. Ron Raposa is his partner. Didn't you ever hear the radio ad? She sang: *Bring-ing a Touch; Of Heaven to Homes; In … Hills-bor-ough Coun-ty*. I thought you grew up here. I told you about him, Danny, I know I did. Paolo and me — the *idea!* You're such a dope. Mrs. Kingsford said you seemed upset. Were you jealous?"

She was mocking me and I didn't care. I was so relieved she wasn't on a real date, it was frightening. "*Worried*, not jealous," I said, pulse banging. I'd been ready for the worst, and it was nothing. A gay cousin.

Bella

She'd practically been out with a girlfriend. My pea brain urged a switch to offense. I glanced around to make sure Ellie was safely tucked away upstairs. Pulled the blanket over my head and said, "Your sitter couldn't tell me anything. What if there was an emergency? If your cell was on, I never would have spoken to her in the first place." I know Isabel was grinning at the other end. She had me; we both knew it. I remembered her by the stove, how she liked to cook. One more turn, a little tenderizer, and I'd be done.

She let it pass, asked why I called. I told her — Clay, the tape, everything. When I finished, the voice at the other end belonged to a different woman. Low. Solemn. No more giggles. I came out from under the covers. The house was dark and quiet. Even the old wooden floors and beams had settled in for the night. Isabel said, "I was reading Hank's last letter. I nearly know it by heart. I keep it in a plastic sleeve so Katie will have it when she's older." She paused. I waited. She read aloud:

Dear Bella, It's been a bad few days. We lost one of our guys, great kid from Rochester, N.Y. Sniper got him. We didn't even see him. There was a shot; we looked around to see where it came from and this kid Richie dropped over dead. Eight feet from where I was standing. Bullet went through his cheek; there were pieces of bloody teeth everywhere. Kid died before he could get a hand to his face. A sniper's the biggest coward there is, honey. Shoots from the shadows and runs away. What kind of soldier is that? It's dirty fighting; this is a dirty war. Richie worked in his father-in-law's plumbing supply business up there in Rochester. He was married to a girl named Christina; they had a daughter, same age as Katie. He always talked about the weather. I guess it's pretty cold in upstate N.Y. He said snow came at the end of August sometimes, and they did plenty of skiing in spring. He loved to ski, talked about racing down a mountain, how even though you were moving so fast, everything seemed still. He hated the heat here. But he liked the fairy tales, Aladdin, magic lamps, flying carpets … I told him my story about the evil sorcerer and Princess Aryana. He got a chuckle because the right people won. Not like here. Anyway, he said he liked it so much, he was going to tell his little girl the story when he got home. He had six weeks left. That still spooks us. Bad stuff can happen any time. One minute you're fine, the next, bam. I'm going to write his wife a letter, tell her what a good guy he was, how we all got a such charge out of him … That's all for now. I want to put down this machine gun and pick up my rackets. I miss you and love you. Thinking of you and Katie is what keeps me going. Always and forever, Hank.

She was crying quietly by the end. I wanted badly to hold her. There were four states and 600 miles between us. I said, "Isabel, I've never really said how sorry — "

" — Hank was dead 19 hours before they told me, you know. Nearly a whole day. Gone from this Earth, and I didn't even know. Katie didn't know. Or his mother. No one knew, except the Army." A flash of anger entered her voice and then abated. "Three of them came to my front door. It was a Wednesday morning, about 9:30. Katie was at school. I looked through the curtain and saw the uniforms. There was a chaplain with them. I knew what that meant." She gasped at the memory, and it was hard to believe I was speaking to the same giggly woman who'd just gotten home from a night of cavorting with Paolo the gay gardener. She said, more slowly this time, reconstructing details, "I leaned against the wall in the foyer and slid down until I was sitting on the floor. I tried to stay very quiet. I thought if I could trick them into thinking I wasn't home, they'd go away. I thought they'd forget and not come back. And then none of it would be true. Katie would come home from school and we'd go grocery shopping. We'd buy some *Sugar Pops* and get something to cook for dinner and everything would be fine. But my car was in the driveway and I realized I had music on, and that they could hear it through the door." She stopped a moment to concentrate. "Luther Vandross. I had Luther on — the live concert. I like listening to concerts. Such energy. Like being there. Sometimes I dance when I'm by myself. I was dancing that morning … They must have known I was near the door. One of them knocked. The first time, they rang the bell. This time they knocked. Someone said in a reasonable tone — not yelling — he said, 'Mrs. Moss, please let us speak to you a moment.' I thought, no, I can't let them in. If I just sit here quietly, they'll go away and leave me alone. They'll forget about us. Let them make their ghoulish deliveries to the wives of other soldiers. I'm not accepting today. *No one home, damn it!* They must have stood outside 20 minutes before I got up and opened the door. I don't remember much else. One of them was a doctor. He gave me a shot. I slept until night. When I woke up, there were people in the house — Hank's mother, the base chaplain, some neighbors, Katie … I walked into the living room and they all came at me. My legs were wobbly; I couldn't think clearly. I wanted to sit down and there was nowhere to sit. I couldn't imagine why everyone was in my house. They all wanted to touch me, to hug me and tell me how sorry they were. I couldn't stand it. I pushed away. *Please don't touch me. I don't want to be touched. Stop. Please.* I ran to the bathroom. Both were taken. I ran outside. I ran all the way down Laurel Canyon Drive. The chaplain came after me and brought me back after I got sick in front of some neighbors I didn't know. When we were walking away, the woman said to her husband, 'Must be drunk. This neighborhood's getting so bad.'"

Chapter 30

Next morning, Clay got permission from Mary to return home, though her consent came with a stipulation: all his crap was in the guest bedroom. And yes, that's where he'd be sleeping from now on. It was Thursday, 11 days since Isabel Moss arrived in my life. I wondered if my initial hunch to dismiss her was born of some primitive survival instinct. Reagan popped into mind: *Are you better off today than you were four years ago?* Was I better off now than I was two weeks ago? Didn't matter. Second-guessing was a waste of time. Plus, the train was speeding along too fast to jump off, not that I wanted to, especially now, with key evidence nearly in hand.

Clay and I wound up at his front door just as the Ohrbach girls were leaving for lacrosse practice. The bouncy teens wore blue skirts and shirts with a white *BCC* (for Bethesda Chevy-Chase High) stenciled on front and turf-stained black spikes that clicked against the tile floor. Both had their curly chestnut hair pulled into pigtails, the ends linked behind their head Dutch style; both were chewing gum; both nodded at me and ignored Clay. Evidently the Ohrbach females were sticking together. Mary had probably told them a sanitized version about Clay's romp with Ellie, enough to draw some anger, not so much that they were repulsed by the sight of him. I doubted she'd said anything yet about military cover-ups or secret videos. For now, the girls were mad about dad cheating on mom. Mom was hurt; dad was the villain. He would pay until mom felt better.

I, meanwhile, had softened. His face when the girls rushed past without a word was pitiful. Eyes bloodshot and crestfallen, he was embarrassed about what they knew, and just as scared of what they would learn in the coming days. Clay's punishment had barely begun; the thought of what awaited poor Double A sapped my anger.

Mary, fussing with the skirt of her pale green suit, appeared and grabbed her briefcase. "Hi. I'm late; we'll talk later. Hello, Danny." I returned the greeting and Clay moved to kiss her good-bye. She brushed him off and walked out, repeating, "Gotta' go. The girls are at a sleepover tonight. We'll talk at dinner." She apparently had an agenda that would specify the conditions for his permanent return, and also include new rules about what was permissible in the area of physical intimacy. For now, he didn't even get a kiss goodbye. He watched her go and stood staring from the doorway even after she'd driven away. "Clay," I said, "let's get started."

He kept staring. He'd done a bad job of preparing for his reception at home. He said he'd been a faithful husband and textbook father 99.5 percent of the time. "Where's everyone's sense of balance? One rotten mistake and I'm a leper." I didn't like the self-pity, and I sure didn't like him referring to Ellie as a rotten mistake. "You were expecting a parade, maybe? They're upset. Give it some time." How absurd that the cuckolded husband was advising the guy who seduced his wife. Yet Clay was no womanizer, and I didn't know for sure it wasn't Ellie who seduced him. All of that wasn't important now anyway. I needed to see the footage. "Where's the tape?"

He breathed against a glass panel on the door and finger-painted a stick house. "I'd like to know how I'm supposed to get them back. I can't un-do what happened." Clay the scientist was looking for a formula. There was none. This was more art than science. My advice most likely wasn't much comfort. "Nothing you say is going to help much. They'll judge based on what you *do*. Tomorrow night, when you're all back at the dinner table, apologize to Mary and the girls. Ask if anyone wants to discuss it. If yes, talk it through the best you can. Stay calm. No self-pity. Be contrite; don't be weak. If no one wants to get into it, tell them the matter's closed and the family's moving on."

He turned back from the door. "That how you're going to play it, Danny?"

"It's different for me," I said with more certainty than I felt.

Bella

Chapter 31

Something was bugging me. Little as I knew about armies, planes, weaponry and soldiering, I'd learned enough to know satellite imagery was to a battlefield commander what economic theory is to a Wall Street trader. The global view might be interesting, but key decisions were made based on what was happening closer to the ground. Senior officers needed to know what the war looked like past the next ridge, forest or mountain-top before sending soldiers forward. So what was the National Reconnaissance Office — the deep space satellite experts — doing with *medium-altitude* surveillance video feeds shot by an aircraft drone? I put the question to Clay as he got the tape from a hiding place deep in the bookcase. It was behind a hardcover dictionary and a paperback I'd never heard of: *Questions from Earth, Answers from Heaven.* "Gag gift from an old MIT buddy," Clay said, seeing my interest. "The only heavenly answers I believe in are the ones you get off of satellites."

The tape I'd expected turned out to be a DVD. He slipped it into a sleek black machine with lots more buttons and dials than any player I'd ever seen. "You're right, though; there's a disconnect." He paused the DVD. I quickly wondered if I should have saved my question. I felt a history lesson coming on U.S. military intelligence. At least Clay had refocused enough to put his marital misery on hold. He touched a shaving cut on his chin. "The NRO opened shop in 1960. Other parts of the intelligence team, like NGA, the National Geospatial Intelligence Agency, are a lot older. The term *geospatial intelligence* actually goes back a couple of hundred years, to Lewis, Clark and their maps of the Louisiana Territory."

Yawn. The main feature was loaded and I had to sit through more commercials. I resolved to be polite for another 30 seconds.

"Spying from space was still science fiction in the 1800's. Now it's routine as a cell phone call. We use satellite data to pick out military aggression. We can keep track of nuts or nations producing nukes and other WMD's. We can hunt down terrorists, enforce arms control and environmental treaties, and even assess the impact of a hurricane, volcano or a nuclear disaster like Chernobyl."

I tapped my chair leg, softly at first, then loud enough to be rude. He didn't notice.

"Thing is, the big intelligence team has a lot of stars and not so much teamwork. Lately there's been a push for us to get better at integrating data and information from all our sources. It's a huge team — the National Security Agency, the National Reconnaissance Office, the State Department Bureau of Intelligence and Research, the FBI, CIA, Homeland Security — and a bunch more players, including the intelligence orgs in the four military services. Improved communication means less duplication, more cohesive intelligence, a better return for the taxpayer." He shrugged. "We all need access to the same info; we need to work together to get the best intel to the national leaders and the generals making the decisions and to the soldiers executing the plans."

"For Christ's sake, Clay."

"Okay, okay, the point is, someone floated the idea of a few pilot projects that draw on the expertise of specialists from the different agencies.

I'm part of a tiger team that works closely with the Air Force and Army groups and J2."

I perked up. "The Intelligence Directorate at the Pentagon. Braxton's outfit."

"Precisely."

I thought about that as the first images came up on a 27-inch flat screen TV monitor. I was roundly disappointed. I was expecting Hollywood and got Hollywood High, not *Saving Private Ryan*, but some young Spielberg wannabe, some ascot-wearing president of the high school video club granted permission to shoot dreary, monotonous footage out of the cockpit of a commercial plane because his Aunt Beverly was chief stewardess. No close-ups, no dialogue, no swelling music, no cutaway scenes, no *action*. "What is this? Does it get better?" Clay spoke as if to soothe a spoiled child. "It's not a movie, Danny; it's *intelligence*. Raw and uncut. It's knowing the other guy's cards before you bet. Think about what you're looking at. It's a spy in the sky, not just an aircraft. More than 50 military people are involved, including the pilot, who's sitting safely inside a ground control station nowhere near the aircraft. The images you're looking at are sent real-time to analysts in communication with soldiers in the field. That means our guys don't get surprised or walk into ambushes. It switches the advantage. And no one's at risk in a UAV. If they shoot one down, no one dies. We just send up a replacement. The smaller drones come in suitcase kits. A single soldier in the field can launch one. And by the way, these systems can also deliver weapons."

"You mean blow stuff up?"

He nodded. It was remote warfare. Spy and kill from the comfort and safety of your own living room. The soundless video kept rolling with the same dull perspective. It was like gazing out the window during a long trip, immensely, intensely boring. The worst director couldn't have made the Afghan landscape less exciting. Time and date rolled along in white letters and numerals against a black background at the bottom of the screen. Other positional data appeared in blue boxes in the upper corners of the screen. It reminded me of vacation footage shot by friends bent on capturing each moment of their fantastic journey abroad. Then they get home and want to share. They insist. *Come over, we'll crack open some of the good stuff. We'll show you the vacation video.* Ten minutes in, you're squirming like you sat in gum and looking hard for the emergency exit. "Clay, when is something going to — "

" — Shhh. Watch."

The drone had approached the edge of a town. A covered truck was rumbling down a dusty one-lane dirt road toward a group of bombed out buildings in the distance. Though our view wasn't as good as the worst seat in a pro football stadium, it was easy to see sudden movement at the back of the truck. Suddenly the cover was thrown back and a bearded man wearing a light-colored *chapan* and turban hoisted a weapon to his shoulder. Moments later, a flash of light trailed by a fuzzy plume of smoke whizzed toward the drone. I felt myself brace for impact, but the missile streaked by, missing by yards.

"Lucky he had crappy aim."

I had almost forgotten Clay, the man of many surprises. Who knew he had a streak of black humor? I guess Ellie knew, or found out. Maybe that was part of the attraction. Meanwhile, the drone, all-seeing yet oblivious, stayed on course and there was no second shot. I started looking amid the rugged and mountainous terrain for signs of the native culture Hank had described to Isabel in his letters — parched nomad camps, with gangly camels tied up like horses at an Oklahoma cowboy ranch, or the festive bazaars bustling with grinning merchants hawking spices, baskets and bright-colored kites. I gazed and saw nothing. War had driven everyone inside or somewhere else.

On flew the drone, recording everything within the line of sight of its color nose camera and reacting to nothing but the unseen hand at its controls. I remembered some of the specs rattled off by Bart Jefferson at the diner in Tampa. The unmanned aircraft was about 14 feet top to bottom with a wingspan of 116 feet, and might have been gliding at minimum speed or clipping along at 90 miles per hour. It was hard to tell. The maximum altitude was 65,000 feet; this one looked to be flying at about 20,000 feet. Drones could stay airborne for 35 hours while sending back surveillance, intelligence and reconnaissance info on an area measuring up to 40,000 square miles. The hour and minutes on the screen crawl turned slowly: 4:51 p.m., 4:52 p.m., 4:53 p.m.; seconds and tenths of seconds raced around like the images of fruit imprinted on the reels of a busy slot machine. The date remained constant: 5/16/02.

That's when it struck me.

Somewhere down there Sgt. Hank Moss was about to die.

Again I found myself looking for Hollywood drama: an anxious glance between two front-line GI's; the soundtrack pouring forth minor chords from mournful violins; cut to the blackening sky; cut to the young soldier's hand; in it, a photo of his girl that he brings to his lips; cut to the enemy tanks massing in assault formation, and to the commander, binoculars in hand as his nod launches the attack; and then, finally, back to the Americans, huddled in their foxholes, checking their weapons, nervously fingering the religious medals dangling from their necks, unaware of the rival forces moving toward them, yet sensing their proximity.

There was none of that. The robot aircraft buzzed forward, seeing all, reacting to nothing, and recording mile after mile of wide-angled monotony.

Until the flash.

"What was that? Down there, on the left? Rewind; play it again."

The doorbell rang, freezing Clay before he could replay the segment. The sound startled us both. I looked at my watch — it was just after 9 a.m. Who would stop by that early? He went for the door; I angled for the living room window, hoping for a peek at the unexpected visitor. I couldn't see anything but a *UPS* truck parked in the driveway. I shot Clay a sign to pretend no one was home. He waved me off like a kid intent on swimming less than an hour after lunch. He opened the door and signed for a small package. I half-expected the delivery guy — a scruffy kid with a Jesus beard, rolled-up sleeves and anchor tattoos on both forearms, to drop his clipboard, whip out a pistol and shoot us both dead. Instead, he politely asked Clay to sign for a small box and said, "Thank you, Mr. Ohrbach."

"Don't open it. Put it in the backyard."

"Don't be an idiot, Danny. It's nothing."

I thought, *his* girls hadn't been tricked into getting in a stranger's car. He didn't come home and get attacked by his hysterical wife while the police interviewed his son. And Clay hadn't been stopped or booted by a phony cop. "Fine. But wait 'til I'm gone before you open it."

"You're being ridiculous."

Clay put the box on a table, produced a pocket knife and cut into the packaging. I fought an urge to back out of the room. It was all too coincidental, a package arriving just as we were viewing the incriminating video. "Clay, wait." His eyes stayed on the box. He tore off the paper and we saw the package had come from a sporting goods store. Which meant nothing, except that the devious assassins were clever enough to disguise their bomb in innocent-looking wrapping. "*Clay.*" He finally suspended the operation. "Will you please calm down? You're freaking me out. *I'm* the one who should be paranoid." He wedged his fingers in the bottom and started to lift the cover. I held my breath and summoned an image of Robbie and Ellie. I would never see my son graduate from high school, meet his fiancé or know my grandchildren. My poor wife would be a widow like Isabel. I could imagine the gory mess when they found our bodies … The cover of the package came off and Clay sneered, "See? I told you." He displayed the contents, two pairs of girls' black soccer cleats.

Clay rewound and started the video. Moments before the sudden flash I'd seen earlier, he tweaked the machine to slow the on-screen drone to the pace of an old pack mule. Another dial etched a white square around the general region where the explosion had occurred, and then filled the screen with the squared-out section. Clay punched a button that drew us nearer the treetops. One more touch landed us even closer. "That's the best I can do. Any more, we'll lose the resolution." I tried to fit the sector below into my limited knowledge of the local geography; Jalalabad was east of Kabul, north of the Khyber Pass and brushed Pakistan's western border. We were looking at an industrial area somewhere on the outskirts of Jalalabad.

The crawl read: 5/16/02; 5:12 p.m. Thanks to Clay's wizardry, even the seconds and tenths of seconds were turning slowly. Outside the cockpit, the weather was overcast; light rain was falling. Still, I could clearly see a team of three soldiers, as if from a traffic helicopter, their weapons drawn, moving in short, crouched bursts around the remains of a row of two and three-story buildings that might have once been warehouses, small factories or apartments. One man led, two followed. The war-torn streets were empty except for several pitiful poplars and a few abandoned vehicles, one of which, an old charred Jeep, had been left on a small embankment and was still smoking. The three GI's reached a wall and suddenly the lead soldier quick-stepped ahead of the other three. Even from my aerial view, I could see he was an athlete. He moved in quick, economical steps, with purpose and without hesitation. In tennis stadiums, Hank's fans had called him *Screech*, a tribute to how hard he scrambled to run down and return well-struck shots, or, in the jargon of the sport, to keep himself *alive* in the point. Though I couldn't hear his footsteps now, I imagined his Army boots quiet as a whisper. He wouldn't want to alert the enemies he thought were waiting. I wanted to warn him, tell him to get back. The only enemy ahead was a scared and confused soldier from South Carolina named Marcus Ravoli. I couldn't see Ravoli, but knew that by this point, he was likely thinking about the grenades in his personal arsenal. His actions in the coming moments would define his future. Within months, he would be dead by his own hand. I wanted desperately to warn him: *Stay calm, Marcus.* What was Hank thinking? Hank was a good soldier and would follow the orders he'd received to assist the American unit his commanding officers thought was pinned down by *Taliban* fighters. How could he know there were no enemies directly ahead? *Go back, Hank.* I reached out to the screen. "Danny?" Clay said. The flash followed within seconds. Smoke billowed skyward and quickly dissipated. Then four soldiers — the two who'd been trailing and a new pair from another direction — met at the spot of the explosion. Three stood in a half circle while the fourth paced in front, talking and gesturing.

In real time, the tragedy that took Hank Moss' life took 11 seconds from start to finish.

Bella

"Again, Clay. This time freeze each frame so I can really get a close look and take notes."

It was just as Bart Jefferson had described it, and yet a vital element was missing. We could not hear the instructions Sgt. Marlin Falk barked at the other soldiers, Jefferson, Osky Sanchez and Marcus Ravoli. I needed to hear Falk's voice, learn for myself what he told the shaken men. Two of the three were now gone. Sanchez was killed in action on another Afghan battlefield and Ravoli shot his brains out just outside the Citadel in Charleston. Only Jefferson could confirm that Falk had ordered the truth suppressed and was singularly responsible for the lies told to Isabel Moss by a grim trio of Army officials who knocked on her door and ruined an otherwise fine May morning of cleaning and dancing to Luther Vandross.

"That's it, everything you wanted to see," Clay said as the drone moved on, its unblinking electronic eye scanning new terrain and sending back the constant stream of raw, objective data that the military men wanted, or at least thought they wanted. I could see the generals huddling once the story broke. *Criminy, boys, do we really want that thing recording everything that happens out there?* Private Jefferson mocked me when I compared the drone to a convenience store surveillance camera, and yet it had pretty much done the same job. In recording every moment without comment or interruption, it captured the accident and the criminal cover-up. The footage would correct an official record that was high fiction. It would allow a grieving widow to move on, and it might just send a few arrogant slimeballs to jail. It was the unimaginable — a reality show that actually served the public interest.

Clay asked if it were possible to keep his name out of the story by saying I'd been given the video by an anonymous source.

I said it was possible.

185

Chapter 32

Traffic was crawling all the way to the office. It was nasty hot and road rage lurked like summer lightning; a cabbie nearly mowed down three teens who tried to beat a changing light at 16th and Roosevelt. One of the kids hurled half a can of soda. The cabbie stopped short. *Dent my cab, punk, I'll dent your ugly face.* The kid grabbed his own crotch in response. I barely noticed. My mind kept replaying the video. Whatever his motive, Falk's sloppy effort at crisis management had spawned one tragedy after another, ruining at least half a dozen lives. And it was about to crush the Army beneath an avalanche of disastrous press.

Falk at some point learned the footage existed, maybe as soon as he returned to base the night Moss died. He likely panicked, since the grim video, if it got around, would shine stadium lights on the secret he'd ordered his men never to reveal. He needed help, so he called his buddy Braxton. Braxton, either because he approved of Falk's strategy or wanted to save his friend's behind, located and squelched the video. I could hear the back and forth between the two Desert Storm buddies.

Falk: *You can't see what happened just by looking at the footage. You gotta' grind down hard on the left corner, the Southwest. Might be that no one would even notice. I just didn't want to take a chance.*

Braxton: *This Moss kid died a hero. We give him a hero's funeral at Arlington, his wife gets a flag, and that's that. We've still got terrorists to hunt. I don't have time or resources to waste prosecuting some hillbilly from South Carolina. What's his name again?*

Falk: *Ravoli — he already feels like garbage. What good would it do to lock him up?*

Braxton: *No good at all. Our story is, Moss gave his life for the country he loved. Put his own interests second to the nation's. Period.*

Falk: *That's better for his wife and family.*

Braxton: *It's better for everyone. Why bum out the whole damned country, to say nothing of the troops still in the Sandbox?*

Falk: *So we're agreed?*

Braxton: *Agreed. Those other three, they'll stay quiet, right?*

Falk: *No problem there.*

Braxton: *Make certain. I don't want any surprises. And Christ, Marlin, don't let this happen again.*

That was close to how it went down; it had to be.

T wo hours later, I found myself, at last, face to face with Sgt. Charles Braxton, Joint Chiefs of Staff, Directorate for Intelligence. "Put all that away for now," he said, meaning my pen, pad and tape recorder. I steeled myself for another argument about what would be on or off the record.

Braxton had casually instructed me to look for a bald guy, mid-40's, standard blue D.C. business suit. I found myself looking for another government geek like Gavin Sussman. I might have looked all night if Braxton didn't find me first. We didn't shake hands. He slid in behind me and said quietly, "Patragno." When I turned, his hands were on his hips, as if he'd stumbled on something interesting in a used car lot. I saw why I'd missed him; his self-description was an under-sell. Braxton was buff and bald; his scalp was polished to the same high gloss as his dress shoes. The suit was indeed blue, but had an expensive luster. The way it bulged at the shoulders, chest and biceps said, or rather announced, that Charles Braxton hit the gym as much as Gavin Sussman hit the refrigerator. Braxton had an animal way of assessing strangers that I felt right off, even before he spoke, before he said softly, with a slight smile, as if he had my wife and son chained to a metal radiator in a warehouse down by the waterfront, their mouths covered by duct tape, "You won't need any of that stuff because you're not going to write this story, son."

Getting the meeting had been easy. Braxton answered the phone himself when I finally reached the office after the murderous traffic and called the Intelligence Directorate. "Dan Patragno," he said thoughtfully, as if we'd once been college roommates. "I was wondering when you'd get around to me." I started to tell him about my story and the video, intending to ask for a comment. He stopped me. "I know what you've got. Let's meet. I like to look at a man when he's trying to bring me down." He laughed. The notion was absurd. I asked if I should bring back-up and he laughed again, a deep, lusty snort that suggested Braxton was a man who'd found what made him happy and would happily squash anyone who tried to take it. "Food court at Pentagon City." I suggested 1 o'clock and he said 2:30. "The *touristas* will be outta there by then. We need alone time."

That left me more than 90 minutes. I rifled through my notebook and found another number I needed to call since seeing the footage from Afghanistan. The phone rang six times and then she answered, just as gruff as I remembered. I felt sorry for any telemarketer who got Louisa Ravoli on the phone.

"Who is this?" she demanded. "How'd you get my number?"

I told her. She remembered Isabel right away. "You were that reporter with her, right, that smartass?" I was. I apologized for being a smartass. I reminded her that my story would hit harder and go further if she allowed us to use the piece about her son — that he was depressed — suicidal — because he'd accidentally caused Hank's death.

"Never could get past it," she said. "Marcus was a good boy 'til then. No trouble, not as a little one, not in high school, not after. Waiting tables there in Charleston was a stop-gap. The boy was whiz-bang at science; he used to talk some about architecture or engineering school. Then this happened. He felt twice guilty. Once for what he did over there, twice for keeping it hidden behind the curtain. We miss him terrible, me and Fred. We're down at that cemetery each Sunday after church."

"Mrs. Ravoli — "

She snapped, "You ought to learn a reporter shouldn't cut people off, 'less it's some windbag politician. It's rude and it breaks the flow of a good interview. You recall I told you I was in journalism a good many years?" I did and told her so. "Well then, you just listen. I'm still not sure what I want to do about this business."

"May I tell you something?"

"Go ahead; be quick."

I could see her pacing around the backyard, pulling weeds from the garden as she listened. "The accident involving Marcus and Hank Moss was caught on tape by an unmanned U.S. aircraft that patrols the region, a robot plane with a camera. I've seen this video; in fact I saw it this morning."

"You saw my Marcus throw that hand grenade?"

STEVE PIACENTE

"No, the aircraft went by very quickly and there are only a handful of frames that show what happened. You can see Hank out in front of his men and then the explosion. You can't see who threw the grenade, or the grenade itself. One or two more frames show four soldiers — one being Marcus, I'm pretty sure — gathering afterward. I'm guessing that's when they were told to say that Hank Moss was killed by enemy troops if anyone asked."

She whistled a low trill that reminded me I still needed to call Canton Spivey. Isabel was also waiting to hear what happened at Clay's. It was the first time since we'd met that I didn't want to speak to her. I just didn't know how to explain all I'd seen. For each detail I could provide, I knew she'd ask for five more I didn't have.

"Mrs. Isabel Moss called me the other day, you know," Louisa Ravoli said, reading my thoughts. "Sharp girl, very persuasive. Real looker, too."

"Yes, she's all that."

"You two an item? I felt something 'tween the two of you when you were here. I'm never wrong about that sort of thing."

"Mrs. Ravoli — "

" — Oh, you can ask questions, you just can't answer any."

"Yes, we're seeing each other."

"And you're a married man."

"Yes, but — "

" — Nevermind. That's your business. You don't need an old woman telling you what's right and wrong." She stopped abruptly. Five beats passed. Then she said, "I made up my mind. I'm going to give you a quote for your story. You can't ask me any questions once I'm done. Deal?"

The woman had an amazing way of limiting my options. "Yes, go ahead, slowly please."

190

"You ought to learn to write faster. What kind of reporter are you anyway?" She sighed and told me to get ready. "Marcus told me he threw the hand grenade that killed Sgt. Moss. He thought there was an enemy 'round that bend. After, he felt awful. No one wanted to know the truth. They *ordered* him not to tell what happened over there. He was very sorry for what he did, even though it was a mistake." I considered asking her to slow down and decided against. "They discharged him, said it was for medical reasons, but it was because they didn't want him wearing a uniform while he was lugging around that terrible secret. He came home and wasn't interested in much. He got more and more depressed until he couldn't take it anymore." Another sigh. "That's it, all I'm saying. "You get it down?" I got it. "You want me to repeat anything?" I didn't. "Read it back to me." I did. "All right, then," she said. "Don't mess with those quotes. Anything inside a pair of quote marks is sacred as Scripture, never forget that." I thanked her and headed for the subway and Pentagon City.

B raxton was right. By 2:30, the food court was empty. Two bored women with hair nets cleaned tables to get ready for the dinner rush. A man mopped in rhythm to music pumping through his white earbuds, breaking every few measures to hoist and twirl his scraggly-ended mop like a skinny dance partner. Though none of the three attacked their work with much enthusiasm, the smell of ammonia solution was strong and competed hard against the aroma of bourbon chicken, baked ziti, steak teriyaki and other dinner fare being prepared by a lively crew of fast food chefs. Braxton looked from a sushi place to a hard rain pounding the skylight above and then directly at me. He laced his fingers like he didn't know where to begin with such a dolt. His cockiness surprised me. He knew I'd seen stark, conclusive evidence that verified the story told by

Isabel, Bart Jefferson and now Louisa Ravoli. I started to lay out facts and proof and took out my tape recorder. Braxton waved me off. "Let's just talk for now. We'll save the *on and off the record* thing for later." He lifted the stained plastic lid from his coffee and stirred, even though he drank it black. He let me speak half a minute and then pointed the thin stirrer like a nun aiming a ruler at an unruly child. "I'm not arguing about the story. You did your homework."

"What are you saying?"

"I'm saying the story is accurate."

"And?"

"And the problem is that all you're looking at it too simplistically, the who, what, when and where. You need to know why. Once you understand the back story, you'll see why you shouldn't publish." I may have let on there wasn't much flexibility there. "Give me a few minutes," he said. "Try to remember we're both Americans." *Oh, brother, where's the Color Guard?* One of the cleaning women wandered over and tried to wipe our table. "Come back after we leave, would you dear?" he said, charming her into a smile that he matched and raised with a silly wink. He sipped his coffee and pulled a cigarette from a fresh pack of *Camels*. "Hank Moss was a pro athlete, Dan. His sister was slaughtered on 9/11. What did he do? He forgot his career and remembered his country. He put the *nation's* security in front of his own security and happiness. Why? He wanted to pay back the kind of scum that would hijack and fly our planes into downtown office buildings. You saw those pictures of people jumping off the Towers, didn't you? That was *America. New York City.* Defending his country was more important to Hank Moss than pro tennis — even though that was his dream. It was more important than staying home with his wife and little girl. No one asked him to enlist. He joined up; he knew the risks." I sat up straight, eager now to fire questions. Braxton didn't leave any space. "Now on the other side of that stairwell in godforsaken Jalalabad, Afghanistan, you had Marcus Ravoli, nice Southern boy from a nice Southern family, in what the poor kid thought was a desperate situation. Don't get me wrong, Dan. We train these men and women hard and thorough before we put them in harm's way. And it's not just how to tear a rifle apart and put it back together. We toughen body and mind. We run all kinds of scenarios to make sure they don't crack under pressure. Hank, Marcus and the rest of them all received the same training."

Leaning in, I told him I knew all that. "What good was the training? Ravoli cracked like spring ice."

Braxton lit his cigarette and the same cleaning lady ran over and made him put it out, ending their brief courtship. Mr. Charming now looked like he wanted to hit both of us. He waved her away and mashed out the Camel after a last, long drag. "Let me finish. Please." Again he was trying to lead me, the blind man, to the light. "Imagine it: Ravoli's scared. He's been scared since he got there, probably. It's just him and Falk; he doesn't want to wind up in a body bag before his 23rd birthday. Understandable. He thinks some Taliban *A-hole* is hiding around the corner with a knife big enough to saw through his neck like it was a birthday cake. Slamming planes into buildings and decapitation — that's how these guys make a point. Ravoli doesn't want to take any chances, so he pulls the pin and lets fly."

Braxton tucked the cigarette behind his ear. I needed to get some of this on the record. I said, "So the dust settles and Falk realizes Ravoli killed another American. And he orders a cover-up. You, a ranking official with the Joint Chiefs of Staff at the Pentagon, help him. You lie to the Moss family, you lie to the country. You stash that video away in a vault somewhere. And somehow you're telling me none of this is worth reporting?"

"If all you're interested in is selling papers, yes, it's newsworthy. Aren't some things worth more than selling papers?"

"Ah, the *greater good* argument. Censor the news for the betterment of mankind. Sorry, I don't see it. A story exposing what you've done won't hurt any Americans other than you and Falk. And by the way, I don't write stories to sell papers."

He tapped the salt shaker against the pepper. He couldn't understand why I didn't get it. "How about troop morale? We've still got thousands of kids over there. You think this is going to pump them up, help them catch terrorists and spread freedom?" He didn't wait for an answer. "Then there's what folks are thinking in Cleveland, Miami, Los Angeles, New York … A story like this would ruin people's confidence in the military. Isn't the national psyche part of national security?"

"I'm going to ask the cleaning crew to come back and mop up some of your bullshit, Braxton."

He gripped the wrought iron table and shoved it into my chest. I was more surprised than hurt. At the same moment I saw a flicker of movement at the far end of the food court. Something clicked. *Suit, black and gray crew cut.* It was the businessman from Lafayette Park, the phony cop, the guy who tricked Robbie into taking a ride. All three were the same guy. I cut my eyes from the mystery man to Braxton. He nodded at the guy and gave me another charming smile. "Jake over there's an old friend. Fact, he was my sergeant when I was in boot camp a hundred years ago. These days he does a little freelancing for us." He patted my hand. "I'm sorry I lost my temper."

"Cocksucker," I said, rising.

"Sit. We're almost done, but not yet." I glared down, realizing nothing had been on the record. I still had principles even if Charles Braxton thought it was okay to cover-up a U.S. soldier's death for the sake of the national psyche. I felt the eyes of the cleaning crew on us. I sat and shoved the table back at him, stopping just before it hit. I wanted to make him flinch; the suit-wearing soldier from Vegas never even blinked. I laid my recorder in front of him. Both of us knew he could make me swallow it whole. "This is your last chance to answer on the record. Otherwise you go down as *no comment.*" I turned it on; he switched it off. "Now look …" I said, hitting the red *record* button. He shut it and slammed the small gray box down on the table. The battery cover shattered; gray plastic flew in five directions. "*You* look," he said, the smile back. "My answer to any question you have is as follows: 'The Army stands by its original position. Sgt. Moss was killed in the line of duty. His death was a terrible tragedy.' But there's no questions 'cause there's no story, Danny-my-boy."

"What the hell are you talking about?"

"You may not understand the ramifications of publishing this story, but your bosses do."

"My bosses — "

"— Your bosses are good Americans. Solid citizens. Go talk to them — Canton Spivey, his boss, Jasper Downing, your paper's law firm, McCraw and Hillebrand, all the way to your publisher, Mr. Ivey. They see it our way, not yours. Sorry. No hard feelings. Try the sushi next time you're here. Guy makes a helluva spicy tuna roll."

Chapter 33

I'd worked for Canton Spivey seven years and never heard him apologize. "You put a lot into this, Danny. I'm sorry."

"Unacceptable."

"Nothing I can do. The Army brass was too convincing. They flew down late yesterday and got us together at McCraw and Hillebrand. I've been trying to call you. Once they won over that bowtie-wearing little prick Bolton Hillebrand, it was over. When the lawyers talk, Mr. Ivey listens."

"What am I supposed to tell Isabel Moss? There's no reason to kill a story like this. It doesn't undermine any government program; it doesn't put anyone's life in danger; it doesn't help the enemy."

Canton agreed on each point except the last. "They argued that negative publicity would hurt troop and citizen morale, which would help the terrorists."

"No, Canton. Yanking out a rotten tooth doesn't ruin the other teeth; it saves them." Lawyers. I wanted to strangle Bolton Hillebrand with his paisley bowtie. "Canton, let me come down and make my case. They listened to the Army; the least they can do is listen to their own reporter."

Canton said the decision was made and final, but I could come if I wanted. "There's a few bucks in the travel budget."

Bella

Three months earlier — precisely one month and two days before an American hand grenade killed Hank Moss — a U.S. Air National Guard Major named William Umbach and his wingman, Major Harry Schmidt, were soaring home after a 10-hour patrol over Afghanistan. When they reached the airspace around Kandahar, they looked down and saw what they thought was surface to air fire. Assuming they were under attack, perhaps thinking about a serviceman who'd recently fallen out of a helicopter and was tortured before being murdered by the Taliban, the Americans pointed and dropped a 225-kilogram laser-guided bomb. The blast killed four Canadian soldiers and injured eight more from the Third Battalion of Princess Patricia's Canadian Light Infantry. It wasn't until later that Umbach and Schmidt learned The Canadians were "friendlies." They'd been conducting an anti-tank and machine-gun exercise. They were not shooting at the American plane.

I tried to imagine myself bouncing around in a dark jet at 23,000 feet with Umbach and Schmidt, dodging what appeared to be Taliban anti-aircraft fire, thinking about the grim men below determined to shoot me from the sky, instead of safe inside a commercial plane 20 minutes from Tampa. They thought they'd flown into an ambush. It was kill or be killed. Keep flying for base and hope for the best or hit the button, drop the bomb and worry about it later.

You'd think it would be different today with all the sophisticated technology. You'd think we could tell friend from foe, even in what experts called the *fog of war*, that in addition to high-tech tactical graphics, infrared reflective markers and other battlefield gizmos, there would be more advanced training and thus better discipline. Thirty-five Americans were killed by friendly fire in the Persian Gulf War, damned better than the 8,000 accidentally killed by fellow soldiers in Vietnam, and the

21,000 in World War II. Those were the official Pentagon estimates; the real numbers were probably higher.

Then there was the true tale I'd learned about Stonewall Jackson. One hundred and forty years ago, the illustrious Confederate Lieutenant General Thomas J. Jackson died at the trigger-happy hands of his own disciples during the Battle of Chancellorsville in northern Virginia. Jackson and his men were returning to camp on May 2 — funny that it was May, the same month Hank died — when they were mistaken for Union cavalry troops. Jackson was shot in his right hand and, more seriously, twice in the left arm, just below the shoulder. They had to amputate, never a happy prospect, but especially dreadful in 1863. The removal of a smooth bore musket ball from his hand confirmed he was shot by his own men. They moved the mighty war hero to a plantation office building in Guinea Station, Virginia, where he died of pneumonia on May 10. The funeral was held three days later in Lexington at the Virginia Military Institute, where Jackson once taught philosophy and artillery, an odd pair of subjects for one professor. VMI's adjutant said in his eulogy there was "not a home in the Confederacy that will not feel the loss and lament as a great national calamity."

Imagine being one of the gray-uniformed rebs who brought down his own general, among the most famous and beloved figures of the Civil War. Me, I would have felt just like Schmidt and Umbach when they bombed the unsuspecting Canadian soldiers a few months ago, or Marcus Ravoli when he threw his grenade and killed Hank — sick, ashamed, miserable — knowing the rest of my life would be marked by one wretched mistake. It would haunt me when I closed my eyes at night and each day, all year, every year, at Thanksgiving and Christmas, on my birthday and the Fourth of July. It would ruin every meal, wreck every vacation, spoil every breath. It would still torture me when my son graduated college and later, when

Bella

Robbie got married and beyond that, when my grandchild was born. The only escape might be the route taken by Marcus Ravoli.

I decided then that I agreed with those who deplored the term "friendly fire." It was too light, too disrespectful to describe events so tragic.

The proper word was fratricide.

Someone tapped my shoulder and I jumped. "Seat belt, please, sir. We'll be landing soon. Sorry to startle you."

The *Daily News* execs wouldn't budge. I argued that there was no valid reason to kill the story. I cited the First Amendment; I invoked Watergate and the Pentagon Papers. I told them there was no cover-up when Confederate doctors plucked the musket ball from Stonewall Jackson's hand and confirmed the storied general was killed by his own troops. I was good — Bob Woodward and Tim Russert with a dash of Jimmy Stewart. I told them I double and triple-checked each fact, and relayed each sensitive point of the story in tortuous detail. I explained how impotent I felt seeing the video, knowing Hank Moss was maneuvering toward his death with every step and that I couldn't do a thing but watch. I begged them to consider Isabel and Katie Moss, Louisa Ravoli, Hank's mother, Osky Sanchez and the rest. Killing the story would dishonor every individual — now and throughout history, from Hank Moss to John Peter Zenger — who fought for fundamental American ideals like freedom of speech and of the press. Oh yes, had they heard me, the white-coifed Founders would have minted a new coin bearing the Roman likeness of Daniel Patragno, angular-nosed champion of truth and justice. "Congress shall make no law abridging the freedom of the press," I said, my own eyes misting a little. I yearned for a gavel and settled for a fist on the table. "Jesus, guys,

199

think of the precedent you're setting here. What will they say at the next ASNE Conference?" The annual American Society of Newspaper Editors gathering, usually held in Washington, brought together the nation's top editors for a look at trends and challenges facing the industry, as well as the year's best and worst journalism. The event was important enough to draw the president as a luncheon speaker. "The story's going to get out," I said. "Isabel Moss will go to someone else who won't be so cautious, maybe *St. Pete* or the *Herald*. Then we'll have to explain to *Columbia Journalism Review* why we didn't go to press. Think of the precedent."

Jasper Downing, the executive editor, said, "That's the second time you mentioned precedent, Dan. We're not setting any precedent. Each story is judged on its own merit, same as always. There's also the matter of publishing classified information. The video you saw was *classified military information*."

He stressed the last three words like I'd stolen money from my mother's purse. "I didn't do anything illegal. Besides, that tape helps expose a blatant abuse of power. Isn't that what we do?"

"Of course, but the lawyers have reservations. And what about your source? You'd be willing to do jail time to protect his confidentiality?"

"I would if it came to that."

The other four executives, including Canton Spivey, sat like dummies and stared at their hands. Jasper Downing lit his pipe. "Very romantic, but I'm not sure this one's worth it."

Downing was a dust dry man with a fondness for vests and the gold tie bars I associated with 1950s high school assemblies, better suited for the courtroom than the newsroom. I accused him of kow-towing to national and local military leaders just like glad-handing, unctuous Congressman Eddie Dwoark. In the end, frustrated by their patronizing hand wringing and head nodding, I walked to Downing's wall-length window overlooking the Hillsborough River, glanced over my shoulder and softly called them a bunch of hairless pussies. Canton Spivey immediately apologized. Jasper Downing cut him off. "You just crossed the line, Dan," he said. "I wouldn't go any further."

I didn't, and that was that.

"Y ou're here? Can you come over?"

She seemed genuinely excited. I told her I'd be there in 15 minutes and to break out the highest-proof liquor in the house.

"It's 10:30 in the morning, Dan."

"We'll need two glasses," I said.

A fat blotch plopped onto the windshield like bird crap as I shifted the rental Taurus (Zodiak. *May again!*) into drive. By the time I reached Bayshore thirty ticks later, the rain was pelting the car hard enough to leave marks. I switched the wipers to frantic mode. No contest. I couldn't see and pulled over. Rain beating down, off on the side of a road I could not navigate, thunderstorms not gathering, but present and stalled overhead, it felt suddenly like I'd come to the end. The story was done, fabulous and going nowhere. My wife was a stranger, my happy marriage a fond memory. My new girlfriend soared and sank like the hot stock of the month, dragging me up and down until I was dazed. For the first time I could remember, I felt old. I'd watched Sinatra the other day. *From Here to Eternity*. Frank was about my age when he played Private *Angelo Maggio* and walked off with the award for best supporting. He deserved it; the acting was outstanding and he looked great. In 1953, at 38 or so, he was heading places, branching out. Great singer, great actor. Unlike poor *Maggio*, Frank could tell the commanding officers in his world to screw off and they'd salute smartly. Not me. I tried to flex and the bosses laughed. They said I crossed the line and warned me to get back on my side, and that's just what I did.

I needed some therapy, to run around a little. How great it would feel to forget about everything for a couple of hours, to pump everything into racing up and down the court, to put in a few jumpers, bang for rebounds, hurl a perfect pass, shut out my man on defense … Except it was still pouring. The courts anywhere within driving range would be wet for hours. I leaned my head against the steering wheel. The hard plastic had ridges that would leave an impression on my forehead. I pointed the rear-view at my face and saw S-shaped ridges atop a pair of brown, frowning brows and the two weary, bloodshot eyes of Dan Patragno, crusading angel with a halo of black storm clouds. I wanted to start fresh and thought of Hank. What would he do? In tennis, the clock never runs out until one of the players wins a fixed number of points. In a best-of-three sets match, you can get crushed the first and come out like a new man in the second. I hadn't lost anything yet but a close first set. I stepped out of the car and sat on the hood, feet on the bumper, elbows on my knees, and let the heavy drops wash over me until the clouds moved on.

Little Katie answered the door, safety blanket bunched and tucked under her left arm. Her hair was twisted into two chestnut braids tied off with a pair of thin rubber bands. "Hey there, pretty girl." She turned for her room. "You're getting the floor wet. Mom's in the backyard." I thanked her, remarked on the rain, which had given way to blazing sunshine, and asked if she wanted to come out with us. She didn't answer and I said, "Katie, did you hear me?" She stopped walking. "Why don't you come out with us, hon?"

Still facing her room, she said, "Henry needs me. I have ...Henry."

Isabel laughed when she saw me. "Come, I'll give you some clothes."
She steered me to her bedroom, checked to make sure Katie was occupied, and joined me, shutting the door with a midnight smile. "Take off that wet stuff." She took a handful of shirt in each hand and ripped it open. Buttons flew and bounced silently on the beige carpet. She laughed and shoved me back on the bed. She climbed on top and buried her face in my neck, hips grinding against mine as she wetly whispered a preview of what was coming. "You're going to be too tired to walk out of here, love." Willpower fading, I called time out. "Why?" she giggled, playfully biting my ear.

I pulled away and she crawl-chased me to a corner of the bed, pouncing again. It took all my strength to push her off. "Wait, Isabel, stop, I have to tell you ... You may not want to ... The reason I said to break out the booze ... They killed the story. They're not going to run it. They're afraid of a lawsuit, of being criticized, of undermining troop morale. I'm not exactly sure why they're so scared." I might as well have said I caught something from a twenty-dollar hooker. Her face fell and the mood plunged. "You're kidding, right? Why? After all this time, the work we did ... We've got proof. You saw the video, right?" I told her about the military's personal appeal. "I'll deliver a personal plea to your bosses they'll never forget," she said, backing off the bed and rummaging through a box of men's clothes at the bottom of her closet. She handed me a polo shirt that was too big and shorts that were too small at the waist. Hank's stuff. "You can try; I think their decision is final. I told them you'd take the story to another

---

paper, probably one of our competitors." She closed the box. "So lame …
What kind of newspaper do you work for?" I didn't have much to offer
there. I was just as disgusted with my gutless editors.

"Who's Henry?" I said, breaking the quiet and changing the subject in
hopes of salvaging the afternoon. She looked at me blankly. "Katie said she
couldn't come out with us because she had to take care of Henry." Isabel
gently closed the box of clothes and pushed it back in the closet.

"Henry is Hank, her daddy doll."

The three of us had lunch. "What are you going to do?" she said,
meaning I'd better do *something*. "Right now I'm stuck. I thought *getting*
the story was going to be the problem, not *publishing* the story." She asked
about freelancing the piece to another publication. I said I could do that
and start looking for another job at the same time. "Would that be so bad?
Maybe you should think about working for journalists with a different
perspective." Nice, I thought. I work my ass off to get the best job at the
paper, and I'm supposed to up and quit over one story. I wasn't ready to
leave the News. But her remark about perspective did make me think of
Wendy Hearn and a quick trip to Tallahassee. Wendy knew a little about
the story from our conversation soon after I met Isabel. She would find
a way to get it into print or tell me why it couldn't be done. "You gave me
an idea," I said, heading fast for the laundry room and my drying clothes.
"Sit tight; call you later." I kissed her cheek and tried to do the same to
Katie, who pulled away, saying, "You shouldn't wear daddy's clothes."

I was prepared to fly up and wait on Wendy's porch if she wasn't around.
I thought of a long-ago frosty New Year's Eve when the two of us, then

student and teacher, squeezed onto her old rocker and made out like runaway teens. Wendy never married. I thought of her as the J-school match of *Bull Durham's Annie Savoy*, who plucked one minor leaguer per season for lessons in love and baseball. Except Wendy couldn't stand baseball, thought the players were petulant men and marginal athletes. I called her from TIA and she answered on the second ring. I was glad our shared history made pleasantries unnecessary. "I'm landing at four; can you get me? Sorry, I know it's short notice." She quickly agreed. "You wouldn't have asked if it weren't important."

The flight was marred by a stray thunderstorm, an orphan of the earlier weather that drenched Tampa, but we landed without incident or apology from crew or captain. The air was heavy; more rain would fall within the hour. Wendy was outside in a noisy VW bug and suggested a bar we knew close to FSU. I buckled in and noticed her peering at me over her glasses. "Who are *you* supposed to be, *Fabio?*" I looked down. My shirt was nearly open to my waist. No buttons. "Long story, not important." I tucked in the best I could, thought briefly of Isabel and the rough lovemaking that never happened, and talked all the way into town, explaining about Hank Moss, the trail of sources leading to the video, and the new dead end in my own newsroom.

I'd barely cleared the head from my beer when she said, "There's a way; you might not like it." She hadn't changed much over the years. I thought of my homeless woman story senior year. Wendy branded me with a *C* that I'd always carried as a reminder that good reporters had to be accurate, fair and plenty skeptical. She still dressed like a college kid, flaxen hair cut short and bouncy, a touch of mascara and pink lipstick, jeans and a V-necked T-shirt that made me think of our special nights in the old house on Tharpe Street. Sometimes we'd come to this bar before our lovemaking, a risky play since lots of FSU students and professors stopped in as well, and we weren't always discreet. She knew where I'd slipped off to and smiled, her teeth straight and white as I remembered, though slight wrinkles had begun forming at the corners of her mouth. I chastised myself for being so critical. She was mid-forties and could pass for a decade younger. "Focus, Daniel." I apologized. She sat quiet a few moments. The *Dixie Chicks* played on a jukebox that I knew was stuffed with country, gospel, and what the music world now called contemporary Christian. The bar had morphed over the years into a concoction of chrome and mirrors, pretty slick for Tallahassee. And yet there was no dance floor; this was a talking bar, one where politicians traded favors and lobbyists hung around to pick up the tab. Wendy put her hands together, prayer position, each slender finger tapping in unison against its opposite. I felt a breeze and looked up at a ceiling fan with old-fashioned tassels that seemed lost in the modern decor. "Here it is," she said, eyes bright with the joy of a puzzle solved. "To get the story published, you've got to end-run your editors. You need an outside ally willing to fight for this woman, someone local, but with enough clout to attract national attention when he starts talking. It has to be your local congressman."

"Dorkman? You're kidding. Eddie Dwoark didn't want any part of this. He nearly threw Isabel out of his office. She had to stick what was left of Hank's burned up uniform in his face before he'd even listen."

"Doesn't matter. You got him half on board; now go the rest of the way. You and Isabel Moss have to convince the Tampa congressman to call out the Army. He has to be outraged. He has to *yell*. He has to charge them with a cover-up and demand an investigation, maybe congressional hearings. In return for giving him all the evidence — and a big political payday — he agrees to let you break the story a day before everyone else.

When the other reporters are playing catch-up, you'll be able to focus on a second-day story that will break more new information. The big papers and even the networks will quote and credit the Tampa *Daily News* for a solid week, depending on how hard you keep pushing. She drank half her beer in a gulp and grinned. "That's how you give your editors cover, get the story published, and reveal what really happened to Hank Moss."

I weighed the idea. "That kind of publicity would guarantee Eddie Dwoark's reelection."

"From what I know about the district, he's a lock anyway."

She was right. "My editors aren't going to like me handing my story over to the Dorkman."

"Your editors forfeited their moral authority when they caved in to the military. Anyway, I think they'll be happy. This way your paper gets to break the story risk-free."

"Will Dwoark go for it?"

"His one worry is retribution from the military, all those servicemen and women and their families voting against him. I don't think that will happen. If the story is accurate, the military can't blame him for exposing a slimy cover-up. In fact, they'll probably jump on his bandwagon. I can hear the top general: *No one's above the law, uniform or no uniform. Anyone who falsified official documents will be prosecuted.* They won't be able to lock up Braxton and Marlin Falk fast enough." A waitress came and Wendy insisted on paying. "I think your Mrs. Moss should go along in case the congressman has any doubts. Sounds like she's got a persuasive quality ..."

Wendy was right; this was the way to go, the reason I spent 250 bucks for a 90-minute trip to Tallahassee. I leaned across to kiss her cheek and she pulled away. Her hands went back to prayer position. "There's something you're not telling me."

Crap, she was good. "I don't think so."

"Daniel. I find this offensive. You call me up out of the blue, tell me your sad story and ask me to help. I do, and you sit there and lie to my face."

This was the one risk in coming to see her. I thought I'd gotten through the traps. "I'm sorry, it's personal."

"Personal. You're involved with her, aren't you?"

The woman knew everything.

"How deep are you in? Did you sleep with her a few times or is it more than that?"

I couldn't answer. She sank back in the booth a second and then pitched forward. Her next words hurt. "My advice — my *strong* advice — is to get back to Tampa and explain to your bosses that you've developed a personal relationship with your source. Apologize. Beg them not to fire your ass on the spot. Do it tonight. Then ask them to reassign the story to another reporter. Then *that* reporter has to go to Congressman Dwoark."

"I can't give up the story."

"Then break it off with the woman. It's already too late, but that would be better than — "

" — I can't."

"You can't write about her and fuck her too. I thought we covered that your first semester."

She stuck a fork in her water glass and fished out an ice cube, not speaking again until it dissolved in her mouth. "Something bad is coming, Daniel. You're putting your paper at risk and fooling with your career. I don't know why. The critics — and that might wind up being quite a cast — Falk ... Braxton's defenders ... the military ... the mainstream media ... even the right-wing talk show nuts ... All of them will say you weren't fair because you were shacking up with the dead man's widow. Whether you actually skewed the facts doesn't matter. You crossed the line and tainted your reporting. Is it true, by the way?"

"Is what true?"

"Have you slanted the story because of your feelings for her?"

"Absolutely not, and no one knows about us except Ellie."

"Your wife. Well, that's another issue and I'm not going there. See a marriage counselor." She sat up straight and suggested I listen closely. "Someone *will* find out. Then it's your career. Change your plans, Daniel, or start thinking about what else you can do for a living."

My feet were itching to get me out of there. I rubbed one worn leather heel against the other under the table, knowing I wasn't going anywhere until the professor said so. My shirt fell open and I drew it closed. I could tell from Wendy's face that she now had a pretty good idea of how the buttons came off. Ears burning, I apologized. I told her I was on guard from the second Isabel Moss flashed her legs the day we met in the Senate. "I thought of you, Wendy. I imagined being in this spot and you saying the kind of things you just said. I never wanted to hear you talk to me that way."

She took my hands. "Let's go. The last flight back leaves in 45 minutes."

Chapter 34

There were seven people on the plane. I sat in a window seat and put my feet up, hogging the whole row. Even so, I felt like a man locked up and dying of thirst. No water, no *prospect* of water. All I had was a carton of milk six days past the expiration date. Should I drink? Pray? Drink *and* pray? I decided to drink. I would drink it all and accept my fate. It might work out. I might be able to cheat the journalism gods, land Isabel Moss and end up happy. Wendy didn't think so. Well, Wendy didn't know everything. The plane hit an air pocket and I gripped the arm rests as we free-fell for maybe six seconds. Once we leveled off, the overhead speaker crackled. "Captain Morris here, folks. Sorry about that; couldn't get around it. Shouldn't be any more turbulence before we land in Tampa."

I walked back into Isabel's house at midnight. We sat at the kitchen table and I asked for a beer. She put a glass of microwave-warmed milk in front of me. "You had a rough day. This will help you sleep." I told her the two options — live with no story or follow Wendy's plan. She decided we would visit Congressman Dwoark in the morning.

Bella

We made tired, perfunctory love that did not live up to the wild promise of the afternoon, when she tore off my shirt and growled into my neck. Afterward, she turned on her side. I gently moved some hair off her face and stroked her cheek. "I love you, Isabel Moss," I whispered. No answer. She was already asleep or faking it. I rolled on my back and, though drained to exhaustion, stared at the dark ceiling a long time, wondering dizzily about old milk. Before I could get sick, I fell asleep and dreamed I was in a clearing in a forest arguing with a talking bear. It was early morning, cool and quiet, except for frogs and fish playing in and along the bank of a nearby river. It was evident from his upright gold crown that the white-muzzled bear ruled this particular forest, and that I was guilty of trespassing. *Don't be ridiculous, the forest is free for everyone*, I said. I might have stopped there had squeaky bird and chipmunk laughter not greeted my words. I stood up straight and waved a finger all around. *Maybe I should call the park ranger.* There was a gasp. The old bear sat on his haunches and smiled. He lit a pipe, the barrel of which bore a carved replica of his royal profile. He puffed a few times, producing small, smoky clouds that smelled like cherry, and said:

Has it occurred to you it's unwise to argue with a bear, even one who can talk?

Watching him, listening to his smooth baritone, I became fascinated and quickly lost track of why we were fighting. I moved closer. I expected breath like tobacco and raw fish. I was wrong; it was actually pleasant. I told him so and he grinned, showing fearsome white teeth.

When I was younger, I liked to hunt for my meals. When I began to get old and slow, I taught myself to speak. It wasn't as hard as you'd think. Now I just say a few words and my meals are delivered free, wherever I happen to be. The humans are too curious to stay away from a talking grizzly. I

*barely have to move. Get it? Barely? Ha! Delicious, he said, putting a paw
to his great mouth as a gourmet chef might kiss his fingers in describing
the nightly special.*

Wrapped up in his black *Capone Uomo*, starched white shirt and
gold-flecked black tie, Eddie Dwoark looked too dapper for a congressman. Too dapper, too nervous. A staffer told me Dwoark said the first
meeting with Isabel Moss two weeks earlier was like getting his foot
snagged in a lawnmower. My subsequent interview with the congressman
also hadn't gone well. Since then, I knew he'd been waiting for a story
to appear in the hometown paper and wondering how he'd come off,
sympathetic or cold, the kindly, compassionate public servant or a well-
dressed asshole graying nicely at the temples. But no story had run, and
now Isabel and I were sitting before him, obviously wanting something.
Eddie Dwoark fidgeted first with the laminated day schedule card his
assistant prepared each morning, and then with his gold initial cuff links.
I tried and could not think of another man I knew whose initials added
up to his first name. Ed was clearly uncomfortable, even in his fancy suit.
"You asked for a meeting."

Isabel nudged me. We hadn't discussed who would begin. She glanced
at a 5x7 of Dwoark and his wife Edie, an ex-Miss Florida with great political smarts. Anyone who wanted a job on the congressman's staff had to
first survive an interview with Edie Dwoark. I once wrote about their
partnership, called it *Adventures with Eddie and Edie.* She wasn't amused
and Ed didn't return my calls for a month. The editors got tired of reading
stories with, *Congressman Dwoark couldn't be reached for comment,* and
forced me to make peace. I apologized and she accepted graciously. Shaking hands to affirm the ceasefire, she said, *We work hard for the district,*

Bella

Danny; you should think twice before you ridicule the congressman. Isabel straightened the photo and picked up a *Dwoark for Congress* campaign pamphlet, smiling a little at the flag motif and corny logo: *Ed Dwoark: First for Florida.* I knew the slogan was Edie's idea. By honing in on the entire state as much as his single district, Dwoark was laying subliminal groundwork for a future U.S. Senate campaign. He did frequent favors for the other Florida congressmen and was warmly welcomed on his make-work visits to Miami, Jacksonville and Tallahassee. "I'd like to tell you what we've discovered about Hank's death and get your reaction, Congressman."

Dwoark listened to her and kept close watch on me. "It may turn out I don't need to ask you any questions, Ed. Depends on your reaction."

He lifted a hand, inviting one of us to begin. I tried to see her from his eyes. Her beauty was undeniable, yet he might have been the one man not affected. Her hair today was swept up, accenting the slope of her elegant neck and a pair of delicate, six-inch rectangular earrings that hung low and sleek like modern art. Where most men would fantasize about helping themselves to her soft lips, now painted with tangerine gloss that matched her sleeveless summer dress, Dwoark would remember her mouth from several weeks back, quivering as she tossed shreds of Hank's uniform on his desk — this very desk — and demanded his help. This meeting was calmer, yet Dwoark was clearly on guard. Isabel sketched the big picture; I filled in details. We told him we'd met and interviewed the anonymous caller, Bart Jefferson, about Marcus Ravoli's suicide and our meeting with his mother. "Sweet woman," I said. "I have a notebook full of quotes." Dwoark nodded, trying for neutral body language. Isabel told how Bart steered us to a critical video, and that I'd found and watched it with an official (Clay) from the U.S. National Reconnaissance Office.

"The tape confirms Hank was not killed by enemy fire," she said.

213

"Marcus Ravoli got scared and threw the grenade that killed Hank." I piped in. "Once they figured out what happened, the highest-ranking soldier at the scene — a Sgt. Marlin Falk from outside Pittsburgh; he's still in Afghanistan — Falk ordered the other soldiers to lie and say Hank was killed by enemy fire. Then he falsified the casualty report."

"I don't understand about the video. Someone filmed all this?"

Were Dwoark only as sharp as his thousand-dollar suit. "No, Ed, the events were inadvertently captured by an unmanned military aerial drone that was flying by on patrol. It's not unequivocal proof, but it's close. Add the video to everything else, and there's no doubt."

"Then why are you here? I already gave you a statement."

Again Isabel kneed my thigh. My turn, and yellow flags were flying. If I said plainly that the newspaper refused to run the story because of pressure from the Army, savvy pols like Ed and Edie Dwoark would never take a chance. It had to be his idea. Would he go for the bait? "What do you think should happen here, Ed? If you were the benevolent dictator, how would justice best be served?"

"Off the record?"

"Yeah, until we decide how to go forward, you can be off the record."

He clasped his hands. Rays of piercing sunlight ricocheted off a gold ring that was worth more than I made in a year. His window overlooked a slice of downtown Tampa where old and new joined in the promise of a glitzy tomorrow. Dwoark intended to parlay the city's sharp rise — all due to dynamics that did not involve him — the surging pro football team, the renowned international airport, the weather, beaches and a dozen other factors — into a lifelong career in politics. He grew stern, as if another Atlantic hurricane were sizing up Florida and his job was to get people the hell out of the way. He tapped his desk a second and stopped. What he said next surprised me, even though sources are always bolder when safely off the record. "If all this is true," Dwoark said, "people should go to jail and Mrs. Moss deserves an official apology."

The three of us gave that some thought. It was nearly statesmanlike. Isabel secretly squeezed my hand. It occurred for the hundredth time since I'd met her that the relationship between reporters and sources was a funny animal. Close is good, because people with information won't feed it to a journalist they don't trust. *Too* close is bad because it suggests bias. It was wrong to sleep with Isabel, but okay to sleep, so to speak, with Dwoark. Isabel and I had already done the deed. Now we were priming Eddie Dwoark to make it a threesome. It was as necessary as it was revolting. Maybe we could get Edie in there too.

"I need you to say it publicly."

It was my turn to nudge Isabel. She was jumping ahead, going too fast. She couldn't demand that Dwoark … She ignored me. She said, "We'll give you all the documentation. Once you're satisfied, you'll write a letter to the Secretary of the Army, the Secretary of Defense and the President. You'll release the letters to the media at a press conference in D.C. the day after Danny announces your intentions in a story for his paper. I can help make sure the local TV stations send someone to Washington or get stringers."

I watched Ed as Isabel spoke and got a glimpse of what life must be like within the Dwoark mansion, with Edie Dwoark ripping off instructions and poor Ed jotting everything down. *Yes, ma'am, I'll get right on it.* He seemed hypnotized as Isabel laid out the agenda point by point. When finished, she said, "Will you do all that for me and my little girl, congressman? So that people can know the truth?"

Dwoark looked my way for the first time in awhile. "Why don't you just break the story, Danny? Why do you need me?"

Isabel answered. "It works better this way, sir. It has more gravitas with a congressman's name attached. Danny and I discussed it. He agreed."

A good answer, though far from the truth.

Dwoark said, "I'll need to talk it over with my ... I'll meet with my team. I'll get back to you."

We rose and shook hands, all but sealing the deal. Dwoark's stall was intended to carve some wiggle room, but Isabel, master huntress, had him cornered. She let the trap snap as he opened the door to see us out. Isabel stepped forward and shut it. She put her back against the door so the two of them were face to face, close enough to make him squirm. I thought of Mr. T and pitied the fool. "Do this," she said, "and when the time comes, I'll do everything I can to help elect you to the Senate."

Eddie Dwoark was pretty speechless for a politician.

"Y ou meant it?"

"I meant it."

"You think Ed Dwoark and his lunatic wife belong in the U.S. Senate?"

"I help those who help me. And Katie. Not every senator has to be a leader. Most don't come close. Look at Kirk Lawton, for God's sake — strolling into a police station with no pants. Not exactly Thomas Jefferson. Dwoark's no worse than anyone else."

Jefferson drafted the Declaration of Independence, served as Secretary of State and was America's third President. He'd never been a senator, but hell, it was too hot to argue. I would write about Dwoark's shortcomings when the time came. Isabel clammed up — I knew she was analyzing each turn of the meeting — and soon it felt too quiet. I turned on the radio and we caught the tail end of the news, sports and weather, all punctuated by the sing-song ad for *Urso & Raposa Lawn Care and Landscape.* Isabel came back to life, chiming in with the chorus: *Bring-ing a Touch; Of Heaven to Homes; In … Hills-bor-ough Coun-ty*, then burst out laughing. She poked my ribs, said, "Me and my gay cousin," and cracked up again. I laughed too, adding, by the way, that she should never, ever sing in public. When the mirth ran out, we were only a few blocks from her house. I mentioned the radio sports guy's tennis note about reaching the midpoint of the two biggest pro tournaments, Wimbledon and the U.S. Open. Isabel said Hank would have been training hard through mid-July and early August, trying to hone his game and build confidence at the hard-court events leading up to the Open. The road to Flushing Meadows ran through several cities, including Indianapolis, Los Angeles, Toronto, and D.C.

I imagined trying to write an important story with 20,000 people applauding good sentences and booing when I screwed up. Having some loved ones in the stands would help.

"Isabel, do you stay in touch with Hank's mom? Does she know what's going on?"

"Of course. She's Katie's grandma."

"Would you help arrange an interview?"

"I'm surprised you waited so long to ask."

"I was saving her for last. I didn't want to disturb her until the story was a sure thing."

"Make sure you're gentle. She's buried a husband and two children."

Anne Moss was frail and petite with luminous light blue eyes that were overly moist, as if she'd just stopped crying or were about to start. She lived east of Tampa in Plant City in the same home where Hank and his sister Catherine grew up. The house, a French colonial with wrap-around porch and three wicker rockers, was too big for one person, so Mrs. Moss kept the second floor closed off except when Isabel and Katie, or Sally, Catherine's daughter, came for a long visit, usually during the annual Strawberry Festival in March. We arrived around lunchtime, and there was a silver tray waiting with tuna sandwiches on toast sliced in quarters and a matching silver bowl of small carrots. Mrs. Moss was in her early seventies. Her home was museum clean; the food arrangement was restaurant worthy. All that and the woman's outfit — a simple blue dress half a shade deeper than her eyes and topped with a delicate sapphire necklace — suggested she'd spent considerable time preparing for our visit. "Hope you two are hungry," she said after shaking my hand and tightly hugging Isabel. "How's my granddaughter?" Isabel said Katie was well and they would visit again Sunday. "That's fine," Mrs. Moss said, steering us to the dining room table. Fresh-cut pink and red roses stood tall in a smoked glass vase beside the sandwich tray. "Child's growing so fast, I have to see her each week or I don't recognize her. She has Hank's eyes and smile, you know. Two middle bottom teeth overlap, just like his. And smart ... She's smart like Isabel."

"Katie's great," I said, thinking of the brooding child and her daddy doll, and wondering if she'd forget her father, or grow up and battle intimacy problems based on an irrational fear that the men in her life would walk out one day and never come back.

But Katie wasn't the reason I'd come to Anne Moss's home.

I tried to imagine Hank racing around the house as a kid, doing his math homework, mowing the lawn, tearing up the stairs to change clothes for tennis practice. This is where he got his first bike, lost his baby teeth, learned right and wrong and pestered his big sister. Unlike Isabel's house, there were few signs he'd ever been here. Somewhere along the way, Mrs. Moss decided she'd keep her memories private and boxed up all his photos, tennis trophies, greeting cards and kindergarten art projects. There were just two pictures on a blonde wood mantle by the staircase, one of Hank, the other of Catherine. Hank's looked to be a formal sitting around the time of college graduation. He was smiling broadly; the two lower middle teeth did indeed overlap. I wondered if he'd been thinking of his secret plan. Everyone thought he was gearing up for a life in business and advertising, when he was really headed for pro tennis.

Isabel and Mrs. Moss were still talking about Katie. I nibbled a tuna sandwich, not sure whether to interrupt or wait for a signal from Isabel to begin the interview. Mrs. Moss sensed my discomfort. She turned and I saw that I'd been wrong earlier. She was small and elderly but not frail; she sat with a straight back and there was elegance in each movement, even when she swiveled her head and said to me, "So you want to know about Hank." I nodded, apologetically, for in truth I felt badly, interrupting whatever peace she had left and forcing her to talk about things she probably didn't want to share. "Let's go to the living room." She rose and we followed; before sitting she went to a wall unit and turned on quiet music. "Hank liked classical, why I have no idea. His dad and I were big country fans. Johnny Cash, June Carter, Loretta Lynn, later, Willie Nelson. And all the kids around here when he was growing up listened to rock 'roll."

"Did he play an instrument?"

Her laugh was low and even, not an old person's laugh. "He tried clarinet in the third grade. Lord, the screeching. Drove *Yogi* clean out of the house. *Yogi* was our cat back then." She looked around as if the practice and reaction had occurred here in the living room. "A little while later we got him his first racket. We didn't play. He must have gotten the idea of playing tennis from the same mystery place he found Bach and Mozart."

Isabel leaned forward as if she'd never heard the story. Mrs. Moss said, "That racket — he always had it in his hands. Played every day, mostly by himself in the beginning. The other boys liked football and baseball. No one around here liked soccer. Most times Hank was off hitting on the schoolyard wall where most of the kids played stickball. I'd have to find him for supper. No cell phones then. Ask me, we were better off."

Little of this material would make my article. She was caught up in the telling, though, and Isabel was listening intently, so I waited to ask my questions.

"We made him a deal. We'd spring for lessons if he made a B-plus average or better." She collected a spot of lint from the sofa and shrugged her slender shoulders. "He kept up his end easy. Hank liked school. Same with Cath. I don't think we ever saw a C, not in high school or college. Hank got good at tennis. We didn't know *how* good. How would we know? We didn't know anything about the game. *Love, deuce, let court?* Sounded like nonsense to Henry — Mr. Moss — and myself. Every few weeks Hank would show up with some little trophy or plaque. There's trunks full of 'em in the attic. End of his junior year at Plant High, letters started coming from different colleges. Scholarship offers. Mr. Moss was suspicious. He couldn't believe any respectable university would pick up the tab for Hank's degree in return for him playing tennis. I admit I thought there had to be some catch. Nothing's free in this world, I believe. We'd spent years saving for his college. It felt wrong to spend that money on anything else. Cath and Hank were going to be the first in the family to go past high school. Mr. Moss worked at *Beall's* forty years. Menswear, mostly, until he became manager." She put her glass to her mouth. "Oh, dear, I finished my water. I'll be right back. You two need anything?"

When she was gone, Isabel reached over and squeezed my hand. "You're being very patient. Let her keep going. She'll run out of steam and you can get what you need for the story."

Mrs. Moss returned with a worn letter from the University of Maryland. "Terps! We knew Seminoles and Gators, not Terps." He could have gone to FSU, Florida State, or a dozen other schools. He picked Maryland because his high school coach was close friends with the Maryland coach. Nice men, both of them. Maryland also has that good business school. By then, Catherine was already set up in New York. Good job, rotten husband, except that together they made my beautiful little Sally." The mention of her other granddaughter tore open the old wounds. She pulled a white handkerchief from her beaded purse and dabbed her eyes. "You'd just think with all the rotten people in the world … crooks, cheats, rapists, and worse that God above would've taken someone else … "

Isabel ran to her side. "Mom … "

"I'm so sorry. I'm okay. Ours is not to question why, only it's hard sometimes. Go sit back down, Isabel."

"Mrs. Moss, you know I've been working with Isabel on a story about how Hank died in Afghanistan." She nodded. "We've found proof that another American soldier accidentally killed your son, and that the Army covered up the truth. I'm expecting my newspaper to publish the story any day. Would you like to comment?"

I wasn't sure she followed. "They killed Mr. Moss when they killed Catherine, you know." I began taking notes, not sure where she was headed. "He died two months after the funeral. He was sick with cancer, but it was in remission. Al Qaeda. They killed him; he might as well have been in one of the towers. They didn't care who they killed, so long as there were a lot of bodies. How many people did they kill, I wonder, who weren't in the buildings?" She folded the Terps scholarship letter and placed it inside the original envelope. "We tried to talk Hank out of enlisting. Isabel tried. He wouldn't change his mind. Hank and Catherine were very close." Isabel started to cry. Mrs. Moss got a box of tissues. Again, I was surprised at how effortlessly she moved.

"I miss my son, Mr. Patragno. I miss my son; I miss my daughter. My husband and I, we had a good life. I know none of them is coming back." She shuffled the Terps letter and brought out a second envelope I hadn't noticed. "He wrote me this soon as he got over there." She turned the short note toward me. The handwriting was neat; even someone with bad eyes could read it easily, as she read now:

Dear Mom, Arrived safely; it's hotter here than any place I've ever been, even Plant City in July! I know you're worried; I won't take any chances, just like I promised. Please keep an eye on Isabel and Katie. I'll be home before you know it. Love, Hank.

She tucked the letter back in its envelope. "This proof you have — that's not going to bring Hank back." She faltered and I thought that was it. I squirmed around a little on the sofa, uncertain if I should collect Isabel and leave. Mrs. Moss held out her hand to stop me. She still wore a modest gold wedding band. "Thing is, they lied to me. Mr. Army Bigshot sat right where you're sitting and told me the other side got him. Hank wouldn't have liked that. It's cheating. Hank hated cheaters. If a boy ever cheated him in a match — called a ball out when it was good — Hank would always end up winning. He wouldn't tolerate cheaters or liars." She pointed at the sofa. "Man sat right there and lied to my face. Lied to the whole country, if you want to look at it that way. So yes, I have a comment. You bet I do."

Chapter 35

U.S. Congressman Ed Dwoark called an hour later. Voice terse and urgent, as if he were agreeing to parachute into hostile territory and snatch the enemy's top-secret war plans, he said, "I'm in. Get me the materials."

My first thought was of the mall at Pentagon City, of Charles Braxton shoving that wrought iron table into my chest at the food court, of his slimy smile, and how good, how absolutely fucking wonderful, it was going to be to call the bulky master sergeant and politely ask him for a comment on the Army cover-up alleged by Tampa Congressman Ed Dwoark in the tragic case of Hank Moss. I felt lousy acknowledging my revenge lust, even to myself. Reporters are supposed to be about facts and fairness and following stories wherever they lead, not payback. Most critics get it wrong. They think journalists push an ideological agenda, as in, the *liberal* media or the *right-wing* press. The real issue is journalistic egotism, an unshakeable sense that *We the Media* are imbued by some higher power with the jury's wisdom and the judge's power. In many ways, it's the same elitism that beat reporters love to write about when they catch politicians, athletes, entertainers, businessmen, fashion designers and restaurant owners getting too cocky. I was there the day

Eddie Dwoark arrived in Congress. He was embarrassed to get in one of those old-fashioned marble-floored U.S. House elevators with the bronze doors because they all had human operators. I heard him mutter, "I can push the damn buttons myself." He saw me jot his words in my notebook and asked me not to use the quote; he hadn't intended to complain out loud, he said. I agreed. By the end of his third term, he wouldn't even walk through a door unless an aide held it open. And look out if one of the junior staffers didn't move fast enough. I noted all this in a column, again incurring the wrath of Eddie and Edie.

So maybe there was a double standard. Perhaps I had the reporter's version of Beltway Fever. So be it. I also had the First Amendment and a barrel of ink. Braxton, that fucker, was going to pay.

Canton Spivey became my new hero. I could almost see him nodding in approval as I explained how we drafted Dwoark. "I'm not supposed to tell my reporters how to bypass the editors, Patragno. I really should be tearing you a new one, but shit, I might've pulled a stunt like this myself back in the day. What's the timing? When am I going to get the story?"

"It's nearly done. I have to insert quotes from Hank Moss' mother and get a comment from the Army."

"You know Braxton's going to try to stop Dwoark, right? He's going to have every military official in Greater Tampa hounding Dwoark to back off. Make sure he doesn't cave."

I assured Canton that Dwoark wouldn't change his mind. I hoped I was right.

"Why don't you come in and write the piece, sit in the newsroom like old times?"

"I've got my laptop. I'd rather be here where it's quiet."

Strained silence. "You at a hotel or the widow's house?"

"I'm at Isabel's," I said, wishing I'd lied, then wishing I'd said Mrs. Moss instead of Isabel.

"It's a bad idea to write a blockbuster story from your main source's private home, Danny. It wouldn't be right no matter *what* story you were writing. Come to the newsroom. I'll find you a desk."

His tenor suggested the conversation wasn't over.

By 4 p.m., Congressman Dwoark had the documents he needed to get started. I plucked some fresh quotes and made sure he understood — and would make clear to the press — that the incriminating information had been provided by Isabel Moss. "Should anyone ask, it'd probably be best not to mention I was part of the meeting, Ed." He agreed and I phoned Charles Braxton. A secretary said he was in a meeting and promised — once I'd made enough of a fuss — that he'd get back to me before close of business. I called Bart Jefferson, who'd left a message a few days ago. I explained where we were to Bart, thanked him for being the first to alert Isabel, and asked for his comment. He was nervous as the day the three of us met at *Mel's* diner. "You already put it all together. Why do you have to quote me?"

"C'mon, Bart, you've seen the lawyer shows. There's hearsay and direct testimony. Hearsay is second-hand info. You were *there*. You're credible. You're going to give the readers a firsthand account. That's why I need you in the story."

He stayed silent. "Plus," I added in the quiet, "I think that deep down you want to be part of making this right."

"True," he said, and started talking.

225

There's no such thing as a tidy newsroom. Narrow, half-filled spiral notebooks, old newspapers, personal knick-knacks and plastic coffee containers are everywhere. There's also no decorum; when editors need something, they need it now and everyone knows it, because the yelling as deadlines approach is nearly constant. Reporters, too, are not shy about speaking up to copy kids or the people they're interviewing by phone. Think of a library and picture the opposite. When librarians have nightmares, they probably dream of newsrooms. And yet there's a current in the air late each afternoon — a controlled, energizing chaos, even on routine days — when reporters are working stories and editors are buzzing in and out of budget meetings, fighting to get their stamp on the next day's section fronts.

Canton Spivey had already secured front-page play for the Dwoark-Moss story. It wasn't a hard sell. Hank Moss was a local kid and the local congressman was making charges that had national implications. There were muscle-headed villains, a brave whistle-blower, a suicide victim, a grieving widow, and a fatherless child. And there was a hero, a handsome, rising politician willing to take on powerful military interests in his own district. At least that's how it would come off. No one need know that Ed Dwoark had to be dragged into the fight.

All I had to do now was finish crafting my fabulous ingredients — dozens of pages of notes, tape-recorded interviews, mental images of sources, situations and the accidental video — into a coherent, balanced, and accurate newspaper story. This is the muck where many reporters get bogged down, slogging details or inflammatory quotes on top of the most important information. As a young reporter, I'd heard more than one editor complain, *Patragno, you buried the damned lead.* Even with years of experience and a clear path to the front page, it was hard to finish the job. This one had to be right: I didn't want any editors screwing with my copy. *Think, Danny. What's the most important part of the story? What do people need to know? It's a complicated piece. Make sure any reader can understand.*

I heard from Canton that the only other local story getting A-1 consideration was a quirky expose about the Tampa fire chief driving his truck home after a day of team drills and using leftover water to fill his swimming pool and water his lawn. The mayor said it was a firing offense. The city hall reporter who uncovered the fiasco sat one cubicle over. I overheard snatches of conversation and clacking from his computer keyboard as he interviewed the bewildered chief and took notes. "*I don't know what you should have done with the extra water, Chief. What were you supposed to do?*" More clacking. "Well I guess you should have dumped it, then."

Stories about on-going fighting in Afghanistan, a big trade by the *Florida Marlins*, and a hurricane forming out in the ocean were also front-page contenders. I had no quarrel and would gladly share the space, so long as the Moss story led the paper. Reporters and editors kept stopping by to congratulate me even though they hadn't seen the story yet. The only sour face belonged to Jasper Downing, the executive editor who killed my original story. I caught sight of him bearing down as I was writing. I stayed fixed on my screen even as I smelled his sea-breeze cologne and pipe breath. He spoke so only I could hear. "I know you gave Dwoark the information, Patragno. When I can prove it, I'll fire you myself. You won't get a job *delivering* newspapers."

"Mrs. Moss provided him the materials when you refused to run the story, Mr. Downing."

He spun around and walked off just as my phone rang. I cradled it between shoulder and ear to keep my hands free and said, "This is

Patragno."

"You self-righteous prick."

People were cursing or threatening me from all directions. How could I not enjoy being back in the newsroom? "Hello, Sgt. Braxton. How are things in Washington?"

"You went crying to your congressman. You couldn't get your editors to run that crappy story so you went crying to your congressman. That's some journalistic integrity."

I gave him the same answer I gave Jasper Downing, that Isabel Moss, widow of the soldier killed by friendly fire, supplied the information.

"Bullshit. You gave the stuff to Dwoark or instructed her to do it."

"This is very interesting, Sergeant, but I'm on deadline. Would you like to comment on the congressman's allegations? Have you heard what he said?"

I imagined Braxton choking the shape out of one of those stress-relieving squeeze balls. He said in a measured voice, "We have a protocol around here. I don't speak to the press. Hold for our communications director." I held. A guy got on and identified himself as Kenyon Steward, director of communications for the Joint Chiefs of Staff. He said, "We have great respect for Congressman Dwoark and will look carefully into the accusations." When I attempted a follow-up, he said, "That's all, Mr. Patragno." I asked for Braxton again. "Can you make Sgt. Marlin Falk available for an interview?"

I believe if we'd been face to face he would have used my throat like the squeeze ball.

"This is not to be quoted: Sgt. Falk is overseas in hostile territory fighting the war against terror on behalf of the President and the American people."

"Got it, thanks. And by the way, Congressman Dwoark knows about your other buddy, the silver-haired gangster who likes to play cop and give little kids rides in his car. He's not happy about Reese Wehrman, if that's the guy's real name. I'd keep your boy on a tight leash from now on, if I were you."

He hung up on me. I put his quote high in the story and read what I had so far:

Army Spec. Hank Moss, a Tampa native and fast-rising pro athlete, was killed by friendly fire and not enemy soldiers as reported by the Army, Tampa Congressman Ed Dwoark alleged Thursday.

Dwoark called for immediate congressional hearings on an "appalling" cover-up by Army officials. He said that lying to Moss' widow and the American public about the young soldier's death on May 15 was "indefensible."

Isabel Moss, 26-year-old wife of the dead soldier and mother of their four-year-old daughter, said, "I can't understand why they did this. They let us have a funeral thinking Hank died fighting America's enemies. I'm very angry."

According to Dwoark, Moss was killed in the Afghan city of Jalalabad by a grenade thrown by a soldier from Charleston, S.C. That soldier, Marcus Ravoli, was honorably discharged from the Army on June 3 and later committed suicide in Charleston. His mother told the *Daily News* that Ravoli was unable to live knowing that he'd accidentally killed a fellow soldier and later agreed to a senior officer's order to conceal the truth.

The order was given by Sgt. Marlin Falk at the scene shortly after Moss died. Falk, from Monroeville, Pa., is still on active duty in Afghanistan and could not be reached.

"We have great respect for Congressman Dwoark and will look

carefully into his allegations," said Kenyon Steward, spokesman for Master Sgt. Charles Braxton, an Army official at the Joint Chiefs of Staff in Washington, D.C.

Dwoark said two factors were critical in bringing the conspiracy to light: information provided by Private Bart Jefferson, who was also at the scene and under Moss' command, and the discovery of an Air Force surveillance video inadvertently captured by an unmanned aerial drone.

I thought awhile about identifying Clay Ohrbach as the source who provided the video. I tried to forget he was a basketball buddy who, by the way, also slept with my wife. Here I was again, judge and jury. Punish Braxton, let Clay slide, I decided, and wrote:

A copy of the video was provided to the *Daily News* by a government source who asked not to be identified. The source said he feared retribution from higher-ranking military officials, and *Daily News* executives opted to grant his request to remain anonymous.

"Patragno, how's it coming? I've got nothing but a goddamn sinkhole on the front page 'til I get that story."

"Ten minutes, Canton."

I stayed until first run. At 11 p.m., the bulky offset presses whirred to life and began churning out the next day's news at a clip of 90,000 papers an hour. A copy kid was dispatched to bring a dozen up to the newsroom. Contrary to the old saying, they came off the presses moist, not hot. At midnight, one of the night editors would post an Internet version of the piece on our website. Then the AP would pick it up, rewrite the top and send it out, and the world would know what really happened to Hank Moss. I was leaning against a wall admiring my work, experiencing mixed feelings about the color photo of Dwoark — it was a huge amount of free publicity, after all — and starting to think about a second-day story — it was possible that Dwoark's college buddy, Senator Newlin, would order immediate hearings on the Hill, I'd have to check with that feisty Asian press secretary, Gemma something — when Canton Spivey touched my back and said, "Let's talk."

As a rookie, I'd spent enough time in the newsroom to know Spivey was one executive who didn't need an office. Instead, he sat at a work station at the heart of the newsroom 10 hours a day and yelled instructions like a marching band director without a baton. *Wilson, get two more sources to confirm this information. Sansoni, you think your mother up in Schenectady would understand this budget story? Patragno, you buried the lead again.* So I knew it was bad news when he led me to his office, still neat as a vacant apartment after all these years, and worse when he closed the door behind us.

He didn't say a word, another omen. He handed me a one-page document I recognized as the Society of Professional Journalists' Code of Ethics. The code is divided into four categories: *Seek Truth and Report it; Minimize Harm; Act Independently* and, *Be Accountable.* There were several specifics listed under each category. Plenty of ethical soul-searching is required of reporters in return for the power they wield. Unlike, say, lawyers or doctors, there's no license that permits someone to be a journalist. You earn respect and build more with every story. Your credibility is your license to practice. Violate the ethics code and you forfeit your license. You might as well step in front of a bus, or worse, run for office. Ha.

Canton Spivey had circled three items in red marker. The first said journalists *should avoid conflicts of interest, real or perceived.* The second, that journalists should *remain free of associations and activities that may compromise integrity or damage credibility.* The third circled item said journalists *should abide by the same high standards to which they hold others.*

"Are you in violation, Danny?"

I stared at the code I knew by heart and by which I'd tried to live my entire career. I thought for a flash of Wendy Hearn, and Isabel, and Ellie and Robin Patragno of the Galapagos Islands, of how I'd insisted my son behave in class and adhere to the highest ethical standards as proscribed by Miss Lipinski.

"Yes," I said. "Terrific story though, huh?"

"Yep, sure was."

Bella

Chapter 36

You'd think Gavin Sussman would love an *iPod*. He doesn't, and it's not because he doesn't know or like music. He does — all kinds — I've gotten to know his collection — Debussy and Dylan to Tito Puente and John Lee Hooker. I guess he'd rather brush up against everything he hates about D.C. than insulate himself with a pair of headphones. Walled off by music, he wouldn't have anything to bitch about. This way he gets to hold forth on rambunctious kids and phlegmy granddads on the subway, or the skinny Asian street performer who "tortures everyone at Farragut North with that thing that looks like a shovel with strings; Jesus, even the *dogs* run for cover," or of course the guys who hose the sidewalks.

One of them got his leg the other day when we were heading to work. The spray struck his calf like a wet bullet, leaving a dark spot in his wrinkled khakis. Gavin stopped dead. "That's fucking *it*!" He dug into his backpack. Gavin carries a generic backpack — gray with red trim — instead of a briefcase. He says leather briefcases are pretentious, and besides, there's no room for his lunch and stainless steel thermos. No way he's spending eight bucks each day for a three-buck tuna wrap at the Pentagon mess. "Or," he'd tell you, "two-fifty for a bottle of water. *Water!*" Gavin's kitchen cabinets are likewise stocked with generic cereal; he uses store-brand soap, dishwasher gel, shampoo, toothpaste and medicine. He drinks tap water and grocery store soda. The closets are crammed with clothes free of designer labels. Even his colored T-shirts bear no logos because, "No one's turning me into a walking billboard."

It was barely daylight and 17th Street was jammed with commuters in suits and jogging shoes. A group of them dashed into a semi-circle as Gavin produced a lime super soaker and furtively tested it against a tree. The spray was fierce, though not as powerful as a five-ply rubber hose fueled by a District of Columbia water line. Weapon in firing position, he quick-stepped up to the hose man, a guy no more than 25 whose name, according to the raised red stitching on his breast pocket, was Lazarus. "Not so funny now, is it?" Gavin said, finger trembling on the trigger. Lazarus' dark eyes opened wide. He flexed his knees, looking, I thought, more amused than scared of the overweight white dude with his big water gun. As the tense moment stretched, it became clear that while he was a mediocre sidewalk cleaner, Lazarus was 25 or so and, despite the beginnings of a W-shaped balding pattern that would require plugs or a clean shave within five years, built like a young *Ah-nald* compared to Gavin, who was nudging 40 and hadn't so much as tossed a football since the second Reagan Administration. No blows were struck. Lazarus somehow got hold of Gavin's wrists and winged him so hard into the stone-faced Barr Building, it must have jarred the loaves of sourdough rising in the bakery next door. Gavin sank fast. It was something to see, like the coyote after a full-speed crash into that boulder painted to look like a tunnel. He wound up on his back staring up at what I bet looked like cartoon canaries, but which were really about two dozen strangers happy for the unexpected morning entertainment.

Lazarus retrieved his hose and grasped the silver pistol-grip handle. His shirt was clinging with sweat now; pecs, delts, triceps and the rest of the upper body arsenal was popping with adrenaline. He aimed at Gavin and the crowd gasped. The soaking would be thorough and brutal. The sweaty black hose was plump and fidgety, the water within an angry, itchy-twitchy snake aching for freedom. Gavin, still dazed after banging into the wall, raised his arms as if under arrest. Lazarus tested the heft of the six-shooter nozzle and pointed at Gavin's heart. He hesitated, wiping one wet hand off on his pants. Was he having second thoughts? "Do *it*, mu-tha-fucker," came a voice from the back. "*Do it!*" The crowd turned. The voice belonged to a homeless woman pushing a shopping cart crammed with metal, wooden and plastic brooms, all in sad shape. She wore jeans caked with dirt, a navy kerchief and a man's flannel shirt torn at one elbow. I stared, not quite comprehending. Someone who spent the day wandering and sweeping city streets should have been on Gavin's side; all he wanted was for Lazarus and his cohorts to clean the sidewalks without water.

Lazarus grinned; these were his 15 minutes. The story of how he subdued and cowed the crazy gringo would be repeated at family picnics for generations. The sidewalk and subway grates, I saw, were not only dirty, but shiny wet. Naturally. Gavin had interrupted the man in the midst of the morning sweep.

Lazarus grew thoughtful. He tugged the corner of his black moustache. He looked to his audience as if expecting thumbs up or down. A small muscle in his wrist twitched and relaxed, and then twitched again. I looked for a cop or a bank guard or even one of those guys in gold and black who tell tourists how to get to the White House and Smithsonian. Nothing.

Lazarus did not fire. Instead, he whipped the silver handle from right hand to left and back, blew softly on the barrel, and holstered it in the front right pocket of his chinos with a cowboy flourish. Most in the crowd applauded. One guy gave him a high-five. Some booed. "Pussy," the old woman hissed and took off with her rusty cart. I rushed to my prone co-worker. We would be late. Marjory Annandale, the associate administrator who ran our shop, would drag us into her office and demand answers. Lazarus glanced from Gavin to me, perhaps expecting a second attack. When he saw I was no threat, he said, "Wuz up with your buddy, man?"

"He thought you got him wet on purpose."

"It was an accident, man," he said, grinning to show that Gavin's analysis had in fact been correct.

My *buddy*. I guess it was true. I picked soggy Gavin Sussman off the ground, just as he'd done for me nine months earlier. I needed a place and we became roommates. I needed work and he recommended me for a public affairs job at DOD, which also worked out after a two-month interview process. One thing the Feds aren't is fast. The pay isn't bad — better than I made as a reporter — though the pace is slower and the material isn't very exciting. I write press releases and edit snoozer publications and brochures. Marge Annandale says if I go a year without screwing up too bad, she'll let me work on speeches for a few second-tier officials. I get two weeks vacation, free Metro farecards and six paid holidays a year.

"C'mon, Gavin, let's get you dried off. Marge is probably getting ready to send out the MP's."

"I'm not going to forget that guy, Danny."

"Hey, he just had a bigger hose; don't worry about it." I tossed the yellow soaker in the trash and pulled him to his feet. He smelled like mildew.

Bella

The Blue Line was jammed, same as always. I stood inches from a kid who seemed headed home after a rough night. Bored with the commuters, shaggy blonde hair a mess. Pierced everywhere — ears, nose, belly-button and tongue. I saw it when she licked her lips. At least I wouldn't have to follow her through airport security. *Foggy Bottom.* No one got off, a dozen more pushed on. More perfume, cologne and bad breath. It would be the same at Rosslyn before the usual tourist exodus at Arlington to pay respects to the dead soldiers. Then one more stop before the Pentagon. A guy in a seersucker suit and Navy tie with gold anchors was asleep with his mouth open, hugging his attaché case like a teddy bear. I glanced at Gavin, caught between a twangy mom towing two kids and a local businessman asking questions about Oklahoma City — *How are folks down there?* She bucked up a smile, murmuring, *Still very sad. The Murrah Building. We lost people. My aunt. A niece ...* I wanted to say, *That fuck McVeigh. The needle was too good for him.* The businessman nodded and offered insider's tips on getting around D.C. "You're a lot better off if you can avoid Metro during rush hour ... "

I shouldn't be here, I thought. I shouldn't be sharing the same air as the pierced girl, or lugging Gavin off the sidewalk, or Metro-ing to a dumbass Pentagon public affairs job that, truth be told, I'm glad to have.

The story hit like *Krakatoa*. Congressman Ed Dwoark's outrage was captured by *CNN*, the *New York Times*, every local news channel in Tampa and daily and weekend political talk shows of every stripe. *Florida Congressman Edward Dwoark: whistle-blowing do-gooder or seedy opportunist? I ask you Eleanor.* No matter if the pundits thought Dwoark was gutsy or garbage, each was talking about him, and what impact the scandal would have on the public's view of the military, to say nothing of those on active duty. Most media outlets were quick to join Dwoark's call for two investigations of Moss's death, one by the Army Inspector General, the other by an independent prosecutor. "This disgrace cannot stand," he told the cameras in a sound bite used by each network that night. I imagined the clip as part of a 30-second spot for his future Senate race. *Eddie Dwoark: Fighting for You, for Florida, for America!* He'd be a senator within five years; Edie Dwoark would be a powerful woman.

The weary and tired-looking Army and Defense Secretaries said yes, of course there would be an investigation, that they were saddened by the revelations, and hoped the allegations would prove unfounded. Sgt. Marlin Falk would be brought to Washington immediately to answer questions with Charles Braxton. Whistle-blower Bart Jefferson was also headed for D.C., and there would be an official inquiry into the death of Private Marcus Ravoli in Charleston, S.C.

"Do you have anything to say to Isabel Moss?" one reporter shouted at the press conference.

The Army Secretary began to answer and was nudged aside by the Defense Secretary, who, reading from a small note card, said, "The President wants Mrs. Moss to know that he and our nation consider Hank Moss a hero. His death was tragic but honorable, no matter the circumstances. Training procedures in all branches of the military are under review. The President has personally directed me to conduct an inquiry that will run concurrently with the independent Inspector General's investigation. I will begin immediately. We of course remain deeply sorry for the loss suffered by Mrs. Moss, and all who knew and loved her husband."

Nearly every story credited the *Tampa Daily News*, an intense ego boost for the editors, owners, and even average residents, like when the

Bella

local pro team makes the playoffs. Your cousin in Boston calls and says, *Hey Jim, those Bucs of yours are playing some kinda ball,* and you say, *Sure are,* as if you were the offensive coordinator or the quarterback's dad. With one story, the parochial paper went from local rag to national player. Sweet, though it wouldn't last more than a few weeks. Reporters from famous newspapers and infamous tabloids called all day begging me for quotes, background and new leads. *C-SPAN* and *National Public Radio* wanted me for special reports once I got back to Washington. *Did Moss live after the explosion? Will Falk get court-martialed? What about that Pentagon guy, Braxton — he going to jail too? Who gave you the video? Does it really show Moss getting blown up?* I planted myself in Isabel's living room and patiently answered each question that didn't violate agreements I'd made with my sources. As in my story, I didn't identify Clay.

Only one guy caught me off guard, the "special investigations bureau chief" from a supermarket tabloid called the *National Exposé.* I was skeptical at first, but he sounded as professional as the rest, asking what had become a usual string of questions about Hank's tennis career and decision to enlist in the Army. So I stayed on a few minutes, even giving a few details I'd withheld from the others about the meetings with Marcus Ravoli's mother and Hank's mom. He was very engaging and told me about another scandal he was working on — this one involving a famous baseball player whose sudden homerun output might have a pharmaceutical explanation — and — maybe I was drained and my radar was down — it soon felt like we were just two professionals having a conversation. I mentioned I started as a high school sportswriter. His first job was police beat reporter for a small daily in Ohio. "Only thing worse than a cranky desk sergeant is a cranky high school football coach," he said. I agreed and told him some about Coach Gooch. Somehow we got around to pick-up basketball. He said he played, and I invited him to join our Sunday game next time he was in D.C. Toward the end, he casually asked how I'd first been alerted about possible wrongdoing by the Army. I told him Isabel called because I was the Washington correspondent for her hometown paper. He paused and I heard papers rustling. "I've got a clip with a picture here. Good-looking woman." I agreed — "yes, she is" — and he said, in the same nonchalant tone he'd used throughout the conversation, "Hey Danny, you nailing that?"

"What?"

"You know, are you screwing her?"

"What kind of question is that?"

"The kind of question my readers like answered."

"What kind of scumbag are you? Maybe *that's* the kind of question they'd like answered."

"So you're not denying it."

"Jesus, no wonder people hate that rag you work for."

He laughed. "They hate it, but it's always in their shopping carts."

On some calls, I referred the reporters to Isabel, who was in the kitchen baking gingerbread cookies with Katie and half-listening to the TV accounts. After half-a-dozen stories, I saw she was losing interest and went back to answering the questions myself. I wondered if she was beginning to realize that exposing the truth wasn't going to bring back her husband. At the end of each interview, I thanked the caller and politely asked that I not be identified as a reporter with the *Daily News.*

"I don't work there anymore."

$\mathbf{M}$arge Annandale found us in our adjoining cubicles. She seemed ready to write us up, stick something in the official record, or do whatever it is bureaucrats do to punish a guy at the Pentagon. *You two slackers are going to spend all afternoon memorizing acronyms. Don't cry. You deserve it for being late again.* After one look at Gavin, though, she threw up her hands and said, "I don't want to know. Just don't let it happen again." She marched off and Gavin, still looking like he'd run through the sprinklers, smiled for the first time that morning. His dignity was back. Dry socks would take a little longer.

"Let's get on those news releases," he said and began humming. I glanced at the clock. Another seven hours and twenty minutes, and I'd be able to get back on the subway and go home sweet home, to Gavin's generic apartment.

The work, as I said, isn't hard. There's lots of time to think about how quickly things unraveled.

"Doesn't your wife wonder where you are?" Isabel said the second night after the story broke. By then, Washington — still toiling through the torpid summer with no rain and no news in sight, thanks to a stagnant weather pattern that pushed in from the South and the usual congressional recess — was suddenly revived by the joint hearings ordered by Senator Newlin, Congressman Dwoark and Florida Senator Kirk Lawton. "That boy was a Floridian," Lawton said gravely, ignoring those who pointed out he'd discovered in the emerging scandal a way to make people forget he'd recently walked bare-assed into a police station. Dwoark was glad to share the stage; Lawton would make a handy political ally down the road.

Meanwhile, the wire services and *Washington Post* reported that Marlin Falk and Charles Braxton were answering questions before a military tribunal in D.C. Congressional hearings would begin soon. Lawmakers from both parties, particularly those up for reelection, wanted the Army to explain how the cover-up could have occurred, and what procedures were being changed to prevent a similar episode in the future. Isabel was asked to testify, as was Hank Moss' mother.

It was exasperating to have broken the original story and not be involved in the follow-up. That's how it goes for a newsman without a newspaper. I'd been suspended immediately for "gross ethical violations" and would likely be, pending final review, summarily fired with two week's severance plus vacation pay. We weren't a union paper, so there was no formal appeal process. Canton and several reporter friends at the paper pressed for leniency, but Jasper Downing was already furious because he believed, correctly, though no one ever admitted it, that we gave Dwoark the evidence he used against the Army. It was my third night at Isabel's; I hadn't called home in four days. I was very tired.

"She knows I'm here."

"I think we better talk, Danny."

She didn't dance around. She let me go like a housekeeper caught lifting grandma's diamond ring. Worse, she tried to give me money, a check for five grand. "I don't want you to walk away from all this empty-handed." I looked at the check. The style she'd chosen from one of those cookie cutter graphics shops showed a trio of Polar bears lounging in the snow, everything white except their black eyes and rubbery noses. They looked clumsy and out of place against her precise librarian's handwriting. I wondered what she'd been thinking when she chose the pattern. I wondered when she wrote the check. Was it this afternoon or the afternoon we first met? Was the idea all along to "hire" me to break the story? "I don't want your money. Isabel ..." We were standing; she was wearing a stupid pink tank top that said, *Flamingos are Fabulous*. I took her bare shoulders and made her face me. It was terrible feeling so helpless, to be hooked as a drug addict, to know arguing would be useless and demeaning, and to still plow on. *Leave now and hang on to a little pride.* Instead, I said, "We get along. We have great sex. Why are you doing this?"

She rolled her eyes. "It's not so great, Danny." She pulled away and began speaking in a distant monotone. "I thought you knew. I don't feel things the same as other people anymore." She let down the curtain between now and then, returning to the weeks after Hank died, filling in painful details she'd kept private. After her tantrum at the funeral home when she screamed at relatives and spit at the Christ statue, she said she was inconsolable at Arlington, sobbing and gasping so violently, a doctor was called and a tranquilizer administered. Hank's mother wanted Katie to move in with her in Plant City until Isabel's strength returned. "I hated her for that. The Army took my husband; now she was going to steal my daughter?" Isabel said she could barely eat or sleep. "I weighed 97 pounds, then 90, then 86. Some days I couldn't move, the grief was so profound. Everyone spoke in front of me like I wasn't there. They talked about hospitals, feeding tubes, shrinks, shock therapy ... I can barely remember. Then they got serious about moving Katie to Florida, so I faked it."

"Faked it?"

"I *recovered*. I forced myself to eat. I started jogging. Three months later I was volunteering to help with school plays and church picnics. No one saw me cry again." She blinked slowly and her eyes returned slightly unfocused. "I wasn't perfect. I told my priest God didn't exist and yelled at the paperboy when the newspaper got wet. Katie's little friends came with their bikes and *Big Wheels* and I wouldn't let her out to play."

"Did Katie ever stay with her grandmother?"

"No, but they kept talking about me, especially the other mothers ... Those cows. It got back to me: *The woman is strange, like she's made of plastic. Yes, you're right, and we all see how she simply smothers that poor child.* I wanted them to trade places for a day so they'd see what it was like."

She went on for some minutes, telling me she took to practicing in the mirror to make herself look natural. She vowed not to let what happened ruin her. She said she stopped praying because God failed her. She took drugs to stop her headaches and sat on her hands when her fingers trembled. In time, she improved. "It's not like there's a cure, you know. It's not like having an injury; it's like having a condition, like asthma. You learn to live with it. You carry an inhaler." After awhile, she felt well enough for a real test run.

"We were out of town at a hotel. I got a sitter for Katie. I put on a black dress and some make-up. I had a glass of wine and went downstairs. The doorman and cabbie made me laugh, fighting to see who could serve me fastest. I went to a club, lied about my name and danced with a guy still in college. Body like concrete. Brain, too, but who cared? I went to his apartment and fucked him silly for two hours. It was great, Danny, except the kid fell in love. He wanted my number; I told him it wasn't going to happen. Somehow I wound up with the same cabbie on the way home. What are the odds? We had a nice chat about men and women. He said the problem with dating was that the girl always fell in love. I laughed. I told him, "I must be starting to think like a man.""

She looked at me for the first time in awhile. "The point, Danny, is we all do what's necessary to get by. It's the survival instinct. I still love Hank, Danny. Only Hank. Always and forev ... "

The tank-top flamingos, pink, beautiful and oblivious, suddenly infuriated me. "Ever think that he didn't choose *you* always and forever? He picked war, Isabel. War and revenge first, Isabel and Katie second. He knew there was a chance he wasn't coming back." I hated myself as soon as I said it. She recoiled. I apologized, tried to comfort her. She didn't need it. Her downcast eyes brightened with new fury. "I'll make up the couch. You can go home in the morning. Reconsider the check." Her mouth became a cruel smile. "Look at it this way. Five grand for five weeks. Plus benefits. You did alright. You're hot now; every paper and TV station in the country knows about this story. You'll find another job, a better job. You'll make up with your wife, get a better job and have a great life. I'll still be a widow. My child still won't have her father. You're right. He didn't pick us."

"Isabel — "

" — Good night. Please be gone before we get up."

Sometime in the night I awoke to muffled sounds from outside. I squinted and felt my T-shirt. The neck was soaked with sweat. I must have had a nightmare; I concentrated and couldn't remember anything but murky fragments. I pulled off the shirt and again heard what sounded like men shifting around outside. Isabel must have heard too. She came downstairs. We met at the bottom step. "What's going on?" It was 3:40 a.m. Katie was still fast asleep. I was about to speak when we heard it again: two or more guys talking. She whispered, "I'll call the police." I shook my head. "They're too noisy to be serious criminals." I walked to the front door. She tiptoed alongside. I motioned for her to stay back. She took my elbow and wouldn't let me loose. "You're not going without me." I should have insisted she stay back, not that she would have listened. If I did and she had, she wouldn't have been blinded by the flash when I pulled open the door.

The photos, a rapid-fire half-dozen of me in my boxers and bare-chested, Isabel in a white silk housecoat opened sexily to the waist, sash hanging, both of us looking like thieves caught in the act when we were really shading our eyes from the incessant flashes, comprised nearly the entire front page of the next morning's *National Expose'*. The block-letter headline screamed, "**ARMY WIDOW, REPORTER GO UNDERCOVER.**"

It might as well have said Dan Patragno need never again apply for a job in journalism.

Isabel was right: I was hot, so hot that no decent newspaper would let me in the front door. The same proved true of my wife.

"Wild guess — she threw you out." It was more statement than question.

"Yes," I said, cell phone hot against my ear.

"And that makes me what, Danny, the booby prize? Sloppy seconds?"

"Ellie." I said her name and said it again. "What, Danny? What do you want me to say, that I'm happy being the winner by default?" I asked if I could move back in; she said I could visit Robbie when I wanted. "That's the best I can do, Danny; it's more than you deserve," she said.

Marge Annandale buzzed me after lunch. She's a smoker, Marge. Smokes and swears like the stiff-haired waitress at a roadside diner in tobacco country. At first I was surprised; there's a certain air at the Pentagon, a respect for rules and authority, even among the civilian employees. Cursing within the vanguard of national defense feels like picking your nose in church. Marge, an Atlanta girl closing in on 60, wears high-collared dresses and keeps her hair short and neat, with little dyed-blonde bangs that cover the lines on her forehead. I'm sure she was acquainted with Charlie Braxton, though she's never said anything to me about the Hank Moss story. No one has; feeding the information to Ed Dwoark raised his profile and left me a minor figure, an anonymous journalist who was first to report the *congressman's* discovery, as opposed to the real story — that I'd uncovered the conspiracy. Marge probably never connected me to the piece, and Braxton's long gone with a dishonorable discharge, so he can't tell her. I suppose he visits Falk sometimes at the military jail in Lexington. Falk got thrown out and five years hard time to boot.

"Okay, where the hell were you two this morning?" I began to answer. "No," she said, "I don't give a crap. First chance I get, I'm transferring that fuck-up Sussman to the Fargo field office." She sighed and closed her eyes; I could see her with a shot of *Jack* in one hand and a *Marlboro* in the other. In the quiet, I heard Elvis singing softly on her computer. It was early Elvis, the slim, romantic version, all wavy hair and trembling baritone. "But you, Dan, putting aside this morning, I'm happy with you. You're coming along fast." She waited for a thank-you; a nod was the best I could do. Any decent intern could handle the jobs I'd been given so far. She laced her fingers. The blueish veins on the back of her hands jutted out so much, I could count them. "Yeah, well, I'm recommending you for a step increase and moving you to a different part of public affairs where you'll be handling inquiries from the media. Don't worry; we'll give you some training before you start."

I know she meant well, handing me more pay and responsibility. *Love Me Tender, Marge. Thanks.*

Truth is, it drove the nails a little deeper, reminding me first that I no longer was a reporter, and, second, insulting me by saying I needed training to assist the reporters who covered us, as if they only spoke Dutch or Korean.

"Appreciate it, Marge," I said and left the building forever. It might have been the first time in Pentagon history that anyone quit for getting promoted.

Gavin and I don't cook much. There's good Mexican in the neighborhood, a decent pizza joint, and a Thai place up the block that makes "Crying Tiger," so named, I believe, as a dare to adventurous diners. I asked once, through my Tiger tears, what was in the dish. The bicycle delivery kid — his name's *Chaiyho*; he has wispy eyebrows and sideburns and pins baseball cards to his wheel spokes with clothespins — he laughed and touched his temple, as if he couldn't remember. It seemed like a routine he'd memorized. "Grilled beef. Red onions. Scallions. Secret ingredient only chef knows. Good deal for six-ninety five!"

There's no dishwasher in the apartment so we usually eat straight from the cartons, which get mushy after awhile.

Bella

Chapter 37

I sold the Honda. Didn't need it in the city, and it would have been a pain to register and park it. Plus I needed the money. Gavin's place is cheap, not free. On Sundays, I Metro to Bethesda, where Clay picks me up for the weekly basketball game. Gavin doesn't play. He signed up for Taekwondo and talks constantly about getting fit, learning some moves, and another, more rewarding encounter with Lazarus the hose man. I told him I wouldn't help this time; he narrowed his eyes and said he didn't remember me helping *last* time.

We played ball last Sunday. Lost four straight. Clay's wife Mary showed up and watched the last one for as long as she could stand it. Funny how aging guys can't grasp that it's a young man's game. Every time the seasons change there are fewer guys and more of those black latex sleeves holding together elbows, knees, ankles and hamstrings. It was a rare cool day in early September. Autumn was in dress rehearsal; eight middle-aged chronically aching men sporting a dozen latex wraps were in the gym. You could almost hear lungs and muscles protesting each trip up and down the court. Ice and *Advil* were in everyone's near future. We'd play 10 minutes, forget the score, and argue for five about who was ahead. Pathetic. I think the arguing was more about resting than winning. And, maybe somewhere, the knowledge that the high school girls who tore up the gym after us would win by 30 if we ever dared play them straight up. It was emasculating to think that these kids, lean, lanky, and still a few years from college, could kick our antique asses so easily. Nearly any of the girls on the AAU team was better than nearly any of our guys. Dara, their tallest at 6-2, could dunk. I could dunk doughnuts. At least we were smart enough to be gone by the time their parents dropped them off.

I hadn't played in awhile and was gulping air. My side ached and the court seemed longer by yards than I remembered. We began anew and I tried to imagine myself as a local sportscaster watching from the bleachers. The first thing I'd do is tell the cameraman to pack his gear. There wouldn't be a single highlight for the news at six or eleven unless we wanted to go for a reel of sports bloopers. Then there'd be plenty. We'd do a whole segment, call it, *America's Ripest Hoopsters.*

When we finished our old man basketball, Mary, once my most precious news source, was leaning against her sleek white *Mercedes* coupe. She looked smart in a light turtleneck and washed denim jacket. The coupe, I knew, was secured in the aftermath of wayward Clay's return to the nest. Good for her; I was glad she got some nice new wheels for all her trouble. She could deliver the girls to soccer practice in style. I could not come up with anything close if Ellie were to change her mind. I had no job and no prospects. I was so depressed, I wasn't even looking. All I looked for — *hid from*, to be honest — was any stranger who came to the door of Gavin's place. I was afraid it might be Ellie's lawyers come to serve me divorce papers.

Mary peered at us the way an orthopedist studies a bad news X-ray. "You two should take up ice fishing this winter." I kissed her cheek. "Wish

Bella

I felt as good as you look." She chuckled. "If I felt like you look, they'd come with sirens screaming."

Clay needed the bathroom. When he left, Mary and I took a stroll down the parking lot. Cars and mini-vans began rolling up with the AAU girls. They were as giggly as any other teenagers and I caught snatches of gossip about a dance after Friday night's game at Bethesda. There was something about Samantha bringing the *special punch*, and *devastating news* about Alex and Mia. I kept my ball under my arm, dribbling now and then as we walked. The gravel did not yield as smooth a bounce as the wooden floor inside the gym. Mary looked around and chuckled at the girls. Though it was warm, leaves were already falling; pumpkins and turkey were coming fast, and then it would be Christmas, my first without Robin and Ellie. The weather guys were beginning to talk about the bad winter I'd seen coming for awhile, the stormy days that Ellie, Wendy Hearn and Canton Spivey had in fact predicted long ago. A few weeks earlier, I watched Sampras take Agassi in the final of the U.S. Open and thought how nice it would have been if the match had begun with a moment for Hank Moss. But no one remembered. Attention focused on the two aging American tennis giants. Sampras was 31; the serve was still intact, the hairline not so much. Agassi, at 32, seemed a shade slower than before. You couldn't see it in his eyes; they were fierce as ever. His mind, too, still saw the court as a speed chess champion sees the board, calculating two or three moves into the future while the rest of us are locked in the present. Where wear and tear had produced more craftiness upstairs, they'd also punished poor Agassi's back and knees. He and Pistol Pete were on their way out, same as the guys I'd just left on the basketball court. Each of us had been permitted to develop whatever talent God and genetics gave us and see where it led, be it the high school gym or Flushing Meadows. Not Hank. Wear and tear was never a factor for Screech Moss.

251

Today the sky was a deep, cloudless blue, and the sun was warm comfort to my aching body. "How are you guys doing, Mary? Things back to normal?" She said she and *Double A* were okay, though his affair had changed them both. She was more jaded and less trusting, which ran counter to her instincts and made her sad. "I want to trust; there's security and stability in trusting." Mary said Clay had become so humble and eager to please, it was annoying. "Normal? Normal is being redefined."

"I know all about it, Mary."

She put her arm around me like I was a little boy. "I saw your friend's TV movie. It was like she did all the work herself; you never existed."

"We didn't end on good terms."

"She's horrible."

"She's damaged, Mary."

"Damaged. Interesting …"

"Damaged, wounded and dangerous. She suffered, and believes suffering earned her the right to hurt anyone standing in her way." I side-stepped some shards from a broken beer bottle. "I didn't get it until too late. I think losing the love of your life when you're young and idealistic can change a person. Different defense mechanisms kick in to get you through. When Hank died, she did too, in a way." I knew Mary was staring. I'd thought all these things and never said them aloud. "Only she came back as a different person. Hank's death certificate became Isabel's license to act with impunity. She let herself be robbed of the capacity to feel shame. I don't know if she feels *anything*. She fooled me, and I was fool enough to let her. I should have gone with my gut and stayed the hell away from her." I realized I was rambling and apologized.

"You should write a book."

"There's enough material and I've sure got the time."

Mary thought about that and we walked on. "Have you spoken to your wife?"

"I tried. She's not interested."

"When did you try?"

"I don't know, a month ago."

"Try again."

I stopped. "You know something I should know?"

"I know you should try again."

We looked back and saw Clay, hands on his hips, clearly wondering what the hell we were doing. I smiled and waved.

Mary put her arms around my neck. I glanced back at her husband. "Now Clay's really going to wonder what's up."

"Look at me, Danny. I see a big comeback in your future. Not in your funky basketball game, but you're going to get your life back together. If I could do it, you can too."

I backed off. No one had touched me that intimately in a long time, not that I'd ever want Gavin Sussman putting his arms around me. I edged back and rubbed my right hamstring, stretching toward my toes, barely reaching the tip of my right shoelace.

"Comeback! I'm pushing 40 and nearly divorced. I've got no job; my kid looks at me like I'm a derelict. Isabel Moss used me and tossed me out ... I screwed up so bad, my old J-school professor wants me to come to Tallahassee and give lectures on ethics and journalism. As in, how *not* to do it."

She hugged me again. I fought a moment and hugged back, eyes clamped, emotions surging. "Come on, now, it's going to be fine," she said. I wanted to ask when. I felt like time was running out. Clay called, "You two about through?"

We swung toward him and saw he was no longer alone. Ellie had driven up with Robin. Mary and I missed her amid all the girls' team traffic. Or was it just me who missed her? Mary poked my ribs. "Well, well," she said. I grabbed her hand and clasped it within mine, mostly out of fear. "Breathe, Danny." I tried to speak to Mary without moving my lips. "Help," I said. She put her hand on my lower back and grinned at her husband, the chastened satellite geek who'd morphed into an annoyingly agreeable lug. The three of them, 25 yards or so away, were standing side by side. Clay slid behind my wife and gestured for me to *do something*. I flashed on the two ex-lovers groping each other in a hotel for just a second. *He had his hands all over her. And she; she …* I didn't realize I'd clenched my fist until I dropped the basketball. It bounced over the curb and onto a little stretch of weedy grass. I fought down the image of Clay and Ellie. Time to move on.

Ellie smiled and gave a timid wave, which I returned. Her hair was getting long, the way I liked it, and I thought fleetingly that she might have let it grow out for me. Mary had predicted a Patragno comeback. Suddenly it seemed possible. Ellie had a hand on Robin's shoulder that he shrugged off. The damned kid seemed a foot taller than when I saw him three weeks earlier. He needed a haircut. She turned him loose and he came toward me at a slow gait, shaggy-headed Robin Patragno of Silver Spring, Maryland, and the Galapagos Islands, his checkered slate with Ms. Lipinksi wiped clean and the fresh year ahead a welcoming haven where he might possibly use his magnifying glass for the benefit of mankind. He wore a blue tank top and matching *Air Jordans*, and looked ready, anxious even, for a little one-on-one with his old man.

I picked up the ball, threw a soft bounce pass and went to meet him.

Bella

Discussion Questions:

1. Bella is one of the strongest characters in the novel. What accounts for her inner strength? Do you agree with Danny that she feels entitled to use any tactics to achieve her personal agenda? What would you say to or ask Bella if you could talk to her?

2. Danny is often conflicted by his duty to be fair and his instinct to pass judgment. Why is it so hard for journalists to be objective? Is it ever possible for reporters to be equally fair to both sides in a controversial story?

3. Clay Ohrbach hurt Danny personally, yet Danny protected Clay when he wrote his story. Why?

4. Sgt. Braxton argued that publishing the real account of Hank's death would undercut troop morale and American support for the war. Was he right, and under what circumstances should the media refrain from reporting on sensitive military matters?

5. Danny is introduced as a confident, take-charge reporter, but is quickly unsettled by the exotic Bella. Would he have begun an affair with Bella if his wife hadn't confessed her own adultery?

6. What does the future hold for Robin Patragno, the son of Danny and Ellie, and Katie Moss, the daughter of Hank and Bella?

Interview with the Author:

Where did this story come from?

Bella was inspired by the death of a close friend's husband, and the courageous way she dealt with the tragedy.

Is this an anti-war book intended to show that technology has made war impersonal and too easy an option?

No, I have great respect for our military and believe war is sometimes an unavoidable option, but that proper checks and balances should always be in place to ensure accountability. One of those checks is an aggressive, responsible media.

Do you admire Bella?

The tragedy that befalls Bella causes profound grief and reshapes her personality. In the end, I view her as a complex but flawed character with many admirable traits.

Describe your writing process, and how you researched this project.

I wrote Bella over a three-year period, and owe a great debt to the many experts, friends and family members who lent their guidance and support to this project. I do most of my writing in a home office in suburban Maryland, and like to think I do my best work in the early morning, usually in two or three-hour stretches that begin around 6 a.m.

What is your own background?

I'm a native New Yorker who wound up spending 25 years working for Southern newspapers. In 2002, I became a speechwriter at a large federal agency. I've since moved into communications management, and also teach journalism at American University in Washington, D.C. My wife is a special education administrator in Montgomery County, Md., and we have three (nearly) adult children. All three played college tennis.

What is the Bella website and what's there?

Please visit **getbella.com** to watch a book trailer, to see what readers around the country are saying about Bella, to read illustrated excerpts, and to buy or gift a copy. I'm also blogging about the story behind our self-publishing adventure and would love for readers to join the conversation.

How were you able to self-publish by yourself while working full-time?

Successful self-publishing requires considerable help and a superb team. I was lucky to find very talented individuals who believed in the project. My heartfelt thanks to: Chris Kelly Cimko, Sarah Millican, Ali Piacente, Dave Haeffner, Jon Haeffner, Felicia Piacente, Danielle Piacente, Patrick Bentley, Lauren Markoe, Wendy Swallow, Dara Padwo-Audick, Josh Redmond, Maureen McCarty, Jade Ryan, and Jess Noonan.

Do you have another book in the works?

Yes, please let me set the stage for Bootlicker:

Their plan is to sneak a few beers in the woods. They must be careful; 1959 is no year for underage black boys to get caught drinking by the sheriff in rural South Carolina. Before the first sip, they come to a clearing. A black man is on his knees, surrounded by white men in robes. One has shed his mask. The local judge. One of the boys bolts. The other, Ike Washington,

Bella

freezes and is discovered. Judge Mac McCauley weighs things and offers young Ike a choice: join the man about to die, or begin hustling the black support McCauley needs to advance in state politics. In trade, Ike will enjoy a life of power and comfort. Decades later, McCauley is a U.S. senator and Ike is poised to become the first black congressman from South Carolina since Reconstruction. Instead, he winds up in the same forest where the hanging took place years earlier, a long rope in hand. The night is noisy, but all he hears is the name his rivals have bestowed upon him: Bootlicker.

Made in the USA
Lexington, KY
14 July 2010